A Place Called

By

Lainy J. Thomas

Copyright

Lainy J.Thomas

2024

1

ISBN 9798860955783

*Dedicated to: Teachers who go the extra mile. *

Prologue

She was still half squatting on the cold, wet concrete. She had no idea how she had come to be so close to the edge of the platform, she could not recall walking from the shelter. If . . . if she had taken a single step more . . .

Aimee dusted off her hands and pulled her hair off her face. She made her way unsteadily back towards the shelter and seated herself awkwardly on her school bag. She wanted to cry but no tears came. The ball of emotion inside her was huge and heavy and Aimee gazed into the silent distance, the train having disappeared as if it had never been there. Was that how it was when you were dead, she wondered. Unseen and forgotten, as if you had never been. How fleetingly was life gone. And made.

Chapter One

An icy wind whipped her long, dark hair free from her hood and the rain lashed viciously against her bruised cheek. Aimee pulled the last of the evening papers from the bright orange bag and pushed it hastily through the letterbox of number fourteen Blueberry Way. With a sigh, she turned and once again the crisp scrunch of her shoes on the wet gravel rudely announced her progress along the sweeping driveway.

It had been a cheerless hour but true misery met her at the top of the road as her nightly departure from reality, walking between the comfortable and affluent looking homes, came to a close. She gazed at the perfectly positioned curtains, the immaculate paintwork and the polished brass of the door furniture. It seemed incredible to her that such homes were a mere fifteen minutes' walk from her own house – she could never bring herself to think of it as "home" – In Deansfield Crescent on Cotwell's most infamous council estate.

Within ten minutes, she had reached the small, run-down shopping centre, whose neglected hoardings and paint-chipped shop fronts offered a forlorn welcome at the edge of the estate. She pushed open the door of the modest shop, which served as post office, general store and newsagent to the small community. As usual and in vain she attempted to close her senses to the familiar smell, a mixture of air freshener, body odours and vegetables.

Leaving her bag on the counter, she retraced her steps and turned towards the row of garages where the usual group of pale, gangly youths hung around idly. Waiting. Waiting for something, anything to disturb the daily dullness, which stretched behind them and before them. Every couple of months, the police would arrive to move them on, following complaints about the various debris left behind as a result of the youths' nocturnal activities. Aimee dodged the remnants of vomit on the pavement with disgust and shoved her cold hands disconsolately into the ripped lining of her coat pockets. She allowed her thoughts to wander back towards the warm-looking houses, imagining the families coming home, smiling and welcoming, enquiring enthusiastically about each other's day.

Too soon, she reached the short, slabbed path and with a heavy heart, she shoved her key into the lock of the door, noticing as always, the slight indentation – a permanent reminder of one of her stepfather's drunken rages.

"Bloody late, as usual!" Jim greeted her menacingly.

Reluctantly, she brought her gaze to meet her stepfather's. She could barely contain her contempt at the sight of him, slumped in "his" chair, nearest the electric fire, clutching his can of lager. Five o'clock already, he would probably be on his second or third can by now.

She forced herself to speak quietly and calmly. "I told you . . . I had to deliver another round before mine . . . "

Just get the bleedin' potatoes on. Yer mother'll be 'ere in ten minutes. . . Pull yer bloody weight, she's got enough to do, you ungrateful bitch."

Aimee felt his hatred burning her back as she moved into the kitchen. As if he cares about my mother, she thought, bitter resentment biting into her chest.

She turned on the tap at the kitchen sink and scrubbed at her fingers, stained from the newspapers and smeared with schoolgirl ink.

Opening the food cupboard, she pulled out the bag of potatoes. Three small vegetables, sprouting in every direction, lay sweating pathetically at the bottom. Aimee closed her eyes, momentarily, in despair. How on earth was she supposed to conjure up chips for five from these?

4

She prayed to God that her mother, returning from one of her cleaning jobs, would remember to bring some more potatoes. Her stomach twisted into a tight knot of dread as she envisaged Jim's rage. It was Monday night: sausage, egg and chips. Lots of chips. His favourite. Carefully, she began pinching off the resilient white sprouts, removing the peel as tightly as she could, lest she should waste any of the precious, albeit softened, potatoes, already a week or so past their best.

* * *

"Jesus Christ! Can't you do anything right?" Jim roared across the kitchen table.

"Where's me fucking chips?"

Aimee saw her mother wince. Even by doing without themselves, there had been no way that they had been able to perform miracles with barely a handful of chips, some of which had disintegrated in the oil, thickened as it was from weeks of heating and re-heating. Stacey, the youngest, already well accustomed to the early signs of her father's temper, blinked away her tears.

"For Christ's sake! Don't *you* start snivelling."

When Jim turned on his own daughters, Aimee knew it was going to be bad. The presence of four year old Stacey and Kayleigh, two years older, was occasionally enough to soften his eruptions.

"Jim ... please ... " Sheryl pleaded. "It's my fault ... I forgot ... "

"Forgot!" Jim exploded, lunging towards his wife. His fist connected with her tiny cheekbone, which, at thirty three, was already prematurely sunken.

5

Aimee's heart raced. The bread knife lay at a sinister proximity to her stepfather's hand. Her eyes moved involuntarily around the room. She imagined him slamming her mother's face on to the still red electric rings just a few steps' away.

Jim's face twitched with rage, his cheeks red with anger, as yet controlled. His family watched him in terrified anticipation. Even Stacey remained silent as, without warning, he flung his plate against the wall, narrowly missing his wife's head. He pushed his chair brutally backwards and it fell with a thud onto the ripped linoleum.

They heard the slam of the front door. For several moments a silence lay over them before Sheryl nervously arose and began to gather the fragments of broken china and scattered food, wiping hopelessly at the wall; another stain, another reminder of her inadequacy. She looked sorrowfully at her children, knowing that she had failed them and that she would continue to do so. Fleetingly, she thought of how it could end; daily she wished him dead. But only the good die young, she reminded herself.

"Mommy," Stacey's small voice broke the silence, "your face is bleeding."

Aimee watched as her little sisters gazed dolefully at their mother's latest wound. She knew it was she who had to find the strength to restore some semblance of normality to their young lives, even if it would be short-lived.

"Hey you two, shall we watch a film?"

Kayleigh looked doubtful, her eye, bright against her sallow skin, darted from her elder sister to her mother but Stacey pulled eagerly at her sleeve.

The ancient machine groaned into life as Aimee pushed in their favourite nursery rhyme dvd. The cheerful sounds filled the room where the air was still thick with the tension of violence and fear.

Aimee returned to the kitchen to help her mother. For a while, neither of them spoke, concentrating on returning the room to a standard that they prayed Jim would find acceptable. They both knew what would happen if he returned to find *his* house anything but ship shape.

"I'm sorry." Her mother's voice was quiet.

"It's not your fault." Aimee returned dutifully. She hated herself for the times when deep down she found herself despising her mother's weakness. It was the new millennium, the age of equality. How could any woman allow herself, let alone her children, to suffer as they did? Inwardly, she vowed that *her* life would be different.

She lifted the crockery from the draining board, carefully wiping each piece dry and smear free and indulged herself in thoughts of her rosy future. Life after school, of course would be completely different. She'd get a decent job, nothing special – there was no point kidding herself – but something that would bring her her freedom – she dreamed of her own little flat, rented no doubt, but her own space, nice little ornaments and a little car parked outside. She closed her eyes briefly and allowed herself to hope. Perhaps she would eventually be able to persuade her mother to escape the tyranny and misery that Jim wreaked daily upon their lives. How she wished that they could all leave now. She no longer bothered to have the conversation with her mother, who reeled off the numerous "reasons" why they had to stay: nowhere to go, not enough money, he would find them and then it would be far, far worse when he did. Aimee knew that it *was* possible, there were hostels for families such as theirs – she'd read about them on problem pages.

A dark and threatening cloud hung over the peace of the next couple of hours for the female members of the Parkinson household. The familiar sounds of Coronation Street filled the small living room; just as in millions of homes around the country and for a while they tried to believe that they were leading a normal life.

Sheryl accepted her elder daughter's offer to get the little ones to bed.

"What would I do without you, our Aimee?" She smiled gratefully, relieved to have a few moments to herself. She hugged her two youngest. "Sleep tight; be good for your sister."

Not that they needed reminding how to behave, little angels that they were, disciplined by the ever-present threat of violence, which, as yet, had not come their way. The sight of Aimee and their mother suffering at the hands, or feet, of their father had sufficiently curbed their childish spirit.

"Night, night, Mommy. We love you," they chorused.

Aimee hurried them out of the room before they could see the tears on their mother's pale cheeks.

The clock struck ten and Aimee stole a nervous glance towards her mother, who sighed resignedly. "You go up, love, you've got school tomorrow."

Reluctantly, she left her mother, both visualising the state he would be in on his return.

Lying in her bed, Aimee knew that she had to stay awake. She had to be awake to listen, to act if things went too far. She often wondered how far too far would be.

How far would he go? Image after image of the catalogue of beatings, those of which she had not witnessed visually, had been audible as she lay rigid with terror. Often, her little sisters would creep under her covers and they would hold each other with bated breath until the sickening thuds and voices subsided. Aimee would strain her ears for the sounds of two sets of footsteps on the stairs. Sometimes it would be a while before

Sheryl followed her husband and Aimee tortured herself with thoughts of the unthinkable.

There had been a time when she would go down, screaming, begging him to stop hitting her mother. And so he would, for a while. And she would almost feel a perverse sense of relief as she endured the pain of his fists on her small body. Somehow, the physical pain released her briefly from her mental agony as she succumbed to the beating that had been meant for her mother.

But experience had taught her that, once he had finished and had flung her back towards the stairs, his attack on his wife would continue with fresh fury at the nerve of her interfering brat.

So, her mother had begged her to stay out of it, leaving her powerless, night after night, dread and fear her constant companions. And whilst she was never allowed to forget that she, Aimee, was the outsider, bad blood, born of her mother's first failed relationship, Aimee knew that her half-sisters suffered no less, the innocence of childhood already lost amidst their father's tyranny.

* * *

"Aimee Parkinson . . . I said . . . "Aimee Parkinson." Her English teacher's irritation seeped into her consciousness. "The answer to question number three, please, Aimee . . . today, if possible."

Aimee ignored the undisguised sarcasm and the titters from her classmates.

"I er . . . " she gazed desperately at the sea of words in front of her, she could not even see question three, let alone answer it.

A wave of misery washed over her. Each day she chided herself for her lack of concentration. If only she could stop herself from drifting off. If only she were not so tired ...

9

"Would you prefer to do this during detention?"

Her heart raced at the prospect of detention, she daren't be late home, it was bad enough when there were extra papers to be delivered; her stepfather would never tolerate any further delay. His shift at the local lighting factory ended at two thirty in the afternoon and he bitterly resented "babysitting" his young daughters during the hour or so before Aimee returned. Aimee often wondered why a man such as her stepfather would ever have chosen to have a family. And God only knew what had possessed her mother to conceive his children.

"Aimee!" Miss Fletcher had finally run out of patience. "That's it: detention!"

It was the last straw. Aimee stared hard at her desk, willing the tears not to fall.

Again the tittering and shuffling as once more Aimee bore the brunt of their amusement until the bell intruded upon the class's enjoyment and Aimee's misery.

"Aimee." Miss Fletcher raised her eyebrow and motioned for her pupil to approach her desk. Her manner softened slowly however as she took in the pale and drawn features of the young girl, who, at fifteen, looked to have the weight of the entire world on her shoulders.

"I'm sorry, Miss. I, er, I've just . . . "

"Aimee, you can do better than this. You're a bright girl."

Aimee stared at the poised young woman in front of her, probably a mere decade older. She watched her lips, with just a hint of lipstick, her sharp eyes, full of expression and hope for the future – her students' as well as her own.

"Well, Aimee, what do you say?"

"I, I dunno, Miss."

"I'm trying to help you, Aimee."

10

"I know Miss." If only she could.

"Take the book and get the work done at home. Bring it to me tomorrow break time."

Aimee breathed a sigh of relief. "Thanks, Miss."

Miss Fletcher watched Aimee's thin frame hurrying from the room. Instinctively, she knew that all was not well with Aimee Parkinson. She made a mental note to have a chat with her form tutor, sooner rather than later.

Aimee stole a glance at her watch. If she ran, she'd get to the shop no later than usual.

"Ouch!" She screamed as she took a sharp turn in the corridor too quickly and on the "wrong" side. "Bloody hell!" she let out an involuntary curse as she dropped her books.

"Here, let me help . . . ow!"

The two heads collided as they both reached down towards the fallen item. Aimee felt hot tears of frustration filling her eyes. Stupid, bloody boy. She wished he would just go away. Jack Davis sensed the state she was in and quietly handed her her belongings.

"Sorry" he mumbled, "just trying to help."

"Well, don't bother." She spat almost venomously. She ignored his hurt expression. "Arsehole." She muttered under her breath.

He threw her a look of exasperation. Who did she think she was? She was the one rushing blindly round corners. *He* was trying to help *her*!

He looked down. He was still holding her English textbook. So she was a swot, or maybe the extra work was not voluntary and that was why she was so angry.

"Look," he began softly, "you seem in a bit of a state. Are you okay?"

Aimee glared at Jack before snatching the book and continuing with a run out of the double doors and towards the school gate.

Her stepfather would be livid.

Jack watched Aimee's hasty departure. Strange girl. He knew her vaguely, they had been in the same English group in year seven. He remembered her as being extremely withdrawn, sullen even. He had never quite understood why she was not more popular. She could be quite pretty if she did something with herself although her clothes were awful, obviously second hand and her hair, well, he would not be surprised if she cut it herself.

He felt sorry for her. He wasn't exactly popular himself, never had been. He had always been "on the edge", never really part of any crowd, let alone the "in" crowd. He was always the last to be chosen for team games, only invited to parties by the lads whose mothers felt sorry for him. He was the only child of a couple who were older than the average teenager's parents. Kath had been forty-five before conceiving for the first time and her husband, Des, at fifty, had long since stopped believing he had it in him. Jack had brought some major changes to their lives. They had done their best to give him everything he wanted, but somehow they never quite got it right. By the time he reached his final school year, it was clear to them both that they had managed to produce a bit of a loner, never really into the right things, never wearing the right clothes. It seemed to them that he was not an unattractive boy but he'd always been tall for his age and he carried himself self-consciously, which gave him a rather gangly appearance.

That evening, Jack could not get Aimee out of his mind. He wondered what it was that made her so nervous, so . . . so desperate looking.

The next day, he found himself looking for Aimee, turning every corner warily, half expecting to literally bump into her again.

"Aimee!" Finally, at the end of the day, he spotted her, hurrying towards the school gate.

Surprised to hear her name, Aimee turned.

"Oh!" she said dully, "It's you!"

"Jesus! What happened to your eye?"

Aimee's hand flew to her face defensively. "It's nothing, just bumped into the door."

"You should be a bit more careful, running round corners," he offered lightly.

Aimee's lashes lowered, contemptuous of his light-heartedness. She turned away and continued quickly on.

"Hey! No! Aimee, wait!"

"Wow! Look out, Jack's after a piece of Aimee Parkinson!"

George Maccleton was the loudest mouth in his class and he rarely missed an opportunity to mock the sensitive Jack. Swiftly, he was at jack's side.

"Fiver says you can't get her on a date on Friday." He nudged his classmate roughly.

Uncharacteristically impetuous, Jack thrust his hand forward defiantly, shaking on the bet.

George's cronies were in uproar as the pair eyed each other scornfully before Jack turned and made a solitary departure from the raucous group. "Hey, Jacky, don't forget Friday night. . . I'll collect me fiver on Monday morning . . . no rush!" he sneered.

Jack cursed as he realised Aimee had now disappeared from sight but realised thankfully that she would not have witnessed the exchange.

Aimee was surprised to see Jack again as she dumped her newspaper bag on the counter. He almost forgot to pick up the chewing he was buying and his eagerness to speak to her did not escape her attention. He caught up with her as she strode across the precinct.

13

"Aimee! Wait!"

She turned towards him, unsmiling.

He waited for her to say something and she allowed him to wait.

"Look, Aimee," God, this was awful. He felt idiotic. He knew he was blushing. "I mean. . . I er was wondering if you . . . ". He coughed, embarrassed, "I mean . . . " He saw her glance swiftly at her watch and sensed her desperation to get away from him. His shoulders slumped in defeat.

She turned away, her thoughts already on what her stepfather's mood would be.

"Aimee!" he called after her desperately. "I'll be at the youth club disco on Friday night – eight o'clock. Meet me there . . . if you like."

His voice rose, relieved to have finally delivered his words, and in such a way that she had not needed to turn him down to his face.

That evening, the Parkinson household was unusually quiet. Sheryl had made a big effort to butter up her husband with one of his favourite dinners – shepherd's pie - and Jim, for once found no fault with his wife's endeavours.

After tea, Jim retired to his chair with a handful of cans and the two youngsters played peacefully in front of the welcome warmth of the electric fire. Helping her mom in the kitchen, Aimee found her mind wandering over the events of the last two days. She recalled the look of concern in Miss Fletcher's eyes as she questioned her about the bruise on her eye and the pitying look as she had handed her the textbook, an unexpected privilege that set her apart from her classmates. The same look she saw in their eyes when she was the only one not going on the school trips, the only one without the "right" trainers, the list was endless. Always, Aimee was the odd one out.

Her thoughts turned idly to Jack and she sighed inwardly. Had he really asked her for a date? Well, it was as good as a date. Aimee had never been asked out before and the thought caused her a strange quiver of excitement in spite of herself. She wondered what she thought of him. Did she fancy him? Did it matter? She was hardly in a position to be fussy.

"You okay, love?" Her mother was normally too wrapped up in her own problems to notice anyone else's and she caught her daughter by surprise. Aimee felt the blush rise to her cheeks. Mumbling something about her homework, she slipped quietly towards the stairs. She paused fleetingly to look back at her mother. A vision of skin and bone, hunched over the sink. God help us, she reflected and God forbid I should ever get involved with a bloke if that's what they did for you.

For once, Aimee completed her homework in peace and she packed her bag carefully, thinking of the times too numerous to mention that she arrived at school with completely the wrong set of books.

The following day, Miss Fletcher again asked Aimee to stay behind but this time her face was smiling as she flicked through Aimee's neat and up-to-date work.

"Well done, Aimee."

Aimee's eyes caught the diamond solitaire on her teacher's wedding finger as she closed her mark book with satisfaction. She imagined her teacher's fiancé, probably slightly older, handsome, clever and with a bright future ahead of him.

They would make a good looking pair, Aimee had no doubt. They would buy a smart looking house and a car, which would be cleaned every Sunday. Their children would grow up secure in the knowledge that they were loved . . . and safe. Aimee longed to be safe.

"Aimee." Miss Fletcher touched her arm gently. She widened her eyes emphatically.

"Aimee," she sighed, "you're miles away."

"Nothing, Miss, I mean, I was listening . . . honest."

"Look," her teacher continued firmly, "I know things can be difficult sometimes. Just try to keep up Aimee . . . it'll be worth it in the end."

Aimee shuffled uneasily. How could she know? How could she possibly know? "Can I go now, Miss?"

Chapter Two

Friday night arrived and with it a belly full of butterflies as Aimee contemplated the possibility of showing up at the youth centre disco. Would he be there? The previous evening had been eventful, as Thursdays often were. Jim had drunk the last of his beer money and to make matters worse, Sheryl had arrived home slightly late. "Maggie was off." She had explained feebly. "I had to do extra."

"I'll give you bloody extra." Jim had spat nastily, spilling his hot coffee as he moved threateningly towards his wife.

It had been seven o'clock before Sheryl had started the evening meal. Kayleigh and Stacey had sat, pale faced, their empty stomachs filled with fear. Even as she made the simple preparations, Jim criticised his wife's attempts and when he had exhausted every avenue of her lack of culinary skill, he moved on to her inadequacy as a housekeeper.

"Call yerself a bloody cleaner!" He ranted, sweeping his hand across the windowsill, bringing the sorry assortment of already cracked and chipped ornaments to the floor.

Aimee tried to keep her young sisters' minds on the jigsaw puzzle, which lay before them. Bravely, she turned up the television in an attempt to protect the young girls, whilst, at the same time, straining her ears, visualising the scene which would await them in the kitchen.

But things were often quieter on Fridays and later the slam of the front door confirmed Jim's departure. With money in his pocket again, he whistled brightly as he strode down the short garden path and called a cheerful "Good evening" to a neighbour a few doors down.

Inside the small living room, the atmosphere of thick tension gave way to a depressing quiet. Aimee stole a glance towards the clock. It was almost eight thirty. That solved her dilemma at least; there was no point in even thinking about the youth club disco. Eight o'clock he'd said. She'd had no intention of going anyway, she assured herself, trying to ignore the niggling twinge of disappointment.

"Who on earth can that be?" Sheryl fidgeted nervously at the sound of someone knocking the front door.

"I'll go." Aimee was already on her feet, her sixth sense causing her stomach to flutter with an uneasy excitement.

She opened the door, conscious that she was still wearing her school uniform. Jack stood awkwardly, a little way back from the doorstep, which had long since lost its last lick of paint.

He cleared his throat, conscious only of his own awkwardness.

"I just . . . erm . . . wondered . . . I mean . . . Are you coming down the disco?"

He saw her look back briefly into the dark hallway.

"Please," he added softly. "Could be a laugh."

She was fifteen years old. She'd not had many laughs. She tilted her head slightly as she looked through the darkness at his young, keen expression. He was not exactly Justin Timberlake but he was interested in her. And that was a first.

"Who is it?" Her mother was curious. They rarely received visitors.

"No one." Aimee stuttered and found herself blushing.

"Wait at the end of the road. I'll be down in ten minutes."

She shocked herself with the sudden decision and noted the smile, which spread across his face.

Sheryl looked up expectantly, awaiting her daughter's explanation.

18

"Mom . . ." Aimee's voice was hesitant, "Could I go out for a little while?"

"What? Now? . . . Where to? Who with?" Sheryl was surprised by the sudden turn of events.

"A couple of the girls from school." Aimee lied nervously. "Just down to the youth centre, nothing special."

"Well, if it's nothing special, why are you so bothered about going?" Her mother regretted her sharp retort as soon as the words left her lips. "I'm sorry, love." She looked towards her daughter, fearful of the trouble this sudden development in her daughter's social life could bring.

"Please, Mom." Aimee herself was surprised by the desperate tone of her voice.

Just ten minutes' later, Sheryl watched her pretty daughter leave the house. She had made it crystal clear that Aimee was to be back well before closing time. Sheryl sighed heavily, wishing it didn't have to be like this. It should be an exciting time for Aimee, she was young and attractive, she should be carefree, fuelled with love of life and hope for the future.

Aimee almost turned back before reaching the corner where she could see Jack waiting anxiously. What had possessed her, she wondered, to risk her stepfather's wrath? Maybe she was a normal teenager after all! Her lips formed into a nervous smile as she greeted her "date".

The disco was in full swing by the time the two slipped into the darkened hall, squinting as their senses adjusted to the flashing lights and the pounding beat of the music that seemed excessively loud.

Aimee stood awkwardly as she noticed a group of her classmate nudging each other and pointing in her direction.

"Come on." Jack commanded protectively. "I'll get us a drink."

They drank coke and shared a packet of smoky bacon crisps before tentatively joining the throng of adolescents who threw themselves wildly into the blare of music, which every so often would give way to an irritating crackle from the antiquated sound system.

Aimee had never enjoyed herself so much in her whole life, forgetting her troubles as she responded to the rhythm.

"You're a great dancer." Jack complimented her later as they made their way home.

"Thanks." The brief abandonment she had experienced was quickly displaced by her habitual awkwardness. Within minutes, she was plagued by so many insecurities. Please God, don't let her stepfather return before her. As if she did not have enough to worry about, her mind moved swiftly on to the question of what was going to happen next. Jack had shown nothing more than a friendly interest in her and yet, well, she had heard the other girls giggling and swapping stories. She feared that he would try to kiss her. She must be the only fifteen year old in England who didn't know how to kiss.

"I'll be fine from here." She blurted suddenly, realising that her house was in sight.

"What, no coffee?" He teased.

Aimee looked towards the house, cringing at the way the curtains didn't quite meet in the middle.

He followed her gaze.

"It doesn't matter." He assured her, moving closer.

Did he mean the coffee, she mused nervously, or the curtains?

A sigh escaped her lips. He inched closer. She could feel his warm breath against her cold cheek.

Jack felt sure that she would hear his heart racing. God, he must be the only fifteen year old in England who didn't know how to kiss! Here goes. His slightly parted lips met hers and their teeth clashed awkwardly. They each pulled away sharply.

"Sorry!" They blurted simultaneously.

Aimee laughed, wishing the ground would open up.

Jack laughed and they both relaxed slightly. This time his lips found hers and they kissed, a sweet, gentle, slightly hesitant kiss.

She was the first to pull away. She looked away. "I've got to go . . . "

He nodded. Had he put her off? Did his breath smell? Had he done it properly?

"I'll see you on Monday then," he offered hopefully.

"Yeah. Great." Aimee smiled as she acknowledged inwardly that he was interested.

Chapter Three

Aimee hated weekends at the best of times. Her parents bickered away the hours whilst the children looked and listened and pretended to play. The worst times were when the bickering spilt over into threats and then the threats gave way to violence. If they were lucky, they'd be sent upstairs after the first few blows. Not so lucky when he sent them out of the house, to the park, or to town. It didn't matter where they went, there was no joy to be found whilst their minds dwelled on the eventualities back at the house. Aimee knew that, as long as she lived, she would never forget the trepidation that filled her soul every time she rounded the corner which brought their house in sight. The sick hand of dread that clutched at her heart, the relief that there was no flashing lights, nor sirens. Not this time.

Following her evening at the disco, Monday rolled around slowly. Aimee had never packed her school bag with such enthusiasm. She could not believe her luck when she spotted Jack just ahead of her on the way to school. Happily, she realised that he had been looking out for her.

"Good weekend?" He asked brightly.

Aimee mumbled incomprehensibly. If only he knew. They walked into school together, each taking turns to steal a sly glance at the other, smiling slightly and looking away when their eyes met.

"Wa hey!" George Maccleton and his mates were quickly on the scene. "Show you a good time, did he, love?" Aimee recoiled in disgust as he leered offensively.

"Oh, by the way, Jacky," The pair were making their way past the group when he called them back. "Nearly forgot. I owe you a fiver."

Jack felt the colour creep into his cheeks. "It doesn't matter," he muttered dismissively.

"No, Jacky," George called, nobody can say I ain't a man of me word." He shoved the five pound note roughly into Jack's chest. "Any road," he added, "was well worth it." He roared with laughter and his mates joined in as if on cue. If George laughed, they laughed, whether or not they thought there was anything to laugh about.

"What's he on about?" Aimee asked quietly. "What's that fiver for?" Her voice had become suspicious.

"Forget it, he's a nutter .... he just owed me a few quid that's all."

Aimee was glad to get away from the unpleasant characters and thought no more about them as Jack moved the conversation back to the events of Friday evening.

"I really had a good time, Aimee."

Aimee blushed as she admitted that she too had enjoyed their time together.

"Can I have your phone number?" He asked just as the bell for registration interrupted their chatter.

"No!" Aimee blurted hurriedly. She thought quickly. She didn't want him to think she was giving him the brush off. "I mean, give me yours, I'll call you."

How could she tell him that they didn't have a phone at home let alone mobiles or internet? What on earth would he think? She thought of everything that normal families took for granted but were still alien to the Parkinson household – computers, wi-fi, satellite TV, mobile phones, I-pods . . .

"Hey, Aimee!" Jodie Lewis' confident and slightly mocking voice trilled across the classroom unexpectedly.

Aimee turned towards the unusual source of attention. She could feel her cheeks burning. On the rare occasions that Jodie Lewis had ever addressed her, it had normally been in order to provide the class with her idea of entertainment.

"You goin' out with Jack Davis?"

Silent suspense hung over the classroom as they all awaited her answer.

Miss Fletcher looked up sharply. Aimee fiddled with her pen.

"Getting pretty intimate at the disco weren't you?"

"Jodie, that's enough, bring me your book and let me see your work."

The warm feeling that she had hugged to herself all morning had gone as Aimee acknowledged that she would never be "one of them". Even if she did get a boyfriend, it wouldn't make any difference, they were in their last year of school, it was too late now for her to be accepted as normal. And bloody Miss Fletcher, she just made her feel worse, with her pitying protectiveness. As the lesson ended, a short while later, to the teacher's bemusement, Aimee tossed her a filthy look as she threw her bag over her shoulder and hurried towards the door.

It was lunchtime and Aimee headed towards the area designated for sandwiches. She was one of the first and sat down at an empty table. She gulped down one of her sandwiches; fish paste on white bread. She had no appetite. Feeling miserable, she spotted Jodie and her gang heading towards her table and not far behind, Jesus Christ, was there to be no peace, came George Maccleton. Aimee pushed her chair backwards noisily and launched the remainder of her lunch angrily towards the bin.

She could feel the huge swell of anger in her chest. She hated school, she hated her life. Why her? Why did it have to be this way? Why couldn't she have been born into a normal family? Why did her bloody mother have to meet her bastard stepfather who was hell bent on ruining all of their lives?

Aimee's inner frenzy was revealed in her walk as she stomped furiously and aimlessly out of the school gates. She had to get away, she had to escape.

"Aimee, wait!"

Already, she knew his voice. Startled from her rage, she came to a standstill, her heart pounding manically. She didn't know whether she was pleased he was there or not.

"What's happened?" Jack's voice was full of concern. Nobody ever spoke to her like that. To her dismay, she burst into tears.

"Hey, come on." She could tell he was embarrassed now, didn't know what to do.

She shoved her arm heatedly across her face, swiping at the errant tears, which continued to fall.

"It doesn't matter, leave me . . . I'll be ok . . ."

Jack hesitated. "Look, come to mine for lunch, it's just round the corner. C'mon Mum and Dad won't be back for ages."

It sounded tempting and she was ever so slightly curious to see where he lived. She nodded, sniffing quickly to prevent the fall of further tears. Her heart sank as they approached Jack's home; it was the total antithesis of her own. She took in the pristine exterior, the polished doorknocker and the shiny windows. How could she kid herself that he could really be interested, knowing where she lived? By the time he led her into the immaculate hallway, the tears had returned. He guided her into the warm living room and somehow she found herself sitting next to him, the sofa luxurious and welcoming beneath her. Later, she could not quite recollect how she came to be in his arms, she only remembered how good it felt to be held in a comforting embrace. He stroked her hair gently, his words were soothing. He smiled down at her and her lips parted in a reluctant smile. He opened his mouth to speak but changed his mind and instead he brushed her lips lightly with his own.

She loved the feel of his warm body next to hers. She felt safe, protected. She didn't feel like Aimee Parkinson, odd one out, misfit, and loner. For once, she felt as though she belonged. Looking back it hardly seemed real, the unanticipated pleasure she had felt as his hands eagerly explored her body, which seemed to come alive beneath his touch and she had responded by touching him until they were pulling at each other's clothes, desperate to be together. The life that she loathed slipped from reality as she heard herself, dreamlike, cry out with the pain and the pleasure of him entering her body. She felt her head and her body explode in a way that shocked, frightened and elated her. She watched his contorted face above her, as his unchecked desire came to a frantic climax. As she felt his body relax beside her, she felt the tension returning to her own as she realised what they had done. She looked down at herself, her school skirt crumpled and twisted. She sat bolt upright, hardly able to look at Jack beside her. She looked at her watch in horror as she realised that they would be late for the start of the afternoon's lessons. She held her face in her hands. What the hell was she doing? She grabbed her bag and fled along the hallway. Before Jack had even sat up, she was gone, running urgently along the street. She arrived at the school gate just as the bell was ringing and slowed to a normal walk as she joined the throng of students pushing their way into the corridor.

It was not long before she was wondering why on earth she had been so worried about being late. The maths teacher was droning on about x this and y something or other and the room was far too hot. She felt sick; she couldn't think straight. She became aware of Mr Jenkins, staring at her impatiently.

"Sorry, Sir, I er . . . I don't feel well. . . " Her voice tailed off and she closed her ears to the usual grumbles about her not paying attention.

She thought the lesson would never end and even when it did, she still had double science to get through. By the end of the day, Aimee must have re-lived the lunchtime events a thousand times, remembering the comfort of Jack's touch, recoiling in horror at the recollection of what they had done. Never had she wished so desperately for someone to confide in; she felt as though her brain were splitting open with the confusion of her thoughts – so happy to feel wanted, so afraid of the consequences. She wondered if that would be it between her and jack, he must surely think her a complete slag; they hardly knew one another. She wondered how many other girls he'd done it with. At least he didn't hang around with anyone in particular, so the chances of him going around telling everyone about her were pretty slim. Or, maybe that was what it was all about, she thought with horror, he was trying to get in with the other lads and she was his conquest, his path to acceptability. With a sick feeling in the pit of her stomach, she recalled the fiver that George Maccleton had mentioned. What the hell had that been all about?

She rushed out of the school gates, needing to be alone, get her thoughts straight before facing the evening and whatever crap that might bring. Jim was not normally in the best of moods on a Monday, having had to work through his hangover from the weekend's binge. She kept her eye open for Jack, half dreading having to face him but knowing that if he didn't appear then that would be it, she would be certain that he had no intention of continuing their relationship. Relationship! Four days ago, she hadn't so much as indulged in an innocent kiss!

He was waiting for her just before the precinct. She froze, feeling foolish.

"Are you okay?" He sked sheepishly.

"Yeah, fine." She shrugged. "Look, Jack, I've got to go . . . my papers . . . "

"Yeah, I know," he answered quickly, "I thought I could give you a hand . . . that's if you want, I mean."

She smiled at his hesitation, wondering if she dared to hope that she had been wrong about his motives for what had happened between them.

27

She collected her bag and they set off together in silence.

"Look, Aimee, " he began finally, "about earlier, I er, I'm sorry . . . I mean, I'm not sorry . . . it was . . . great."

She looked sideways towards him and saw him redden. She too felt her face flush with embarrassment, wondering for the millionth time that afternoon what he thought of her.

"I er, I've never, y'know . . . before."

"Really?" she blurted. The fact that he was confessing this to her suddenly filled her with a huge sense of relief. She felt special, chosen.

"I just want you to know . . . I do respect you Aimee. I didn't plan it . . . honest."

She giggled, relieved to be freed from the anxieties of the afternoon. And yet . . . there was still the biggest matter of all, which she hadn't even allowed herself to acknowledge. She pushed the thought from her mind. She knew the risks, well he was hardly likely to have Aids was he? And she knew you *could* get pregnant the first time, but it wasn't likely was it? Not even she could be that unlucky. She vowed that she would not be so careless again. If it happened again and somehow, Aimee knew that it would, then they must be sensible. Jack would have to use something.

Jack revealed that he had not been back to school. "I fell asleep actually." He laughed. "My mum will write me a note, no problem, I just said I'd been sick."

"So where does she think you are now?" Aimee questioned incredulously.

"Said I needed a breath of fresh air. Chill out." Again, he laughed, his voice warm and friendly.

Aimee sighed. How different his life was from her own. And yet, it was the fact that they were both different from their classmates that had somehow brought them together.

"Shall I call for you later?" Jack asked eagerly as they dropped the paper bag back at the shop.

"No!" Immediately, she saw his wounded expression. "Shall I phone you then?" he ventured hopefully.

Aimee sighed heavily. She wondered how it would feel to have a normal life. Briefly she considered the possibility of confiding in him, telling about what went on behind the closed door of the place she couldn't call home. Immediately she dismissed the idea as being totally impossible, she would choke on the words. Even to her, her existence was surreal, comparable only to the worst TV dramas which, to most, provided inane escapism. Often, at school, she overheard kids complaining about their parents, bemoaning the restrictions placed on their freedom. How could anyone compare the hassle they believed they had with their parents with the hell inflicted on her by hers?

"Look, Jack, my mom's not well. If I can get out later, I will. I'll come to the youth centre. I'll have to go now though." She hurried away from him before he had chance to respond.

Several minutes later, she turned her key in the lock. The house was in silence. No comforting drone of children's TV, no background radio, nothing. She stiffened, the atmosphere was not good. She hung up her coat and tidied away her shoes and bag as she always did, desperate not to antagonise her stepfather, who hated their clutter. She stood at the living room door from where she could see Jim, slumped in his chair, can in hand. As she expected, he did not look round. A heavy malaise had crept through the house and Aimee followed it, up the stairs to the small bedroom she shared with her younger sisters. She whispered through the shadows before turning on the light, in order not to alarm them and discovered them crouched in the darkness beneath the shabby cover of the top bunk. She climbed the small ladder to sit beside them and gently pulled back the bedclothes, to reveal their tear-stained cheeks.

"What's happened?" Her voice, no more than a whisper, seemed to echo around the silent room.

At the sound of her eldest sister's gentle voice, Stacey, who had just managed to bring her silent sobs under control, felt the return of hot, salty tears spilling from her lashes.

"Ssh . . . . ssshh." Aimee tried to keep her tone comforting but she could not disguise the anxious edge to her voice.

Kayleigh was silently, repeatedly biting her lip.

"Did he hit you?" Aimee's voice rose slightly as her concern turned to anger.

Stacey's little body began to heave desperately as emotion again overcame her.

"Tell me." Aimee insisted, frantically.

Slowly, Kayleigh turned towards their little sister and lifted her jumper high above her tummy. Aimee stared, horrified by the sight that lay before her. Tears sprang to her eyes as the depths of misery to which their lives had sunk confronted her in the form of a dark, purplish bruise spreading across Stacey's shoulder and chest.

Silently, Aimee screamed at her stepfather. "Bastard! Cowardly, Fucking Bastard!"

She screwed up her face against the pain of what he had done to his own child, hardly more than a baby. Never had she felt so helpless. She knew, as did Kayleigh and Stacey, that there was nothing to be done. Nothing. She thought of Childline but dismissed it instantly, as she had so many times previously. What was the point? Apart from the fact that telling anyone, anyone at all, would enrage their father further, the consequences of the authorities taking over and the possibility of their being taken into care and most probably split up, was something that Aimee had attempted to explain to her young siblings over and over again.

"Aimee!" The three of them jumped visibly as their stepfather's voice roared up the stairs. Aimee hugged her little sisters before forcing an expression of indifference to her face. Quickly, she shot into the bathroom and flushed the toilet. Her stepfather must not suspect that she had been with her sisters and knew what had been going on. She seethed with anger towards him, murderous fury possessed her and it took every inch of willpower within her to disguise it from him.

Jim glowered as she entered the living room.

"I'm going to start the tea." Aimee informed him icily, anticipating his question.

"About bleedin time."

As she turned, Aimee could not help but mutter sarcastically: "Can't even have a pee in this house." Immediately, she knew that she had risked his wrath and the hairs on the back of her neck tingled in expectation of his attack.

But Jim's aggression had temporarily abated and his assault now was merely verbal.

Aimee steeled herself as he bellowed behind her: "Cheeky, bitch. Mind yer mouth else I'll give you what for." But his voice tailed off as he muttered half to himself. "Fuckin kids, no fucking respect."

Relieved that at least he had calmed down, Aimee methodically began to peel potatoes at the sink, her heart heavy and her mind filled with the horrible picture of Stacey's bruises. She did not even know what the little girl had done to incite him. It didn't matter. Nothing. Nothing excused him. He was the lowest of the low. She wished, as she did almost daily, that God, or the Devil, would take him from them, release them from the clutches of his insanity.

That evening, Jim remained quiet and, to their regret, in the house. He demanded his meal on a tray in front of the fire whilst the three children and their mother sat in virtual silence in the cold kitchen, their nerves shattered and their mood despondent. After silently helping her mother to clear up, Aimee followed Kayleigh and Stacey upstairs. Full of love and the desire to protect them, she cuddled them and read to them before putting them to bed. She took her school books to the kitchen table and stared at her homework. As yet, their mother knew nothing of her husband's act of violence towards their daughter and Aimee wondered whether it was better that she were kept in ignorance. There were times when Sheryl's timidity and fear gave way to a reckless reproach but her attempts to verbally defend herself had always ended in further brutality and Aimee knew that there was no good to be gained from involving their mother.

It was not long before Jim appeared in search of more beer and he glared at Aimee long and hard, willing her to challenge him. She felt his eyes on her, her body taut with tension. When she did not give him the satisfaction of meeting his gaze, he approached her unsteadily. The beer on his breath filled Aimee with disgust. Finally, she raised her eyes that could no longer conceal her hatred. She thought he would strike her and steeled herself for his blow but instead he gave a hollow laugh. He leaned towards her and she froze. Aimee wished that he had hit her because his next action repulsed her more greatly than his fist could ever have, although the physical pain would have been worse. He lowered his body towards her and spat forcefully into her face.

* * *

Jack soon became accustomed to the times when Aimee stood him up. Like a grateful puppy, he simply accepted her attention when it was available. He did not understand her. The first few occasions when she had failed to show up, he had assumed she had changed her mind, that she did not want to see him, but after a while he realised that this was not the case. Whatever the reason for her staying at home without any explanation, he felt sure that it was nothing to do with him. It was clear that the Parkinson household was not normal; Aimee practically had a heart attack whenever he had mentioned calling for her or spending some time at her house and it was not long before he had learned that they had no phone. In fact there were quite a number of things missing from the Parkinson household which Jack took for granted; there was also no computer for example and no internet, no mobile phones and no music systems. He could tell that she became embarrassed whenever the conversation turned towards her family and where she lived – she never referred to it as home – and because he liked her, it was not long before he took the hint and stopped prying. He felt sure that before she had become his girlfriend, she'd hardly been out, apart from school and her paper round. Usually, they met up once or twice a week, normally at the youth centre, but Aimee always warned him that it would be like moving heaven and earth to get out of the house on these occasions and quite often she didn't turn up The one day when he could be sure of her company was Mondays. Mondays were special, very special. Monday lunchtimes at his house, they were just something else. Every Monday, come rain or shine, his parents would spend most of the day with his ageing Aunt Carol, his mother's only sister, where they would spend the day running errands and doing jobs.

After that first time, Jack had hardly dare hope that Aimee would have the nerve to be alone with him again. After all, the first time had just kind of happened, neither of them had planned it and to repeat the act in cold blood so to speak seemed way out of his league. Except that by the time they reached his house on a Monday lunch time, neither of them was in cold blood at all. Jack spent the morning watching the clock, burning with the manly desire to take Aimee in his arms and lose himself in the pleasure of her body. Beneath her rather shabby and ill-fitting uniform, Aimee's body had filled out in all the right places and flushed with excitement, her normally pale face was surprisingly pretty. In spite of her peculiarities and her unpopularity, Jack was quietly pleased with his girlfriend. He'd had to pluck up the courage to obtain precautions. Aimee had been insistent and of course he knew she was right but it was still nerve racking every time he used one of those machines, for ever worrying that George Maccleton would suddenly appear to humiliate him.

The teasing had gone on for a few weeks at school and both of them had suffered the cruel taunts of Jodie and George. But as the weeks passed by the novelty of the two loners becoming an "item" had seemingly worn off and they were mostly ignored, which suited the pair perfectly.

Jack was looking forward to the Christmas holiday, now only a few days away. He was no great fan of school and he eagerly awaited every holiday but Christmas of course had the added advantage that his parents indulged him even more than usual. He had persuaded them to invite Aimee for Christmas lunch and he was already fantasizing about the two of them escaping to his room whilst his parents and the usual cluster of ancient relatives dozed in front of the tv. Persuading Aimee, however, was proving to be not quite so easy as she fobbed him off with the now familiar mumblings about her mother needing her help.

For her part, Aimee was, as usual, dreading the Christmas break. Much as she hated school, and she did so more than ever this last fortnight when Year 11 were subjected to the tedium of mock GCSE's, at least school was a welcome release from the tensions created by Jim. The last few weeks had been especially fraught, with her mom vainly pleading with her stepfather to part with some of his beer money in order that she could scrape together a few presents for the youngsters. Aimee herself had long since given up thinking of Christmas in terms of receiving presents. Jim, as she knew, had a heart of stone and it was as much as she could hope for that they all got through it in one piece.

She wished that Jack would stop going on about her spending Christmas day with him. There was no way she had any intention of even broaching the subject. The last thing she wanted was to meet Jack's parents and all that entailed. He had finally stopped suggesting that he call for her or spend time at the Parkinsons and that was the way she wanted it to stay.

When the last day of school arrived, Aimee's spirits were at rock bottom. She was mortified when Jack presented her with a large pink envelope and carefully wrapped present.

"Jack," she had stuttered, her face crimson, "I'm sorry . . . I never thought, I haven't got you anything."

She tried to work out whether he was disappointed. If he were, he hid it well. It had just not occurred to her to buy him anything. She had little spare cash available; most of her paper money went on toiletries and school necessities and as Christmas approached, she always scrimped together whatever she could, in order to add to the few toys her mother managed to obtain for her sisters.

He smiled and pointed to the gift she was now holding awkwardly. "I hope you like it, Aimee." He kissed her warmly and she realised just how much he was starting to mean to her. She felt furious with herself for not thinking to buy him something, silently reproaching herself for her selfishness.

The few days at home before Christmas Day were quiet enough. Jim did not break up until Christmas Eve and the girls feigned normality with their mother, putting up the small, artificial tree that they had used since Aimee could remember. She tried not to think of the rich looking firs that she glimpsed through the windows on her paper round, just like the one she had seen in Jack's living room on their last Monday lunchtime rendez-vous. The lights had twinkled above them as they lay secretly in each other's arms, stolen, greedy moments of youthful lust which Aimee pushed from her mind whenever the memory returned to her. As she studied their own sparsely and cheaply decorated version, it seemed incredible to Aimee that she had entered into the forbidden, adult world of sex and all its emotions when here, with her family, nothing ever changed. Would she, she wondered ever escape for more than a stolen hour? It seemed impossible to her. Kayleigh and Stacey also snatched eagerly at the rare

35

moments of delight, shrieking with excitement as their mother produced cheap chocolate novelties to hang on the tree.

Peace on earth however did not reign long for the Parkinsons and on Christmas Eve, Aimee truly believed that it was Satan who had entered their household.

Jim stormed into the kitchen, fury bursting from his every pore as he slammed the door violently behind him, swearing obscenely. They had not been expecting him, he was due to finish at mid-day but they had anticipated that his first port of call would be his local. Aimee was at the kitchen table, where the little girls were delighting in their first attempts to make mince pies and the rare pleasure of being allowed to make a mess. Their mother was upstairs putting the place in apple pie order, desperate not to give "him" the slightest excuse to ruin their Christmas. Keeping the peace, as usual, was her sole purpose in life. She need not have bothered, Aimee reflected later, nothing she did was good enough – always it seemed that something beyond their control would come along to shatter their short lived tranquillity, the lulls were always before storms.

But this time, it was more than just a storm in a tea cup. Ranting like a madman, Jim cleared the table of "this shit" as he sent their baking tins scattering and clattering to the floor.

"Get out of my sight, you snivelling brats!" he rasped towards the little girls whose giggles, which had filled the kitchen moments earlier, were gone in seconds, replaced by stifled gasps of fear.

"Where's yer mother?" The question was flung menacingly towards Aimee.

"I'm here." Sheryl had quietly made her way towards the chaos.

"Are you fucking deaf?" I said "GET OUT!"

Jim lunged violently towards Stacey and Kayleigh.

"No!" Aimee screamed with equal venom and flung herself between her step father and her sisters. His fist caught her violently between her shoulder blades and she winced as she pulled the girls towards her, ushering them towards the kitchen door. The terrified children fled to the top of the stairs where they turned and sat stifling their tears as Jim's rage reached them and appalled them.

"Do you expect me to work all year round to come home to this SHIT?"

Jim filled the last word with the full extent of his fury and it was quickly followed by a terrifying smashing of crockery. Aimee held her face in her hands for seconds before summoning up the strength to comfort her sisters. The three of them held each other silently, each of them willing the nightmare to be over. Aimee's emotions see-sawed from despair and resignation to hateful and murderous loathing. After a long half hour of Jim's ranting and their mother's whimpering, they heard the back door slam and an eerie silence filled the house. Kayleigh looked fearfully towards her elder sister.

"Come on." Aimee whispered, motioning the two towards their bedroom. She held her fingers to her lips. "Sshh." She stroked Stacey's hair with a reassurance that she wished she felt. Carefully, Aimee tiptoed down the stairs and listened carefully before rounding the corner into the small hallway. Through the open door she could see Sheryl slumped over the kitchen table, surrounded by broken crockery. The kitchen floor was littered with utensils, bits of pastry, broken glass, mince meat . . .

There was no sign of Jim. Aimee hastened towards her mother who had not stirred at the sound of her daughter's approach.

"Mom . . . " Aimee could not keep the tremor from her voice. Her hand shook as she reached towards Sheryl's thin shoulder, her cardigan splattered with food. Her daughter felt the small rise and fall of her breathing and realised that her biggest emotion was relief.

"Mom. . . are you all right?" the question seemed ludicrous to her, of course she was not all right. But what else was there to say?

Aimee tasted the salt of her tears as they spilled over her lips. She sat carefully beside her mother on the battered kitchen bench and placed her arms protectively around the woman who should have been the one protecting *her*, looking after *her*.

Sheryl turned towards her daughter, hopelessness and shame overwhelming her as she saw the expression on Aimee's face turn from concern to horror as she took in the bloody lip and the ugly purple bruises that were her eyes. The front of her blouse was ripped open and there were heavy marks across her chest. Aimee felt the bile rise in her mouth and her bowels heaved. She ran to the toilet.

Jim did not return that day. Nor the next. Christmas day, for Aimee, her mother and her sisters was the worst they had known. Sheryl's battered face served as a constant reminder of their misery. They opened their few gifts joylessly, listening with dread for the sound of his return, glad that he was out of their way, half wanting him to walk in so that they would at least know what mood he was in.

"Should I cook the turkey?" Sheryl raised the question pathetically.

Aimee shrugged, what did she care? She could not eat. She had retched at the very idea of breakfast and waves of nausea had continued to wash over her. But then she considered the possibility of his returning, expecting his meal and so silently she had prepared the vegetables. She hated sprouts. Jim loved them. Love. Jim. Two words had never been so far apart, in every respect – he was incapable of loving and how could anyone love him? What, in God's name had possessed her mother? Hatefully, she sliced the end off each vegetable, pulling the outer leaves cruelly away. Another wave of nausea gripped her and she fled, heaving, towards the bathroom.

Finally, late in the afternoon, the four of them sat down forlornly to eat their meal and Sheryl produced the cheap, gaudy crackers with a forced, high-pitched laugh.

"Is he coming back?" Kayleigh voiced the question tentatively, her voice full of fear.

"I don't want him to come back." Stacey declared conspiratorially. "*I hate him.*"

"I do too." Kayleigh looked from Aimee to her mother, seeking their approval. "All he does is hurt us. I don't like it."

Aimee's thoughts drifted back over what her mother had told her yesterday as she had bathed her face. Jim had been laid off, permanently. The consequences were disastrous. Apart from the actual financial implications, the idea of Jim with nothing to occupy him all day filled her with horror. He would drink what ever money they had, that was for sure, and God only knew what it would do to his temper.

Aimee looked pitifully at her mother and the two young girls. Hopelessness and despair filled her heart. She craved peace. Her own childhood had been ruined, there was nothing that could be done to change that, but as she watched Kayleigh and Stacey picking over their vegetables, their pale faces reflecting the stress of their little lives, Aimee wished again that there was something she could do to alter the course of their future.

Chapter Four

The immediate future for Aimee seemed to be increasingly stressful. Life under Jim's roof was hell, but that was nothing new. Now, however, there appeared to be no respite to be found at school. It was nothing compared to being "at home" of course, but it seemed that Aimee's days of daydreaming were well and truly over. Not a day went by when some teacher didn't go on and on about coursework deadlines, completed portfolios, modular exams and now that January had arrived, the summer exams were also looming large. Aimee had never been hardworking, she was always far too distracted, but deep down she suspected that if she were to escape the misery of her life then qualifications were the answer. There was no chance of her staying on after sixteen, Jim would never stand for that idea, but Aimee had a half considered notion that if she could get a job – anything that gave her some independence, then she would be able to go to evening classes, better herself, escape.

So, Aimee for the first time, started to work to her potential or at least she tried to. It was easier said than done to concentrate on anything when Jim was around and these days he was around a lot. Jim had returned, menacingly sullen, on Boxing Day. There had been no scene, no discussion, no apology. He was just back. Back in his chair, with no job to go to and no one to answer to, day or night. His drinking began earlier and earlier each day and by the time Aimee arrived home, his temper was generally foul. The weeks since Christmas had been depressing. The air of gloom was palpable and for Aimee, her mother and the two girls, treading on eggshells became second nature.

Aimee knew that she was stressed. She had not felt well for weeks. She had heard the phrase "sick with nerves" and knew that it applied to her. And she was so tired all the time, exhausted by the time she fell into bed most nights. Even Jack had commented that she was looking pale. The pair had continued to meet secretly at his house every Monday lunchtime but apart from that, there was little opportunity for spending time together. Aimee's sudden determination to pass her exams had seemed to rub off on Jack and he reluctantly had stopped pestering her to get out of an evening, which was just as well because Aimee knew that right now she did not have the energy.

It was Monday morning – P.E. The girls groaned as their PE teacher informed them that it would be hockey.

"But it's bloody freezing." Jodie Lewis was the first to protest.

Mrs Johnston glared. "We don't have foul language in school, thank you, Jodie Lewis."

Foul language!" Jodie spluttered, "Jesus Christ, stuck up cow!"

Mrs Johnston went red as she ushered the girls outside, insisting that Jodie stay behind.

The cold air assaulted Aimee's cheeks and she shivered at the prospect of forty minutes out in the biting wind. She looked longingly back towards the PE block. Perhaps she could waste five minutes or so in the toilets. The crowd of girls sauntered reluctantly towards the field but Aimee hung back. Mrs Johnston was looking decidedly flustered as she pushed open the door of the PE block. "And what are you doing here, Aimee Parkinson? You should be on the field with the others."

"I, erm. .. I need the loo, Miss . .. please." Aimee ventured hesitantly.

Mrs Johnston opened her mouth and closed it again. She had been about to take out her frustration with Jodie, who was lolling insolently in the doorway, on Aimee and she knew that would be unfair. She liked Aimee. "You're not supposed to go to the toilet during lesson time, Aimee." She reminded her, too gently. "But go on then, just this once."

"Just this once! Humph! That's a laugh! She's in the toilet half the day, that one," sneered Jodie.

"I know what it'd have been if I'd have asked."

Mrs Johnston sighed. Roll on lunch time, she had year seven all afternoon, at least that would be bearable.

Aimee did not hurry herself as she made her way towards the girls' toilet at the far end of the building. The changing rooms seemed excessively hot. It must be because it was so cold outside, they were never normally so hot, she was sure. Aimee sank down on to the toilet. She did not feel that well, she really didn't think she could face hockey. She bent over, allowing her head to fall into her lap. Apart from the faint buzz of voices, which travelled from the gym, there was an air of silence and Aimee relaxed, for a short while forgetting her troubles. Eventually she realised that she had been longer than she should have and stood up. God she felt awful, her head was so light and every time she opened her eyes all she could see was dazzling lights. She had to sit down again or she would fall down. Somehow she managed to pull open the door.

And then, something hit her on the head. A female voice was asking her if she was all right. Gradually, her eyes focused on Miss Collins, one of the other PE teachers, whose face was concerned as she offered her a glass of water.

"Have you fainted before?"

Aimee realised suddenly that she was sitting on the floor, propped against one of the changing room benches. She had fainted. How embarrassing. Still, at least she might get away with not going out on to the field. Miss Collins was waiting for an answer.

"No, no Miss, never."

Miss Collins was still looking serious.

"Have you eaten this morning?"

"Yes Miss . . . toast." Aimee lied, breakfast was the last thing she could face these days.

42

"Hmm . . ." Miss Collins pursed her lips. She supposed the girl was at that stage, girls often fainted at her age, it was probably nothing serious. Still, she'd have to inform one of the first aiders and the incident would have to be recorded in the medical book. Then there were the girl's parents, they would have to be made aware. She really could have done without this. She thought of the pile of marking she had been just about to sit down to; bang goes my planning time, she thought despondently. Still, she looked kindly at the girl.

"What was your name?" She recognised her but had never taught her.

"Aimee. Aimee Parkinson."

"Is someone at home, Aimee?" It might be best if you go home and rest this afternoon, you've had a nasty bump to your head. Someone probably should take you rather than you walk"

"No!" The little energy that Aimee had was forced into the small protest. Panic set her heart racing. No way on this earth was anyone taking her *there!* Good God, could you imagine the scene, Jim, drunk, answering the door to one of her teachers.

Miss Collins was taken aback by Aimee's reaction. Most kids were dying to skive off. She was puzzled by this one.

"Do you think you can get up?"

Aimee nodded and allowed Miss Collins to help her. The teacher led her towards the PE teachers' small staff room and guided her into a chair.

"You need to sit there for a while Aimee; here drink this."

Aimee took the glass of water silently, feeling self-conscious.

Miss Collins ran her finger down the list of telephone numbers above the desk and dialled thoughtfully. To Aimee's dismay, she realised that Miss Collins was asking someone to come over and "have a look at Aimee Parkinson, year eleven."

"But Miss . . . I'm okay, it's nothing, really." Aimee protested when Miss Collins had replaced the receiver.

"I'm not taking any chances, Aimee, you've had a nasty fall. You could be concussed, I'm not a first aider, you need to be seen by someone who is."

"Who?" Aimee asked flatly.

"I don't know . . . does it matter?" Miss Collins was beginning to feel slightly less than patient. Time was ticking on and covering her own backside was also fairly high on the agenda. "For goodness sake, you're not in any hurry to get out on the field are you?" She winked gently, a faint smile returning.

The "someone" was Miss Fletcher. Aimee didn't know whether she was pleased or not. There were worse teachers in the school, there was no doubt about that, but there was also something about Miss Fletcher which unnerved her. She had a strange way of looking at her, kind of knowing, and bloody nosey.

Miss Fletcher was satisfied that Aimee was not concussed but was not convinced that she should not ring the girl's parents as Aimee insisted.

"Honest, Miss," she said adamantly, "there's no-one in."

"Well, what about mobiles?"

"Yeah right", Aimee responded silently, as if they had actually entered the twenty first century. But she thought quickly; she'd had practice. "They're not allowed them on at work."

Miss Fletcher sighed.

"Look," Aimee added, "You could just give me a note and I'll get them to sign it so you know they've seen it."

Miss Fletcher looked uneasy. "Okay, that should cover it." Like Miss Collins, she too was only too aware of the consequences of not doing things by the book. "But you'll need one for your teachers this afternoon as well if you're staying in school. Now

44

sit here quietly until the bell goes and I'll come back and walk with you to the dining room. What have you got for lunch?"

Over her own lunch, Miss Fletcher contemplated the incident. There had always been something odd about Aimee, but now she could not dismiss the uneasy feeling that there was something else amiss and she was starting to worry about the teenager. She logged on to her computer and typed in the codes to search students' records. She would not feel happy until she had at least spoken with the girl's mother, made her aware of what had happened. She quickly found Aimee's file. No telephone numbers.

"Very unusual," she muttered, surprised.

Pat Brown, the school secretary looked up briefly a short while later when Miss Fletcher approached her desk. She appeared to listen distractedly, whilst Miss Fletcher asked if there were any records of parental numbers that were not on the system. She explained why she was looking for Aimee's number.

"Well, the Parkinsons. No number, that doesn't surprise me."

"What do you mean?" Miss Fletcher was curious.

"Strange family." Mrs Brown nodded knowingly. "Dad drinks and knocks the mother about from what I've heard."

"I see." Miss Fletcher paused. "Thanks anyway." She closed the office door, deep in thought.

"Oh, Julie!" She spotted Miss Johnston just about to turn the corner towards the staff room.

"Hi Helen." Julie Johnston was not eager to chat, she'd spent most of her lunch hour supervising the swimming club and she was starving.

"I was just wondering about Aimee Parkinson."

Julie frowned. It had been a long morning. "Oh yes, sorry, the girl who fainted."

45

"Yes . . . I just wondered, if you know, if you'd noticed anything strange?"

Julie shook her head. "Not really. She just asked to go to the toilet and that was the last I heard until Miss Collins sent a message to say she had fainted. "I don't normally let them back into the PE block," she added defensively, "but she seemed genuine . . . mind you, actually, Jodie Lewis did make some snide remark about Aimee always skiving off to the toilet. Not that I'd take her word about anything." Julie looked pointedly at her watch. "Look, I'm sorry, Helen, but I've not had my lunch yet."

"No, I'm sorry, Julie. Thanks for your help."

Miss Fletcher stood where she was for a moment. Her mind working overtime.

The following day, Helen Fletcher sat in front of her Year 11 group as they worked fairly quietly on their essays. Aimee was sitting by herself. She still looked very pale.

About half way through the lesson, she rose from her seat.

"Please Miss, could I go to the toilet?"

"Do you feel all right, Aimee?" Miss Fletcher's tone was gentle.

"I'm not going to faint Miss if that's what you mean." Aimee tutted.

At the end of the lesson, Aimee was tempted to try to slip out before Miss Fletcher noticed but she thought better of it. Knowing Miss Fletcher, she would come and find her, embarrass her even further.

"Sit down, Aimee."

Aimee did not want to sit down, she wanted to get out of the classroom, out of the school, away from Miss Fletcher and her knowing look. She sat down. Miss Fletcher had that kind of effect on people, they did as she told them.

"I'm a bit worried about you Aimee."

Aimee was silent. Her head slightly bowed towards her chest. She avoided Miss Fletcher's gaze.

"You don't look well . . . is something bothering you?"

"No, Miss . . . nothing." Inwardly, Aimee reflected upon the things that "bothered" her; the beatings she regularly saw her mother taking from her drunken bastard of a stepfather, the terror in which they all lived, the fear that one day something unspeakable would happen to her mother, or God forbid to one of her little sisters. Something that you read about in the newspapers or on the TV. Something that should only happen to other people, strangers, not to people you know, not to people you loved, not to you.

"Did you give your mum the note?"

"Yes, it's in my bag, she signed it." Aimee made no attempt to retrieve it.

"Is everything ok at home, Aimee?"

Aimee did not respond. Miss Fletcher breathed quietly.

"Have you made an appointment with your doctor?"

"There's nothing wrong with me!" Aimee looked up momentarily but meeting Miss Fletcher's sharp eyes distinctly unsettled her and she quickly looked away.

"How do you know if you don't go to the doctor's? Aimee, I've known you for a long time. You are not the kind to go skiving in the toilets, so why the constant trips to the loo? And fainting like that, you should get it checked out properly. You could have an infection. Or . . ." Miss Fletcher paused. It wasn't easy and she was conscious of the repercussions – parental complaints and all that, although to be honest, she considered that highly unlikely. "Or . . . could you be pregnant?"

Aimee pushed the chair back forcefully. Her pale face had filled with colour.

"I'm not pregnant," she hissed vehemently. "It's impossible . . . " Aimee was so angry. Who did she think she was? Bloody, interfering cow. None of it was any of her business.

"Aimee . . . come back! . . . Damn!" Miss Fletcher cursed under her breath as Aimee made for the doorway. "Aimee . . . please! I just want to help." The last words were muttered as if to herself as she acknowledged that she had totally failed, probably distanced the girl even further, the total opposite of what she had intended to do. Damn, damn and bloody damn.

Aimee could not think straight, her head seemed to be spinning and her legs were like jelly. Please God, don't let me faint again, she thought desperately. It was lunch time. There was no way she could face going to the dining room. She had to be by herself. She hurried towards the school gates, oblivious to the crowds of students around her, familiar faces, all of them strangers.

The park was practically deserted, it was almost February and it felt as though it had been winter for ever. Aimee made her way towards a bench. She was breathless with hurrying and anxiety; she was glad of the chance to sit, even though the cold had already bitten into her fingers and her feet were like blocks of ice.

"Could you be pregnant? . . . Could you be pregnant? . . . Could you be pregnant? . . ." Miss Fletcher's words rang through her head, over and over.

Deep down, of course, she had known; but now that the words had been spoken, the reality and the enormity of her situation had hit her hard, as hard as any blow from her stepfather. She was shaken, shocked, sickened and utterly terrified. Aimee and Terror were old friends, oh yes, she had known Terror, or so she thought. But this . . . this was something else. God Almighty, this could not be happening to her, not on top of everything else, there was no way she could face this and live through it. She imagined telling her mother. Sheryl would no more be able to cope with the news than she could. Sheryl couldn't sort her own problems out, let alone her daughter's. More than ever before, Aimee yearned for someone to turn to, someone to tell her what to do. Someone to look after her, keep her safe, make everything all right. She thought of Miss Fletcher, "trying to help", maybe she should have confessed, maybe it would have been a relief, sharing the burden that she had been trying to ignore, hoping it would go away. She dismissed the idea almost as quickly as it had entered her head. The very idea was insane; she imagined Miss Fletcher taking her to tell her parents! Jim would be outraged beyond the realms of all she had previously thought possible. She shivered at the thought of what he would do – to her, to her mother . . . to the life inside her.

For weeks, she had refused to acknowledge the truth, hoping, praying it was a false alarm, a mistake, clutching at every straw which came to mind and ultimately convincing herself that it could not possibly be true. She could not possibly be pregnant. But she was. She was pregnant, carrying a child. What kind of mother could she possibly be to a child? Childhood? She didn't even understand the meaning of the word! And what about the father? What about Jack? He had hardly seemed to feature in her thoughts, in all her turmoil he had been irrelevant. What could he do? What could anyone do? Nothing. That was the answer: nothing. She tried to consider how she felt about Jack – the father of her child. The answer too was nothing. She was numb now that she was faced with the consequences of her actions.

She had no emotion left that included the boy who had featured briefly in her life, who had helped her fleetingly to escape the misery of her existence and who now, she realised, had destroyed the only thing she had had, the only thing that had sustained her from one miserable year to the next. He had taken away the one thing that she had clung to, that she had believed no one could take from her – he had taken away her hope, her hope for the future. It was gone. Her future was gone. There was nothing left, nothing . . . nothing . . . nothing.

An elderly couple were walking towards her, their dog scampering ahead of them, yapping stupidly. Aimee realised that she had tears streaming down her face. She stood quickly, throwing her uneaten lunch into a bin. She walked quickly away. Aimee walked and walked, oblivious of the time, of the cold. Aware only of the pain inside her, the fear and the pain and the hopelessness in her heart.

There was a shelter on the railway platform. It was covered in graffiti and it stank but maybe it would be warmer and she needed to sit down again. She was so tired, so weary. But the seats were broken, one hanging from its hinges, the other had a huge chunk missing from the middle. The sound of the train was a distant rumble, which trickled into her consciousness and she closed her eyes as the noise came louder and louder. Clickety click, clickety click, clickety click. The rhythm was almost comforting. Nearer and nearer, louder and louder. The thoughts that had filled her mind were dispelled. Over and over her mind chanted with the clickety click of the approaching engine. Clickety click, clickety click. Suddenly, she felt herself being flung backwards; she gasped and let out a small scream as she fell away from the edge of the platform. Shaking, she squinted ahead of her, now fully conscious of the huge gusts of air being blown into her face as the seemingly endless succession of carriages roared by. Without warning, the last of the carriages passed, battering her with a final, brutal blast of air.

She was still half squatting on the cold, wet concrete. She had no idea how she had come to be so close to the edge of the platform, she could not recall walking from the shelter. If . . . if she had taken a single step more . . .

Aimee dusted off her hands and pulled her hair off her face. She made her way unsteadily back towards the shelter and seated herself awkwardly on her school bag. She wanted to cry but no tears came. The ball of emotion inside her was huge and heavy and Aimee gazed into the silent distance, the train having disappeared as if it had never been there. Was that how it was when you were dead, she wondered. Unseen and forgotten, as if

50

you had never been. How fleetingly was life gone. And how fleetingly was it made.

Aimee felt herself slipping towards a blackness that overwhelmed her. What was the point? At fifteen, there were no happy memories and now, no hope for the future. The railway stretched in front of her, endlessly. From here, you had no way of knowing where it would end, no matter how hard you looked.

Chapter Five

The automatic doors opened in front of her and she stepped into the cold, damp air. Her bag pulled heavily on her arm and she bowed her head as she fought against the dizziness that threatened to engulf her. Her spirits, never high, were at rock bottom. It seemed to her that she had walked miles before she eventually arrived at the bus stop, which had seemed so conveniently close to the hospital when she had arrived that morning. The street was deserted and she took a seat gratefully inside the shelter. She stared down at her boots, which had seen one winter too many and wondered how long she would have to wait for the next bus. Part of her hoped to delay her return for as long as possible but, at the same time, she knew that the wisest move was to get back as quickly as she could. He would have no sympathy of course. She had come to expect nothing which resembled compassion or humanity from Jim Parkinson. In all the years she had known him, he had never shown the slightest sign of remorse for anything he had subjected her to. And he would show no sorrow now. Nor would he allow her to indulge her grief. The loss of her child was irrelevant to him, except for the inconvenience it would cause if she were late home. Inconvenience which would invoke his rage and she could not face one of his rages. Not today. She looked hopefully, willing the bus into sight and when, eventually, it came, Sheryl rose and walked slowly across the pavement.

The bus driver looked through her in a manner which bespoke boredom and disinterest and Sheryl poured the correct change into the ticket machine before sinking thankfully into the nearest seat. She paid little attention to the small number of other passengers as she tried to come to terms with the grief that threatened to crush her. Counselling – they had offered her counselling as a matter of course, but she had declined. Words - that was all they could offer her and what good were words? Words would not bring back her baby. Her baby was gone. It was too late. Too late to change anything. Not that she had ever been in a position to change anything. None of it had been within her control.

Had she ever been in control, she wondered sadly. It was the twenty first century, women had it all, according to the television and the covers of the magazines she would not dream of buying. She was thirty three years old. She should have a proper job, a mortgage, a pension fund and child trust funds. She had had dreams, years ago, just like all the other young girls. Not too much to ask for surely – a nice house, a husband, a couple of kids, that was all she'd expected. Not exactly ambitious, but still way beyond what she had managed to achieve. There was a time when Sheryl had believed her life was going to plan. Aimee's dad had been nothing like Jim. They had been no more than kids when they first got together, Sheryl had just left school and had considered herself lucky to get a job in a local newsagents. Martin Fisher had been a regular customer, every morning he would call in for his daily paper and twenty cigarettes and she had been flattered when he had asked her out. From the first date he had assumed that they were an "item" and Sheryl hadn't objected, playing the field had never been an option available to her. They had drifted along together unremarkably and uneventfully until a year later she had discovered she was pregnant, just six months before her eighteenth birthday. She was not displeased, she was not the first in the area to get herself into trouble and Martin was not bothered one way or the other. They both knew that the council would find them a flat eventually and in the meantime, Sheryl moved in with Martin and his mother. By the time Aimee was six months old, they were nicely settled on the fourth floor (a stroke of luck when you considered that there were another twenty floors above them) of one of the local tower blocks. It was damp and scruffy, but Martin soon walloped the walls and with the addition of a few cheap ornaments and pot plants, Sheryl was proud to consider it "home". Money was always short, of course, and she found being a mother demanding, but Sheryl was fairly contented with her lot. She had never really wondered whether Martin was happy. She knew he didn't want any more kids and he checked her pill packet rigorously but he was not a bad bloke. He had never suggested marriage and so Sheryl had not mentioned it either. There was no real point, she reminded herself occasionally when the thought occurred to her, they were fine as they were. Martin enjoyed a pint on a Friday after work so Sheryl was not unduly alarmed when, one Friday, he did not appear for his tea. She never saw or heard from him again. Martin Fisher, Aimee's father, just simply disappeared.

For a while, it was just Sheryl and Aimee, who, at two years old, had quickly forgotten that Martin had ever been around. It was not so easy for Sheryl. Martin had not exactly been great company, but she missed him nevertheless. The days were long and the nights were cold. The weeks rolled into months and somehow two lonely years passed by, each day much the same as the next. A girl called Whitney, who lived a few floors above one day casually remarked that Sheryl should join her and her friends for a night out and Sheryl had jumped at the chance. Whitney was a single mum, with two kids by different fathers and Sheryl had thought her a bit rough. But Sheryl was lonely and when Whitney had suggested that she bring Aimee upstairs so that her babysitter could take care of the three kids, Sheryl couldn't resist the thought of a "bit of a laugh" as Whitney put it. Soon, their Friday nights out were a regular event and for the first time in years, Sheryl actually felt young and carefree, even if it was only for a few hours. She was not yet twenty-three but sometimes she felt ten years older.

It was Whitney who had introduced her to Jim Parkinson. He was tall, broad and handsome in a swarthy kind of way that appealed to Sheryl and she had been bowled over to think that he was interested in her. Before long he was staying over on a Friday night and gradually he moved in on a semi-permanent basis. As a lover, he was rough and demanding and expected things of her which she had never dreamed of with Martin. But his powerful build and his charming smile swept her off her feet and she told herself that he was a real man with a man's desires; she knew that she would do whatever it took to keep him.

Aimee was such a good girl, no trouble at all and Jim was pretty indifferent to her. At least her child's existence had not put him off altogether and so Sheryl asked for nothing more. Jim was a drinker and he had a lively temper that always rose to the bait when discussing important issues such as football with the lads, but Whitney assured her that he was "the salt of the earth" and she considered herself very lucky not to be completely on her own.

She blamed herself for her foolishness because it was only when she had told him that she was expecting his child that Jim Parkinson had first displayed the foul temper which was eventually to ruin her life. She had never forgotten how, lying in his arms in the early hours of one Saturday morning, she had chosen her moment. She had delivered her news in a loving whisper shortly after he had rolled off her slightly swollen body. At first he had been silent and she had smiled stupidly into the darkness, desperate to know his reaction.

"Jim … ? Are you ok? Are you pleased? Just think, we'll get a house when we have two kids. It'll be great … a garden and everything."

Without warning, his hands were around her throat and she thought that he was going to kill her as his fury erupted in a stream of abuse.

"You stupid, fuckin' bitch. Pleased! Why would I be pleased? Jesus Christ, it's bad enough having one bastard in the place let alone two."

She had struggled powerlessly beneath him, convinced that she was about to die.

"Oh I know your game. You conniving little cunt and if you think I'm going to spend my life shelling out for your fucking bastards, you can think again." He released his grip as brutally as he had taken hold of her and as her head fell back, helpless against the pillow, he slapped her hard with the back of his hand before rising in one movement from the bed. She froze in the darkness, gripped by shock and fear, as she heard him throwing on his clothes.

She did not hear from him for a week and she assumed that it was over. She was disappointed but tried not to be afraid. Whitney and plenty of others brought up their kids alone – why should she be any different? She might still get her house if she were lucky. Although it might take a bit longer. The bruises on her neck reminded her that she had had a lucky escape.

And then he was back. He walked through the door the following Friday night as though nothing had happened. Sheryl took Aimee upstairs to Whitney's as usual and they all went down the local just as they always did.

After a few pints, Jim had put his arm around Sheryl's shoulders and instructed the crowd they drank with to raise their glasses as he announced that they were getting married.

Sheryl did not know whether to laugh or cry. She looked at Jim's drunken smile, his handsome eyes gleaming and his huge hands gripping his pint glass. She rubbed her hand involuntarily over her stomach and she shuddered at the recollection of his hands around her neck.

Whitney was hugging her excitedly. "You lucky cow! Why didn't you tell me?" she shrieked. Sheryl had smiled weakly. Yes, of course, she was lucky. Last week was just one of those things, everyone lost their temper occasionally and she *had* provoked him, after all. She should have been more careful, waited until he was ready. Everything would be fine. She thought of Whitney, alone with her two kids, constantly looking for Mr Right. Oh yes! She was very lucky.

The wedding had taken place in the register office, celebrated in the local with the usual crowd. It was not exactly what she'd dreamed of, but it was more than some had had. For a few weeks, Sheryl had basked in the belief that soon they would be moving into a little house; she daydreamed about the new baby, which she was convinced would bring out the best in Jim. After all, it would be his own flesh and blood, not like Aimee. Sheryl dismissed the sadness and the guilt that she felt about the way Jim continued to treat her little girl. At barely five years old, Aimee fetched and carried for her new stepfather, eager to earn his approval. Never, ever, did he utter a kind word in her direction or show her anything but disapproval and irritation. Sheryl told herself that everything would be different when the new baby arrived. Jim would be a proper dad. Aimee could take his name and they would be a proper family.

From the very first violent twinge in the pit of her stomach, Sheryl and known she was losing the baby. It had started just after Jim had left for work and she had suffered silently all day. By the time he returned, the worst was over and she said nothing. The loss she felt was enormous but the fear of Jim's reaction was worse. Instinctively, she had known that he would blame her and that he would consider that he had been trapped into marriage. She remembered the mistake she had made when announcing her pregnancy. She would not make the same mistake twice. This time she would choose her moment, do nothing to incite his anger.

He had come home in an unusually jovial mood after "winning a few quid" on the horses at lunch time. Sheryl was mentally preparing herself, maybe tonight would be the right time after all. Over and over, she mentally rehearsed her speech, "just one of those things . . . nature's way . . . try again soon . . ." She tucked Aimee up in bed and walked into the living room, drained and exhausted by the day's events.

Jim looked up and gestured for her to join him on the sofa. She snuggled gratefully against his strong shoulder and allowed herself to relax into his body. Jim took a loud swig of his beer, his eyes focused on the television. He seemed not to notice her pale face, the dark circles under her eyes and the weariness that filled her body. But Sheryl did not blame him for his lack of attention. He worked all week and at least handed over enough for her to provide a decent meal every night and that was more than you could say for some men. She closed her eyes and snuggled closer, it felt so good to be held in his powerful arms. She tried not to think of her baby, flushed from her womb, life snatched cruelly away even before life itself had begun. Sheryl could feel the threat of emotion washing over her and when Jim's arm tightened around her shoulder, she felt sure that he would sense her hurt.

She froze as his hand clutched at her breast and his intentions towards her became clear. Oblivious to her troubled feelings and her drained state, his hand groped her body, his movements devoid of thought or sensitivity. Sheryl's mind raced as she confronted the course that events were about to take.

"Jim . . ." The word came out as no more than a whisper.

Jim drained his can of lager and let out a loud belch. He was ready to give her his full attention. He'd had a good day and it was about to get better. That was one bonus to Sheryl's pregnancy, he thought coarsely, at least he didn't have to worry about what time of the month it was and she had bigger tits! A self-satisfied smirk spread across his face as he leaned towards his wife.

"No! Jim! Stop!" Sheryl recoiled as his hand moved eagerly under her skirt. The beer on his breath nauseated her, she felt weak with fear as she struggled to free herself from his grip. She had to explain . . . Jesus Christ, this was not the way he was supposed to find out . . .

"What the fuck!" Jim shrank back in disgust as his hand felt the soft pad of material which filled Sheryl's underwear.

"Jim . . . it was today, the baby . . ." The tears spilled down her face. "I've lost it. I didn't know how to . . ."

Sheryl gabbled hopelessly as she watched his face fill with rage.

"No!" She was aware of him, standing over her and then his fists were on her face. Somehow, she turned and crawled into a ball, desperate to protect herself. She felt his foot in her back and she thought he would never stop . . . part of her hoped that he wouldn't, as her mind, too, crawled into a black ball of despair.

"Mommy!" Aimee's cry came from somewhere by the door and the beating came suddenly to an end as Jim turned towards her child. Sheryl raised her head just in time to see him send her daughter flying towards the wall with the back of his hand. Sheryl could taste her own blood on her lips as she begged him not to touch her daughter. She watched him take a further step towards Aimee who stood with her hands half covering her face in dread of what was to come. Jim raised his hand and Sheryl closed her eyes.

He let out a cruel and callous laugh as his hand dropped to his side before walking slowly towards the kitchen and opening the fridge door. He returned seconds later, pulling harshly at the ring on the can of lager in his hand.

"Get the fuck out of my sight, the pair of you," he hissed venomously.

Sheryl gathered her daughter in her own weak arms and somehow made it to her daughter's bed.

"Mommy," Aimee had begged in a terrified whisper, "please don't make me stay here. Take me somewhere safe."

"Shush, baby, don't worry. Mommy's here. Everything will be all right."

She cuddled her daughter to sleep and lay in the darkness. She had known he would be upset. Everything had gone wrong. Again. If only she had had the chance to explain properly. Weakly, she found herself making excuses for her husband; he was not a bad man most of the time. . .

Deep down, she knew she should have left him. She was young. Aimee was at school now, she could get a job. But somehow it seemed easier to stay, why should *she* leave the flat? And so the weeks turned into months and the months became years. Gradually, it took less and less to send him into one of his rages until eventually he needed no provocation at all. Mentally, she became accustomed to his beatings and neither questioned his motives nor made excuses for him. It was just the way things had turned out. Sometimes you got lucky, sometimes not.

Four years and two miscarriages later, Kayleigh was born and Stacey two years after that. By the time Sheryl got her house, she knew that she would find no joy there. She had stopped dreaming of happy families years ago. But she loved her kids and for their sakes never stopped hoping that he would change; knew that he would not.

And now, sitting alone on the bus, she told herself that, in a way, what had happened today was for the best. Though she hated and despised him, she acknowledged at least that you should not bring children into the world to suffer. Her heart ached as she remembered how she had felt the very first time she had held Aimee, her first born, in her arms, full of love and hope for the future.

As familiar buildings came suddenly into focus, Sheryl realised that the bus was almost upon her stop and she rose hastily from her seat, immediately regretting her hasty movement as a weak feeling washed over her. She clung gratefully to the metal bar in front of her as the bus jerked to a standstill. A few minutes later, Sheryl was walking towards her road, her heart heavy and her body weary. She prayed silently that he would be out.

"Mom!" Aimee reached out and took her mother's bag, ushering her into the hall as if she were the concerned parent.

Sheryl looked gratefully at her eldest daughter and reminded herself sadly of how lucky she was. Aimee was a good girl who did not deserve the life she had brought her into but she did not know how she would cope without her.

"Take your coat off, mom, I'll get you a cup of tea."

Sheryl raised her eyes questioningly.

"At the pub."

60

Sheryl breathed a sigh of relief. Kayleigh and Stacey who had been given firm orders from Aimee not to pester their mother, looked up as Sheryl entered the living room. At the sight of their bright little faces, filled with relief at her safe return, Sheryl finally gave way to the tears which she had bottled up all day. The little girls were immediately at her side and were joined swiftly by Aimee.

"I'm sorry." Sheryl whispered hopelessly.

"Ssh, mom. Don't worry." Aimee soothed her mother as she guided her towards the sofa, motioning Kayleigh and Stacey with a skilful movement of her head, not to get in the way. "Put your feet up . . . I'll fetch your tea."

Aimee returned to the kitchen and as she walked towards the table, her mind filled with thoughts of the child growing inside her against her wishes whilst her mother sat and mourned her own aborted foetus.

Chapter Six

Each day, Jack contrived to bump into Aimee and each day Aimee gave him the brush off. Initially, she had kept him at bay with complaints about school work and worries about their exams. He had begged her to come round to his house where he assured her they would study together. As it was, he was doing very little school work and no revision whatsoever. All he could think of was Aimee and wondered hopelessly what he had done to upset her, dreaming and scheming of ways to win her back. Soon Aimee had stopped even providing excuses, simply looking irritated by his presence whilst Jack tried to hide his hurt and disappointment. Of course, to make matters worse, George Maccleton was normally around to witness the displays of rejection and Jack was left silently incensed by the bully's taunts and mocking words.

He thought of the happy hours he had spent with Aimee; she had made him feel special and normal. Even if they were not part of the in-crowd, at least they were a couple and the knowledge of this left him walking on air. The icing on the cake had been that Aimee appeared to feel the same and, for a brief while, life had been perfect. Admittedly, there was something odd about Aimee, or at least her family and he was disappointed that she had been so adamant about keeping their relationship from her parents. They would be leaving school in a few months, he could not understand how her parents could expect her not to be leading her own life. Nevertheless, Jack had felt quietly confident that Aimee felt the same way about him as he felt about her. It had, therefore, come as an unpleasant and unexpected surprise when Aimee had suddenly begun to avoid him. He did not believe that it had anything to do with school work and suspected that it was something to do with her family. She looked increasingly tense and pre-occupied whenever he saw her but nothing he said would persuade her to open up to him, in fact, she hardly spoke to him at all.

It was the Friday before half term. Jack vowed that before the day was out, he would confront her and this time he would not allow her to fob him off with excuses. Whatever it was, he meant to get it out of her. He found her during morning break. He saw her face as she spotted him and her desperate bid to avoid him wounded him but he was determined.

"Aimee, I need to talk to you."

"Not now, Jack, I'm busy."

"You're always busy." His voice was reproachful and Aimee turned with a look that told him to mind his own business.

"Aimee, look . . . I'm sorry." He caught her arm and as she turned from him he held her more forcefully than he had intended.

Angrily, Aimee snatched away her hand. "Don't you dare . . . I said I was busy."

He was shocked by the coldness in her voice.

"Falling out again, lovers?" George Maccleton as usual was on hand and Jack was left feeling foolish and small as Aimee stormed off along the corridor.

He knew that he should let it drop. She was making it perfectly clear that she no longer wanted him around and he was making a fool of himself to continue to hanker after her. But it had been so good between them, so special. He could not accept that it was over, just like that, without a word of explanation. Carefully, he planned his next move.

Jack had accompanied Aimee many times on her paper round and knew the route she always took. There was a gully he could use to wait for her; she would have no time to get away from him. He felt sure that, away from the prying eyes of the other kids, he would be able to get her to talk.

He watched her approaching. She looked so sad. Why didn't she let him help her? He knew that she had enjoyed being with him.

Why was she denying herself the pleasure their relationship gave her? Girls were a mystery to him, there was no doubt about it.

He stepped out silently, suddenly blocking her way, appearing as if from nowhere.

"Aimee."

"You stupid idiot!"

Immediately, he realised the idiocy of his action as alarm swept swiftly across her face, quickly replaced by anger, which she directed towards him for the second time that day.

"I'm so sorry, Aimee . . . please . . . I just need to talk to you."

Her eyes looked coldly into his and he recognised the deep, deep sadness which frightened him.

"I don't want to talk to you, Jack. I don't want to see you. Not now, not ever."

"But . . ."

"Leave me alone. You're harassing me, Jack. Go away. And stay away."

He saw finally that she meant what she said. He wanted to tell her that he loved her but the words would not come. He felt foolish. She made him feel like a stalker. He turned and walked away and never had he felt smaller. He should have known that it would not last. He would just go back to being the odd one out again, the loner, the misfit, nobody's best mate and nobody's boyfriend. He felt a sudden surge of anger towards Aimee. What gave her the right to do this to him, just pick him up and drop him again. Bitch! If that was what girls were like then you could keep 'em. He'd rather be alone. He kicked a stone furiously and stomped angrily home.

His mood had not improved by the time he reached his front door and he simply glared at his mother who greeted him happily in the hallway. Kath Davis had said many a silent prayer of thanks that her son had never brought home any trouble and he did not seem to suffer from any of the usual teenage moodiness and awkwardness. He had never been rude to her. She did not recognise the person who had come home this evening. Jack glowered silently; he could not bring himself to speak as he turned and stamped noisily up the stairs.

"Jack?"

Jack slammed his bedroom door shut, ignoring his mother's calls. Damn Aimee Parkinson. Damn everybody! Stupid, bloody women! Why couldn't he have a normal life? He thought of his mother, downstairs, painstakingly preparing a nutritious evening meal. How many mothers wore bloody aprons? She was more like his gran. No wonder the only bloody girlfriend he had managed to get had turned out to be a psycho.

For a while Jack vented his anger with hate-filled thoughts of people he could blame. He stared blankly out of the window, a slow drizzle was misting up the windows and defiantly he scrawled his name in the condensation that was forming inside. That would give his stupid, old mother something to do with her life, clean some more bloody windows. God, he felt stifled, he had to get out.

"Jack! Where are you going? Jack . . . your dinner's ready! Jack . . . It's rain . . ."

Jack slammed the front door as his mother's voice tailed off behind him. He took his bike from the garage and pushed it down the drive. He knew his mother would be at the window, watching anxiously. Let her worry. He flung himself on to the saddle.

Jack pedalled aimlessly, the soft rain falling on his face. He pedalled away from the estate, away from the claustrophobia of his existence and thrust his anger-fuelled energy into pushing himself harder and harder as he fought to control his confusion and disappointment. He wanted to shout and scream and make

Aimee listen. He wanted her so badly it hurt and to his horror he felt salty tears mingling with the rain.

Slowly, after he had pedalled for some considerable time, his anger subsided. It was not his nature to be angry or hateful and it had exhausted him. Wet and out of breath, Jack found shelter under a large oak. He propped his bike against the gnarled trunk and leant against the saddle. He no longer felt angry, simply miserable. And lonely. He was constantly niggled by thoughts of Aimee. He went over and over the course of their relationship. Aimee had always been erratic in terms of when and where she could see him but he had accepted that this was due to her weird family. Now, he just didn't know. What was going on in Aimee's mind? What was going on in Aimee's life that had caused her to want to block him out completely? He was filled with frustration, knowing that he had no choice but to accept her rejection. Eventually, hunger registered itself in Jack's stomach. It was dark and he was cold. He wanted to be at home. Guiltily, he remembered the way he had behaved towards his mother. His poor, lovely mum, who waited on him hand and foot, doted on him completely. He imagined her, pacing up and down, peering through the window, worried to death by his uncharacteristic moodiness and knew that she would be ringing his phone, which he'd left lying on his bed, on silent. Only mildly irritated, he realised that he would be lucky if she hadn't already organised a search party. As he swung his leg over his saddle, he sighed heavily. His parents annoyed him at times and if he were honest with himself he was embarrassed by them, blamed them for his unpopularity. But he knew that he was their world and he did not want to let them down. He thought of his exams, which were looming closer and closer. If he did not take drastic steps to catch up on his revision and coursework, then he was heading for failure. His parents would be so disappointed. And so, he realised, would he. By the time Jack pushed his bike into the garage, his head was clear. Aimee Parkinson was history. Much as he wanted her, much as he wished he could help her sort out her unhappiness, she had chosen to end their relationship and from now on there was only one thing that mattered to him, passing his exams and showing the world just what he was made of.

Sheepishly, he walked towards his mother. He saw her biting her lip, relief flooding into her face, he knew that she was forcing herself not to ask questions or admonish him.

"Mum . . . I'm really sorry. " He put his arms around her small shoulders and hugged her.

"You're all wet, love." It was as much as Kath could manage.

"Is dinner ready?"

"Five minutes." Kath smiled at her son. "I thought I'd do your favourite . . . cheese salad."

"What?"

"Just kidding. Go and get those wet things off, you're dripping all over my floor."

Five minutes later, Jack was tucking into his mother's home made steak and kidney pie.

"Delicious, mum, thanks."

His father looked on silently. Des was a quiet man but not much went un-noticed and he was concerned by his son's earlier, unusual mood.

"Going out later, son?"

Jack shook his head. "Too much work to do. Exams to pass . . ."

He noted their approving looks. It might not be what the likes of George Maccleton sought in life, but it was enough for him. "Any more pie, mum? I'm still starving."

Chapter Seven

Aimee had watched him walk away.

"Jack . . . come back!" She had screamed the words silently in her heart and closed her eyes to fight the temptation to call his name, to let him take her in his arms, to tell him everything. She had to be strong. She would trust no one and she would need no one. Look where that had got her mother.

Aimee turned and continued walking, her paper bag weighed heavily on her shoulder even though she was more than half way through her round. She walked up and down drives mechanically, her mind elsewhere. No way was she going to end up like her mother, she would be dependent upon no man, let alone a man who abused her. She tried to imagine how Jack would react if she were to tell him that he was to become a father. They were to be parents at barely sixteen years old. In a way she wanted to protect him from what had happened. It was clear to Aimee that Jack had led a very sheltered existence. How would he cope with something such as this? She knew that he would not and she felt sure he would blame her. Even if he stood by her, she would dread that he would turn against her eventually for ruining his life. And how on earth would his parents react? He had told her how old they were and so the chances of them delightedly welcoming her into their family as the mother of their grandchild did not seem high.

Then there was the matter of her own family. Taking Jack to meet her parents had never been an option as far as she was concerned. She imagined Jim's reaction as she casually dropped in "Oh and by the way, we're expecting a baby!" She shuddered at the thought of what her stepfather would do.

"Hey!" The voice behind her startled her. "What do you call this?" The man walking towards her was waving a sodden newspaper. "I'm going to be ringing the shop about this. You're supposed to push them all the way through the letter box, especially when it's raining, you stupid girl."

"I . . . I'm sorry." Aimee reached inside her bag. "Have this one." She held out a fresh copy of the evening paper. Her heart sank as she realised she'd have go back to the shop for an extra paper in order to complete her round.

The man looked at the young girl, getting soaked for the sake of a couple of quid. He noted her worn shoes and her shabby coat. He shook his head, feeling pathetic. He probably wouldn't even find time to read the damn paper, anyway. "No, go on, you'll be a paper short. It doesn't matter."

Aimee nodded gratefully. "I won't do it again. I'm sorry, I wasn't thinking straight."

She turned and hurried towards the next house, the rain falling even harder, her bag feeling heavier than ever. She was so weary. She was close to tears, close to the end of her tether. In spite of the rain, she leaned thankfully against a garden wall. For years she had dreamed of a brighter future, believed that there would be light at the end of the tunnel. She had always felt that she was waiting for her life, her real life, to begin. Now she was facing the fact that this was her life and it was not going to get any better.

It was a miserable half term holiday, worse than any she had known. Her stepfather was still out of work, still drinking too much, his violent outbursts needed no invitation. Daily, he rounded upon her mother, nothing she did was right and there seemed to be no lull between the storms these days.

Stacey seemed to be developing a stammer. Aimee knew the little girls were deeply affected by their home life. She feared for their safety and their sanity. Since the abortion, Sheryl had been even more dependent upon Aimee's help around the house. She couldn't seem to cope with even the simplest of household tasks; cooking a meal for the five of them seemed an almost

69

insurmountable task each evening. Her nerves were in tatters and she was physically exhausted.

Aimee took the little girls to the park whenever it was dry, just to get them out of the house and for a short while they were normal children, delighting in the speed at which they sped down the slide together or shouting for Aimee to push them higher on the swings. Aimee, herself was wretched inside, fearful of the future and what it would mean for all of them. She had no doubt that Jim would throw her out when he found out about her pregnancy and she had no idea where she would go. Afraid as she was for herself, her thoughts however were still filled with the dread of what would happen to Sheryl and the little ones without her.

Aimee was finding it increasingly difficult to ignore her swelling stomach and if there had been anyone taking an interest in her then they would not have failed to spot her growing size. She could no longer fasten her waistbands, merely pulling up the zip as far as it would go and then hiding under a baggy jumper. She was conscious that soon the weather would be getting warmer and she wondered how long she would be able to disguise her bump under layers of clothes.

The weeks were passing more quickly than ever and Aimee felt as though she were sitting on a time bomb. She heard the teachers going on and on about exams and applications for college courses or sixth form or apprenticeships and it was as though she were on a different planet. None of it seemed relevant to the nightmare of her own existence.

It had been a particularly unpleasant weekend, three weeks before the Easter holidays. Jim had been in the foulest of tempers and there had been an almighty scene on the Sunday afternoon. He had surpassed himself in the tirade of abuse that he had flung towards Sheryl, and Aimee had believed that this time he would carry out his threats, that he would finish her off. She had lain awake long into the night, her body rigid with fear. Eventually, she heard Jim climb the stairs but Sheryl had not followed him.

Aimee could hear nothing but the ticking of the clock. What had happened to her mother? Risking Jim's wrath, Aimee crept from her bed. She knew the location of every creaking floor board and made her way downstairs as softly as possible.

Her mother sat motionless in the chair nearest the living room door. Her face was bruised and her clothing torn. A broken cup lay behind the chair, its contents splattered up the wall where he had flung it.

"Mom." Aimee fell to her knees beside the chair and placed her hand gently on her mother's hands, which lay still in her lap. Sheryl turned towards her daughter, but she did not appear to see her; her expression devoid of recognition or acknowledgement.

"Mom." Aimee's voice was soft but urgent.

"Okay, love, I'm okay."

It was clear to Aimee that her mother was not okay. She did not know what to do. Desperate thoughts passed through her mind. There was no one to turn to, no one to sort things out. The people who should be looking after things, providing the love and support that she needed were the ones who were wreaking havoc upon her life. Her stepfather was causing the physical hell and her mother was heaping a huge emotional burden upon her. What was she supposed to do? Her brain throbbed with the huge weight of worry and despair. Her own problem was beyond the experience of most teenagers but on top of that, she had the weight of her parents' disastrous relationship to contend with.

"Mom, are you going up to bed?" Aimee did not know what else to say. She thought of the brute upstairs, with whom, her mom was expected to share a bed. Aimee thought suddenly of Jack, how his arms had held her so lovingly. She could not contemplate how her mother could climb each night into bed with the bastard who was her husband. Her mother nodded and finally appeared to focus upon her daughter. "Go to bed, love.

You've got school in the morning. I'll be all right. I'll go up in a minute. He'll be asleep."

Aimee looked at her mother; she was filled with sorrow. "Night, Mom," she whispered, "I love you. See you in the morning."

Sheryl smiled as far as her bruised lips would allow. "Night, Aimee. I love you too."

Aimee tip-toed upstairs, carefully avoiding the creaking floorboards. She crawled back between the covers, jaded by the day's events, weary of her life. For a while she listened to the noises of the house, familiar but still somehow menacing. Eventually, stinging with fatigue, her eyes closed and she fell into a troubled sleep.

She dreamt of babies crying, her stepfather shouting, her mother screaming and her little sisters whimpering. Then, suddenly, in came Miss Fletcher, demanding to know what was going on and why she wasn't concentrating on her schoolwork. She dreamt that she was on the toilet, her swollen belly resting on her legs, the door opened slowly and she looked up in horror to see who had discovered her terrible secret. But before she could see who it was, the bell was ringing for the beginning of lessons, or maybe the end. The bell would not stop ringing. It was getting louder and louder and Kayleigh was shaking her awake.

"Aimee, wake up. It's the alarm, I can't turn it off." The desperation in the little girl's voice far exceeded the gravity of the situation. The unspoken fear of the alarm waking Jim was etched upon her pallid features.

Aimee was still wondering what Kayleigh was doing at school and inwardly panicking in case she had seen her stomach.

"Aimee!" Kayleigh's voice was urgent. "Aimee, turn off the alarm."

Aimee realised that she was in bed and that she had been dreaming. She reached out and took the clock, silencing its persistent ringing. She sighed, shattered before the day had begun.

Sheryl was not downstairs. Aimee frowned as she looked at the clock. Her mother must have left early for her morning cleaning job. She noted thankfully that at least she had cleared away the devastation of the previous night and she busied herself preparing the girls' breakfasts. There was no one to notice that she herself ate nothing. It was Monday morning and there was the usual rush of sandwich making, PE kits and book bags. It was normal for the necessary preparations to fall to Aimee. Kayleigh and Stacey were obedient and helpful but the air was tense, all of them anxious.

It was time to leave. Stacey had diarrhoea. They were going to be late for school. Aimee knew that her sister should be kept at home, but leaving her with Jim was not an option. Stacey was crying and complaining of pains in her stomach.

"Please let me stay home with you, Aimee."

"Stacey, be a good girl. You'll be okay. You'll feel better when you're with your friends."

"Please Aimee, you can stay here with me. Please Aimee."

"For goodness' sake, Stacey. Stop bloody whining at me! You're going to school and that's the end of it. Shut up!"

Stacey looked at her big sister, shocked by her outburst. Fresh and fuller tears fell from her eyes, her nose was running and Aimee crumbled inside at the pathetic sight.

"Come on Stace." Kayleigh put her arm around her sister, only slightly smaller than herself. "I'll look after you, I promise."

"I'm sorry, Stacey." Aimee cuddled her little sister, ashamed of herself. "I'm so sorry, I'm so tired. Look, be a big girl and I'll do your hair in a nice pony tail, that'll make you feel better."

Aimee dropped the little girls off at their school, feeling guilty and anxious. She looked back towards the playground, the other children were playing games, laughing and teasing one another, just being children. She saw Kayleigh leading Stacey towards a bench at the end of the playground and the two of them sat, holding hands, huddled together.

Miss Fletcher was looking at her, exasperated. "For heaven's sake, Aimee, you are supposed to be writing this down. You haven't even picked up your pen."

Aimee focused on the whiteboard and the list of exam questions which, apparently, she should be copying. "Sorry Miss." She scrabbled in her bag for a pen; the first one that she took out did not work. "Damn." Miss Fletcher was still watching her. "Sorry." Finally, she found a pen that worked and hastily endeavoured to catch up.

There was a knock at the classroom door. An undercurrent of chatter rippled around the classroom as Mrs Brown, the secretary, spoke quietly to the teacher.

"Aimee, Mrs Brown would like a word with you."

Aimee's stomach lurched as she scraped back her chair, a hundred possibilities as to why she was wanted racing through her mind.

"Don't look so worried dear." Mrs Brown smiled kindly. "It's just your little sister, Stacey, she's not very well and the school can't get hold of your mum. Is there a telephone number we could contact her on?

Aimee shook her head.

" A mobile?"

Aimee reddened. "No. . . it's broken."

Is your mum normally at home, Aimee? Only Stacey couldn't remember. I think she was a bit upset."

Aimee shook her head. "No, Miss, she's at work."

Sheryl had a variety of cleaning jobs and Aimee could not remember which particular one she would be at just then. She reflected guiltily on how she had shouted at her little sister that morning and sent her off to school when she knew she should be at home.

"What about your father, Aimee? Is there somewhere we can contact him."

Aimee bit back the desire to say that he was not her father. She shook her head emphatically. Whatever was wrong with Stacey, she would be better off at school than with Jim. "No, Miss."

Mrs Brown shuffled awkwardly. She had a list of jobs to do without having to sort out problems for the primary school as well. She sighed, in spite of herself.

"Miss, I can go and get Stacey. I'll take her home."

"No, dear. I don't think that's a good idea."

"I'm old enough."

"Yes . . . but . . . you have to be in school. . . it's an important time, year eleven. Look, go back into class and I'll ring the school back to see how she is."

Aimee returned to her seat.

"Aimee, I've copied this down for you . . . don't lose it." Miss Fletcher handed her a sheet of paper with the work she should have copied. "And here is the list of your exam dates." Aimee's stomach churned in response.

"Thank you." Aimee's answer was vague as she pondered what to do. It was PE after break, they were supposed to be swimming. Aimee was intending to scribble herself a note to get out of it.

She slipped out of the school gate, knowing that she could easily be caught on the CCTV; she was half expecting to be called back. She walked quickly away from the school and within ten minutes, was at the gate of the primary school where she had left Stacey and Kayleigh a couple of hours earlier.

Mrs Bentley, the secretary there, recognised Aimee and looked up in surprise. Aimee explained that she had come to take Stacey home, assuring her that she would be returning to school at lunch time, when her mother returned. The secretary looked dubious.

"You should stay in school, really, Aimee."

Aimee looked at the older woman levelly. "And who's going to take care of my sister?"

Mrs Bentley hesitated as she thought of poor little Stacey. She had needed one change of clothes already and the poor little thing needed cleaning up and putting to bed.

"I'll just have a word with the head, Aimee, wait there."

Aimee nodded, reflecting upon the absurdity of the situation. Apart from the fact that she would be leaving school in a couple of months, the reality was that she was the one who took the most responsibility for the two girls normally anyway. The other irony, which she hardly dared even to acknowledge, of course, was that she herself would be a parent before the exam results came out.

"Aimee, I'm sorry." Stacey rushed towards her, her arms open, her face full of distress at the trouble she was causing.

"Sshussh, shush, Stacey, it's okay, don't worry. It doesn't matter, I've come to take you ... home."

"But what about ... "

"Don't worry, everything will be fine." Aimee interrupted, conscious of Mrs Bentley, who was still looking on anxiously.

Aimee heaved a sigh of relief as she pushed open the front door. Jim's coat and shoes were gone. He was out. She smiled down at Stacey. "Come on." she said brightly, "Let's get you sorted out." Expertly, she had soon got Stacey cleaned up and took her to bed. "Cuddle up to this hot water bottle." she advised, "It'll help make your tummy better."

Stacey snuggled beneath the sheets. "I'm sorry for causing a fuss, Aimee."

Aimee smoothed her hair kindly. "It's not your fault, don't worry." She planted a kiss on her head and walked towards the door. "Call me if you need anything. I'll just be downstairs. It was as much security as she could offer.

Aimee did not quite know what to do with herself. It felt odd not to be at school when she knew that everything would be going on there as normal. She tidied away a few bits and pieces and made herself a cup of tea. She could safely bet that Jim would be out of the house for a few hours at least. Since he had lost his job, Sheryl had changed her cleaning hours and it was she who now picked up the little ones after school. Jim had decided that he was too busy "job hunting" to be burdened with this undesirable responsibility. In truth, he was normally sleeping off his lunch time drink by home time, in preparation for the evening's indulgence.

Aimee took out the pieces of paper that Miss Fletcher had handed to her that morning. Exams. She studied the dates. There were only eight weeks left before they began properly. How on earth was she going to concentrate on her revision? Miss Fletcher had been saying something about a revision timetable. Perhaps that's what she should do. Somehow, Aimee had to pass her exams. She had not performed brilliantly in her coursework subjects but it wasn't too late. Maybe she could scrape together a few reasonable grades.

Half an hour later, Aimee had drawn up a timetable which included all her subjects, placing extra emphasis on those in which she thought she stood a chance of getting a decent grade –

maybe English, history, geography and computer studies, she was good at that. From somewhere she found the strength to feel positive about her prospects. Obviously, she would be unable to work immediately, but she knew that she would be better equipped to face her future if she were able to prove to a prospective employer that she was not entirely stupid. Just unlucky. Very.

Stacey slept soundly and apart from occasionally checking upon the sleeping youngster, Aimee became engrossed in her studies, the house unusually calm. It had just turned three o'clock when Jim stumbled through the door. Aimee jumped, the tension returning to her stomach.

"What d'yer think you're doin'?" He slurred.

"Stacey's sick. I brought her home."

"And where's yer mother?"

Aimee frowned. "At work, I suppose. Then she'll be picking up Kayleigh."

To her relief, Jim merely grunted and climbed the stairs. He did not, Aimee noted bitterly, enquire about Stacey. Aimee hurriedly packed away her books. She wondered why Jim had expected to see her mother, she tried to remember what her mother did on Mondays; she couldn't recall whether she cleaned the pub or somewhere else. And did she normally come home during the day at all? She couldn't remember. She realised that when her mother arrived at the primary school, she would be expecting to pick up Stacey. She sighed as she remembered telling Mrs Bentley that her mother would be home in the afternoon and that she would return to school. Her lie would be discovered when her mother went in search of Stacey. She had no doubt that Mrs Bentley would be on the 'phone to Mrs Brown and she would be in trouble for not going back to school. She walked to the kitchen. Monday night, sausage, egg and chips. She'd peel the potatoes before leaving to do her paper round. Hopefully, her mom would be back by then so that she didn't have to leave the poorly Stacey alone with Jim.

It was twenty to four. Sheryl was not back. She would have to get to the paper shop or she would be in trouble there. She peeped in at the bedroom door. Stacey was still sound asleep. It would only be a few minutes, she'd probably meet her mom and Kayleigh coming down the road.

Sheryl was not coming down the road. Probably that bloody, nosy Mrs Bentley, Aimee thought with an annoyance that turned to a wave of anxiety as she remembered her mother's bruises. Sheryl had become a master of disguise, with make-up, dark glasses, scarves and excuses. Whatever it took to conceal the truth, Sheryl somehow managed it. Aimee trudged the familiar streets, posting the papers through familiar letterboxes. She was uneasy. Something, she didn't know what, was nagging away at her, causing her to worry. Worry, for Aimee, was a way of life, part of her everyday existence, as natural to her as breathing. But, for some reason, she felt that there was something else. It had been a strange day, but it was more than that. There was a sense of foreboding that she could not explain. She returned her paper bag with a heavy heart.

"Cheer up, love," Mr Turner, the newsagent greeted her, "might never 'appen."

Aimee managed a wry smile. Might never happen. That was a laugh. She closed the door of the newsagents and walked towards Deansfield Crescent.

"What's goin' on? Where is she?" Jim was bawling at her the minute she stepped through the door. Aimee looked around her, bewildered. Kayleigh was peeking nervously from behind the kitchen door. Her stepfather was pacing the living room floor, ranting like a lunatic, spit gathering at the corners of his mouth, his fists clenched in fury.

"I've had bloody school teachers round 'ere. Bloody interfering scum! School teacher bringin' back me daughter! Just you wait 'til she gets back. That's it this time. I've had enough. Enough's enough! Where d'yer think *you're* goin'? I' m talking!" He roared menacingly as Aimee turned away.

She eyed him evenly, quaking inside. "I'm going to put the chips on. Kayleigh, go and see if Stace's okay, would you?"

Kayleigh nodded dutifully and started to walk towards the stairs. She turned back and mouthed the words . "Where's mom?" to her big sister, her expression fraught with anxiety.

Aimee shook her head. She didn't know. She waved her sister up the stairs and attempted what she hoped was a reassuring smile.

The chips were on. Jim had emerged from the living room. Kayleigh had reported that Stacey was sitting up and was hungry.

"She'll just have to have dry biscuits, I'm afraid, 'til we're sure her tummy's better."

Kayleigh tugged at Aimee's sleeve as she placed three plain biscuits on a plate. Again she mouthed the words "Where's mom?"

"I don't know." Aimee whispered. "Go on, take these to your sister and do some colouring or something with her until I call you for your tea."

"Shall I bring your tea in here?" Aimee spoke quietly to Jim, who was sitting sullenly in his chair.

He grunted his response and Aimee brought him his tray of food, which he took from her without thanks. Aimee shuddered inwardly as his huge, ugly, dangerous fists neared hers. She was turning to walk away when he called her back.

"Oy!" He waved his knife towards her to emphasise his point. "If you know what the bloody hell's goin on 'ere, then I want to know."

"I don't know anything." And if I did, she added silently, I wouldn't tell you, you pig.

Sheryl did not return that evening. Aimee put the little girls to bed. Stacey was much brighter and she had at least kept the biscuits inside her but this latest development filled the three of them with wordless terror.

"When's mommy coming back?" Stacey finally whispered the question tearfully as Aimee stroked her hair and said goodnight.

"I don't know, sweetheart. You're just going to have to be good girls until she does. Try not to worry. I'll look after you."

Aimee sobbed herself to sleep, gripped by fear and exhaustion, her stomach an enormous knot of tension. She awoke with Jim's hand on the back of her head as he yanked her face towards his. She breathed in the smell of his beery breath; he repulsed her.

"Where is she you little bitch?"

Aimee attempted to twist herself free of his vicious grip. "I've told you," she hissed quietly, fearful of waking her sisters, "I don't know." He was hurting her head but she faced him squarely. "But I tell you this . . . if you're expecting me to look after these two," she inclined her head towards the bunk bed which contained her two sleeping sisters, "and you and this house . . . then you'd better leave me alone. And if you don't want social services round here as well as school teachers, you'd better sort yourself out and pick your daughters up from school every day until she gets back."

He jerked her head further backwards; he was pulling her hair. "Don't you threaten me, you cheeky little bitch." But his grip loosened and he retreated from the room. He had heard her and he realised that he had no choice but to leave her alone.

Stacey did not complain the following morning when Aimee packed her off to school. The little girls said little. Their faces said it all. Aimee had hardly slept. She had lain in the darkness, trembling inside, barely able to believe that she had stood up to

Jim. But she knew that there had been no choice. God knows what had happened to her mother, but the only way she was going to be able to cope was if he left her alone. If he thought that she was going to replace her mother as a punch bag as well as everything else, then he could think again. She had reflected back to the previous night and she rebuked herself for falling asleep before Sheryl had climbed the stairs. What could have happened afterwards? She asked herself over and over. Could Jim have gone back down? He seemed genuinely shocked by her disappearance but could it be an act? She wouldn't put anything past him. But what could he have done with her . . . Aimee almost retched at the thoughts which were colliding in her brain. If she'd just walked out, where could she have gone? Sheryl had had very little to do with her parents, gradually falling more and more out of touch over the years. Aimee could barely remember them and they had never seen Kayleigh or Stacey. Then there was an older sister, Aunty Margaret. Aimee remembered her as a miserable, chain-smoking woman who would for ever be dishing out advice to Sheryl on what she should or should not be doing. Again, Aimee had not seen her since she was small. Jim had put a stop to family visits long ago. The Parkinsons didn't go visiting and visitors were not welcome. As for friends, as far as Aimee knew, Sheryl just didn't have any. She'd never even possessed a mobile phone never mind belonged to any social networking sites.

Aimee had thought back to the previous evening and her mother's state of mind. She imagined how she would feel in her position, ground down by years of abuse. What did she have to look forward to? The sickening thought of what her mom could have done to herself had haunted Aimee throughout the night. Aimee could not face losing her mom. Sheryl had failed as a mother in so many ways but she loved her children and Aimee had always adored her, idolised her. The hurt inside at the prospect of never seeing her mother again, never feeling her arms around her again, was not just mental, she could actually feel the pain of it tearing at her insides. She did not blame her mom if she had walked out. It was beyond credibility that she had stayed for so long. But Aimee could not accept that Sheryl would be happy without her children.

Confused and fretful, Aimee had stayed awake long into the night and as she prepared breakfast for her sisters, their sad, brave expressions tore at her heart and Aimee wondered if life could possibly get any worse.

* * *

The class was silent as they studied a past paper. Aimee remembered her determination of the previous day, her resolve to succeed. It seemed impossible, she was so tired. A year eight student knocked and walked timidly to Miss Fletcher's desk. The teacher nodded and read the note that she had been given before walking quietly towards Aimee and placing the piece of paper before her. She was to see the head of year at morning break. Aimee nodded and looked quickly away from Miss Fletcher's inquisitive eyes. Unbelievable how bloody Miss Fletcher always seemed to be around. Although there had been no more confrontations, Aimee always felt uneasy around her English teacher.

Geoff Ruskin had been Aimee's head of year since she had come to the school at eleven. She was one of those students, however, with whom he had had minimal contact. She was insignificant in that she was neither a trouble maker or a star pupil. He knew practically nothing of her family and he could not remember ever having met her parents.

He had frowned at the note from Mrs Brown, which explained briefly the events of the previous day. It was not exactly what he would call truancy, but still it would have to be looked into. Aimee Parkinson, he reflected thoughtfully, he hadn't even known that she had a sister.

"Ah, Aimee, come in." He looked up as she knocked on his office door.

"So, yesterday, Aimee." He fixed his eyes on the young girl standing hesitantly at the other side of his desk. "Can you tell me what happened?"

Aimee was not quite sure what he meant. So much seemed to have happened yesterday, she wondered what exactly he was referring to. What did he know?

"I . . . er. I don't know what you mean . . . Sir."

He was slightly irritated. He had several other pupils lining up outside to see him, he had lost his free period due to having been put on cover and he had a whole list of phone calls to make, not to mention the fact that he was supposed to be teaching for the rest of the day.

"I mean . . . " He rubbed at the side of his head, he did not mean to snap at the girl. She was very pale, she looked as though she had the weight of the world on her shoulders.

"I mean, " he began more kindly, "that you apparently left school to take your little sister out of school and that you did not return. Is that correct?"

"Yes, Sir. " Aimee was taken aback at the reason for her having been called to his office. In the light of her problems, taking her little sister home when she was poorly did not exactly seem to be the crime of the century and she wondered what all the fuss was about.

"Well, you see, Aimee. The thing is that you are legally obliged to be in school unless there is a valid reason for you to be absent." He hesitated. "Looking after your little sister is not considered a valid reason."

"She was ill, Sir, and there was no one else . . . "

"Yes, Aimee, I do understand, but you see it's not your responsibility. Your parents should have other measures in place. Now, I'm going to have to speak to Mum or Dad. Do you think you could ask them to telephone me?"

Not her responsibility! He was having a laugh. What did he know? Oh yes, she could ask her Mom to phone him, all she had to do was find out if she was still alive.

"Aimee, are you all right?" The girl in front of Mr Ruskin was simply staring into space, as if completely in a world of her own. He didn't even know if she had heard what he had said. "Aimee . . . I said are you ok?"

Aimee blinked slowly. "Yes, Sir."

"So will you do that then?"

She looked at him blankly.

"Ask your parents to 'phone me." He stated with as much patience as he could muster. Aimee nodded. Yes, of course, she'd ask.

Chapter Eight

Geoff Ruskin replaced the receiver. Only half way through his list of phone calls and just twenty minutes left of the lunch hour. He unwrapped a ham salad baguette and took a large mouthful as the door opened.

"Geoff, have you got a minute?"

He raised his eyebrows.

"Sorry to disturb your lunch. I just wanted a quick word with you about Aimee Parkinson."

Helen Fletcher was not somebody who would be fobbed off by a raised eyebrow and a stressed expression. Purposefully, she pulled out a chair.

Geoff pursed his lips and re-wrapped the ham baguette. "Aimee Parkinson," he repeated.

"Yes, I just wondered if everything was all right, only she's been called out of my lesson both yesterday and today. Is there something I should know?"

Geoff frowned. There wasn't really much to say but if he were honest with himself his conversation with Aimee Parkinson had been nagging away in his mind since break. The facts of the matter were not significant but there was something about her that was troubling him, something he couldn't quite put his finger on. He quickly outlined the story of Aimee and her little sister.

"Oh, I see."

Geoff looked questioningly at Helen, her response seemed to imply that she was expecting something else. He glanced at his watch and picked up the baguette. Helen watched him take another mouthful. She looked as though she were about to speak but thought better of it. She rose to her feet, "Sorry to interrupt your lunch."

Helen could not settle all afternoon. Aimee Parkinson was in her head and she could not get her out. And it was not the first time. She could not help but reflect back to the conversation she had had with Aimee several weeks ago now. She had felt at the time that she had handled the situation badly and had said nothing to any of the other members of staff. But she had been keeping her eye on Aimee and she was not comfortable with what she saw; the girl was more than simply quiet, she was completely withdrawn. There had been no further issue with Aimee's work, she had met her deadlines and the quality of what she had done was in keeping with the standard of her band two class. Helen, had, in fact, been pleasantly surprised as there were still times when Aimee seemed not to have listened to a word she had said. She barely spoke to her classmates and they did not seem to even notice her presence.

She tried to remember exactly when her conversation with Aimee had taken place, had it been before half term or after? Before, she decided, but she couldn't be entirely sure; there was always so much to do, the weeks seemed to disappear. She remembered noticing that Aimee had stopped asking to go to the toilet in her lesson. She had come to the conclusion that she had been wrong to question the girl so persistently. She had even been relieved that nothing had come of it – she had been half expecting Aimee to complain about her. But now, once again, she was perturbed. She made a mental note to find out from Geoff what the conversation with the parents revealed.

Geoff Ruskin was not unduly surprised to hear nothing from Mr or Mrs Parkinson. He was surprised, however, by Helen Fletcher's obvious interest in the girl. Today, it was a cheese and pickle sandwich, he'd managed one bite and there were just ten minutes until the bell. At least he had a free period after lunch – he was aiming to get on top of things by the end of the day. Roll on Easter.

"Helen." He tried not to sigh audibly. "What can I do for you?"

Helen smiled; at least he seemed to be a bit more approachable today. "Any joy with the Parkinson parents?"

He shook his head. "Nope."

Helen waited. It was clear that she did not expect him to leave the matter there. Bloody hell didn't she have anything else to do? Get a bloody life, woman. He picked up his sandwich. "I'll draft a letter this afternoon, see if we can get them to at least make contact."

Helen nodded approvingly. She made a mental note. Today was Thursday, the letter should be in the post by Friday afternoon. She'd give him until Tuesday.

* * *

"Penny for 'em?" Paul Horden reached across the table and took his fiancée's hand.

Helen sighed. "It's nothing. Just work."

"Come on, get it off your chest. " He was used to Helen bringing her work home, both mentally and practically. Sometimes it drove him crazy. He could not understand why anyone would want to spend their days with hundreds of irritating adolescents and then bring home a pile of work to mark. It seemed to him like a thankless task. Not to mention all the politics that went on behind the scenes in the staff room. Helen was a dedicated and talented professional, she could be earning double her salary in a proper job and he had told her as much, frequently. He, for example, worked a normal working day in his job as manager of a computer software company. He came home and forgot about it, he had weekends to himself and earned considerably more than Helen. But she loved it, he knew that and he loved her for her commitment and drive.

He listened as Helen told him the Aimee Parkinson story, about how she had practically accused her of being pregnant, about the girl's withdrawn and distracted manner, about her having time off to look after her little sister. There didn't seem to be much substance to the story and he wondered why Helen was so disturbed by it.

"It's not all your responsibility, you know, Helen." He advised softly. "You're not paid to take on the concerns of each and every pupil."

"I don't." Helen replied testily. "That's the point, everyone's so busy with everything else, bloody paperwork and God knows what. There's no time to take on the concerns of each and every pupil and some of them fall by the wayside."

She swallowed a large mouthful of wine. "I'm sorry, Paul. I don't know what it is. I just feel that this girl's in trouble and . . ."

Paul stood up and walked behind her. "I know. Come on. . . you need to relax." He led her away from the dining table and guided her towards the sofa. He sat her down and handed her her wine glass.

She smiled gratefully and watched him move across the room...

"What do you fancy?" he asked her, nodding towards the i-pod dock.

She sighed. He was right, now was not the time to be worrying about Aimee Parkinson. She beckoned him towards her. "You, Paul Horden. I fancy you."

* * *

Geoff Ruskin was not having a good day. He had spent half of the morning sorting out three kids who had been caught smoking down in the precinct half way through period two. His head of department was off sick and had sent a message asking him to set some work for this afternoon's year eight and nine lessons. His wife had just phoned to remind him that he was supposed to be taking his two girls to the dentists after school and he was not pleased to see Helen Fletcher. Surely she could not still be going on about Aimee Parkinson. What was wrong with the woman?

"Geoff," Helen could see that she was an unwelcome intrusion and her smile was deliberately bright. "Aimee Parkinson?"

He sighed. "Not heard anything, I'm afraid."

"So, what next?" Helen asked lightly.

"Helen, the girl skipped a few lessons to look after her little sister. It probably won't happen again and in any case she'll be off our hands in a few more weeks.

"So, you're going to do nothing?" She didn't intend for it to sound like an accusation.

"Jesus! I have done something, but it's not exactly number one on my list of priorities."

He ran his fingers through his thinning hair. "In my professional opinion, the case . . . the situation, does not merit the kind of time you are expecting me to spend on it."

Helen's eyes widened. Pompous git. "Understood," she conceded.

Yet, she knew he was right. There really wasn't that much of a big deal. Most of her concern did not stem from Aimee's absence from school. She wished that she had something more concrete to go on because she also felt sure that there *was* an issue.

The following week was the last before the Easter break. Year eleven would be going on study leave just two weeks after that. Then that would be it. Aimee Parkinson would be just another ex-pupil and whatever was going on in her life would be no concern of the school's.

Monday morning arrived and there were four more days to go. The end of term atmosphere in the staff room was a mixture of exhaustion and euphoria – two whole weeks off. Helen passed Geoff Ruskin who suddenly appeared to have something urgent to say to the person just behind her. She made her way to her first class. Year eleven had started collecting each other's signatures and counting down the days in a state of nervous anticipation. Only Aimee did not appear to be part of the excitement. Helen noted that she sat with her head bowed, her arms crossed around her waist. Helen sighed inwardly. She would see her at the end of the lesson, there must be some way of getting her to talk about what was bothering her. As the bell rang, a cluster of students gathered around her desk, one had missed last week's hand-outs due to being absent, another had a problem with homework and Aimee had disappeared along with the remainder of the class by the time Helen had dealt with the various issues.

By the time she walked into Geoff's office at lunch, Helen was on the defensive.

"Geoff, look, I'm really sorry to trouble you but I do need to talk to you."

Geoff cast a hungry glance towards his lunch tray – jacket potato with lashings of grated cheese. He didn't even care that it was the rubbery school dinner cheese that you didn't come across anywhere else, he was ravenous.

"Please, eat your lunch. I just want you to listen and then tell me what you think at the end of it."

Geoff nodded. "Of course." He waved her towards a seat. He paid her little attention as he plunged his knife and fork into the middle of his potato, mashing the butter and cheese earnestly.

Helen wrung her hands in a wave of uncustomary nervousness. "Several weeks ago, I had a conversation with Aimee Parkinson in which I virtually accused her of being pregnant."

Geoff looked up, fork poised in mid-air. This was not what he was expecting.

"What made you think that she could be pregnant?" He tried to picture the girl. As far as he could remember she was one of those who appeared to be totally shapeless. Year eleven girls were a strange bunch, they were either flaunting their newly acquired assets in clothing which marginally passed for a school uniform or covering up completely in totally unflattering baggy garments.

Helen recounted the fainting episode and the frequent trips to the toilet. "And she looks so pale, worried to death. She's become totally withdrawn."

"You mean she's become withdrawn since you spoke to her?"

"Well, more so, yes."

"So, it could be more to do with the fact that you've upset her."

Geoff nibbled his bottom lip thoughtfully. " Let me get this straight. You accused her of being pregnant, based on gut feeling. I mean, come on, Helen, girls of that age have fainting fits all the time, especially when they want to get out of PE."

Helen met his gaze defiantly.

Geoff took a mouthful of potato. "So, then what, what did she say?"

"Well, she denied it, obviously."

"Obviously?"

"I mean, it's obvious now, otherwise it'd be all out in the open wouldn't it?" Helen was becoming flustered. As she'd expected, this was not going well. Why did he have to be so bloody awkward? He really didn't like her, she was sure.

"So, then what did you do?"

Helen shifted awkwardly in her seat. "I didn't do anything."

"Well, did you speak to anyone else about it?"

"No . . . I, er . . ."

"So now what do you want me to do? The girl's leaving school in a few weeks. Do you really want to upset her again just before her exams?"

Helen leaned forward angrily. "What you mean, Geoff, is do we really want to bother getting involved when she'll be off our hands in another few weeks. You said as much the other week. Well, yes I bloody well do want to get involved. For God's sake, anything could be going on for all we know. There's no response from the parents when we try to contact them, the younger sister is dumped at school without any contact number . . ."

Geoff shoved his lunch away. Bloody hell. "Helen, calm, down. That's not what I was saying."

He looked away; they both knew that it was not true. He would have been more than happy to push the whole thing under the carpet.

He placed his hands on the table in front of him. "I'll speak to Aimee, this week, okay?"

"Today?"

He sighed. God she was like a bloody Jack Russell. "I'll do my best."

"Can I be present? You should have a female member of staff with you."

He would prefer that it wasn't her. He breathed deeply. "Yes, Helen. Afternoon break suit you?"

93

"Perfect."

She replaced her chair quietly and walked out into the corridor, relieved to have unburdened herself of her troubled thoughts and satisfied that she had talked him into taking action. But she was not looking forward to afternoon break.

Aimee received the instruction to see Mr Ruskin with mixed emotions. She didn't dare hope that maybe her mother had been in touch with the school. It was what she had been hoping for every day of the past two weeks. At the end of each day, she crawled into bed, unable to believe that another day had passed without any news, clinging to the hope that tomorrow would be the day when she heard from her missing mother.

As bad as she thought her life had been until now, the last fortnight had been far, far worse. Stacey and Kayleigh looked to her for love and reassurance more than ever and Aimee was determined to provide them with whatever she could. But her own needs went completely unheeded and unfulfilled. At the end of the Easter holidays, she would be sixteen years old and it felt as though she were entirely, entirely alone in a world that she could not begin to fathom and to which she felt completely unsuited.

She had surprised herself in her resourcefulness and initiative in the steps she had taken to try to find her mother. Two days after she had last seen Sheryl, Aimee walked into the local police station. The PC had listened sympathetically but had explained gently that there was nothing that they could do. Sheryl was a grown woman, free to go where she pleased. People walked out on relationships all the time and unless there were genuine grounds to believe that they had been taken against their will or reason to believe that something violent had happened to them, then the police were not in a position to take action.

"Do you have any brothers or sisters?"

Aimee nodded and continued to answer the police officer's questions but she was bright enough to be careful about how much she disclosed. The last thing she wanted was police or social workers knocking on the door.

"Look, love, your mum probably just needs a bit of space, you know. She'll most probably take a little while to sort things out in her head and then she'll be back, I'm sure."

Aimee had not looked convinced.

"I tell you what; I'll give you some contacts. There's a number of hostels – refuge type places for women in your mum's position. You could start by ringing those. That's if you're absolutely certain there's nowhere else she might have gone?"

Aimee shook her head. She took the piece of paper and thanked the officer.

Over the course of the following few days, Aimee had explored every possible avenue. She had slipped out of school at lunch time in order to use the nearby public phone box. She had made contact with each of the organisations given to her by the police officer. They, in turn, were able to provide her with the numbers of other, similar establishments but none of them had any record or recollection of anyone answering her mother's description. They were at pains to point out that they were bound by confidentiality regulations but Aimee had had the foresight to leave her name, as well as that of her school, begging them to please ask her mother to contact her, should they come across her.

The days, however, turned into a week and there was nothing. During the second week, Aimee had searched everything of her mother's that she could lay her hands on in the hope of finding some evidence of where she could have gone. Eventually, in the bottom of her wardrobe, Aimee came across a bundle of what appeared to be old greetings cards, Sheryl's eighteenth birthday, her wedding certificate and the birth certificates of her daughters. Amongst them was an old, battered address book. There was probably no more than about a dozen or so entries in the whole of the book. Aimee leafed through, trying to find names that meant anything to her. Under "M" was an entry for "Mom and Dad", giving the full name and address of Sheryl's parents and underneath was an entry for "Margaret Sawyers." Aimee had hidden the book under her mattress and the following day had once again made her way to the public phone box. She dialled with bated breath and asked the automated response for the number of the two names scrawled on the slip of paper in her hand. Her heart sank as she learned that there was no record of anyone matching the information she had on Sheryl's parents but moments later she found herself writing down the number for her Aunty Margaret, her hand trembling so much that she feared she would be unable to read her own writing.

Nervously, Aimee had dialled the number. The ringing echoed dully in her ear over and over and, deflated, Aimee had replaced the receiver. A few hours later it was the same story, no reply. Aimee recognised the address and had a vague idea of where it was. It was a ten minute bus ride away. There was no way that she could get there. She had managed to convince Jim that unless he picked up the girls from school, then she would have no option but to bring in the authorities. He had to take some responsibility for his daughters, she had reasoned. Even if she hadn't had her paper round to do, the fact remained that her school finished ten minutes later than Kayleigh and Stacey's primary, there was no way that she could pick them up. Nevertheless, each afternoon, Aimee half expected him to forget or simply not bother and there was the worry of the two little ones being left alone with him. So taking extra time to go chasing up possible relatives was not an option.

Aimee recalled the afternoon of the failed phone calls to her aunt with odd emotions. She had walked into the house to meet the usual air of depression. The girls were normally playing quietly in their room at this time and their father was generally dozing in his chair. Aimee was well used to arriving home and starting their tea. On this particular afternoon, Aimee was feeling especially low, following her failed attempt to contact the woman she believed to be her aunt. As she quietly removed her coat and shoes, she became aware of muffled and erratic breathing coming from the living room. She stepped inside the room. Her stepfather lay along the length of the settee, his arms covering his head; he was snivelling into a cushion, his body heaving great racking sobs. Aimee recoiled from the sight, which shocked and repulsed her.

She moved quietly into the kitchen, where she stood by the window staring out into the small, untidy garden. The grass, she noted, badly needed cutting, the flowerless borders were nothing but hardened soil, brightened only by unruly weeds, growing out of control. It was how she, herself, felt: untended, unloved and . . . out of control. It seemed that each day brought a fresh challenge; always there was some incident which arose to make her feel incapable of going on, with no one to turn to and no one to guide her.

She could still hear him, blubbering like a child. She despised him but she pitied him also and the pity in turn made her despise him more. Despising him caused her to despise herself and all that she was. Because, until now, her miserable life had been entirely down to him. But now. Because of her own, cheap and careless actions, she had reaped yet further misery, for herself, her sisters and for the baby, the innocent baby, which kicked away inside her.

Her own sense of worthlessness was echoed in the pathetic sounds, which still emanated from the living room. She wrapped her arms about herself and closed her eyes, longing to be free of the wretchedness which enveloped her. Eventually, she heard the creak of the aged settee as he moved. She felt herself freeze momentarily and then automatically moved around the kitchen, busying herself with preparations for the evening meal. She expected him to come in but he did not and she continued uneasily. She switched on the kettle and located Jim's mug, one of the few which was neither chipped nor cracked, and another for herself. She stood with the two steaming hot mugs of tea before her and took a deep breath. She picked up Jim's and walked quietly out into the next room.

He was sitting now with his head in his hands, bent forward over his knees. He was unshaven and unkempt and to Aimee he was a despicable sight, a reflection of their pitiful existence, a reminder of all that they were. She placed his drink on the wooden fireplace and he raised his head slowly.

"Thank you." The spoken words of gratitude were unusual, unexpected and Aimee was uncomfortable. She could not look at him, though she knew that he was looking at her. It was as though he wanted her to see his sorrow. But Aimee did not understand it and she did not want to be part of it. She could not, would not be a part of it. His misery was his own doing and he must suffer it alone.

"Aimee." The sound of her name on his lips was repugnant to her. "What are we going to do?" His voice was broken, desperate.

His use of the word "we" implied to her that he thought that they were united in some way and she resented it bitterly.

"How are we going to find her, Aimee?" He was looking at her, seeking an answer which she could not provide.

"I'll do anything, Aimee. I'll . . . leave if that's what she wants . . . I just need to know that she's not . . . that she's safe."

"Safe?" Aimee spat the word. "Safe? She's never been safe since the day she met you." Her face twisted into a contemptuous sneer and she averted her eyes from the sight of him, which incensed her.

"I'll be different. . . I promise you . . . I'll not harm her no more. . . Aimee. Oh God, I just want her to be all right."

It was more than she could bear. It was the last thing she had expected and she could not cope with the confusion and the burden of his emotion. She walked away and he broke down behind her, sobbing uncontrollably.

That evening, Aimee had attempted to write to Margaret Sawyers at the address in the tattered looking address book. She had spent hours, trying to word the letter, tearing up page after page of abandoned attempts. She was not even sure that the person she was addressing was her aunty. She did not know how much of their lives she should disclose, she had no idea whether Margaret even knew that Stacey and Kayleigh existed. It was impossible, it was second nature to Aimee to keep things to herself, the face she wore for the outside world was emotionless and distant, there was no way now that she could disclose her truest emotions, place her trust in a complete stranger.

She had taken a final, fresh piece of paper and almost involuntarily had begun another letter.

"Dear Mommy

I love you and I need you. We all need you. I am nothing now you have gone. I have nothing and no one now you have gone. Please come back to us. He said that, if you want, he will go. Please, mom, or we could go somewhere, just the four of us. I will do anything to be back where I want to be and that is with you, Mom. Please come, it is awful without you and I can't bear it any longer.

You always told me that my name means "loved." If that's true, then please, please come.

Kayleigh and Stacey need their mommy and so do I. It's like a nightmare and every time you want to wake up you find out it's true.

Please come, mom.

Love Aimee."

She re-read the letter. She did not cry. She was numb. She placed the letter carefully into the envelope, which she sealed deliberately. She then wrote another note:

"Dear Mrs Sawyers

99

My name is Aimee Parkinson. My mother is Sheryl (nee Thompson). I think she might be your sister. If Sheryl contacts you, please would you give her this letter.

Thank you.

Yours sincerely, Aimee."

* * *

Helen was the first to arrive at Geoff's office. She spotted Aimee dawdling towards her. Where was bloody Geoff?

"Sir sent for me." Aimee offered the explanation as she arrived at Helen's side.

"Yes." Helen smiled tensely, "I know."

Aimee observed her suspiciously.

Geoff Ruskin ambled towards them, a mug of coffee held out in front of him.

"Ah, Aimee . . . Miss Fletcher, come in." He pulled out two chairs before seating himself behind his desk; hopefully, this would be a storm in a tea cup and he'd wrap it up in no time at all. He thought longingly of the mars bar in his top drawer.

"Now, Aimee, Miss Fletcher. . . well, we . . . are a little concerned that there may be something bothering you?" He raised his eyes questioningly.

Aimee's lip curled slightly. "No, Sir."

"No." He mulled the word over as though he had not considered it an option. Helen rounded in her chair, towards her student, her shoulder turned slightly away from the head of year.

"Aimee," She began gently, "We asked your parents to contact us a couple of weeks' ago regarding the incident when you left school to look after your little sister. Do you remember?"

Aimee nodded.

"Well, the thing is Aimee, they haven't been in touch and we, well, wondered if everything was all right at home?"

Aimee tried not to look at Miss Fletcher, whose soft, kind voice unsettled her. It was what she longed for: someone to be kind to her, to treat her gently, to look after her, but she was so afraid of giving in to the raw emotions that such treatment exposed. She wanted so much to unburden herself of her troubles but so afraid of the consequences; she fought to contain her emotions. She had had years of practice in hiding her feelings from the world. She stared impassively ahead.

Helen looked at Geoff. He too was unnerved by the girl's steely composure, her almost inhuman expression that warned them to stay away. The brick wall that she had erected around her was solid.

Helen reached out and took Aimee's hand. It was against the rules. There was no choice. Helen had to get through to this girl, this child- woman whose need for help was so well concealed and yet so clear to her. She did not doubt her instincts; she could not fail in her humanity. It was why she had become a teacher, not simply to quote Shakespeare and correct grammar.

"Aimee," her voice was barely a whisper. She squeezed the girl's hand. "We want to help you . . . let us help you."

Did they? Aimee wondered. Could they? She needed someone so badly to help her but she was so, so afraid.

"We can't help you, if you don't tell us."

Aimee was fighting to control her emotions. She knew that she had to remain silent. She knew that she could not trust them with any of her problems. If she were to tell them about her little sisters in the care of her drunken, violent stepfather, they would have procedures to follow and that would mean bringing in the authorities. Kayleigh and Stacey could be separated from each other, she might lose them for ever. And what about herself? And her unborn child? She was still under the age of consent. Had she committed a crime? She didn't know. Could they take her baby from her?

"Aimee, if you can't talk to us, then is there someone else you can talk to? A friend? Your mum? Can you talk to your mum, Aimee? Whatever the problem is, it can be sorted. Please let us help you."

To her dismay, Aimee realised that she was crying. She felt the tears falling freely over her cheeks. She tried to check them. She used every ounce of strength that she could muster to bring her emotions back under control but Miss Fletcher had moved out of her seat and was crouching next to her chair, her arms holding her, her words soothing her, letting her believe that everything would be all right if she told them her problems. And so somehow she did. The words came tumbling out and once she had begun to speak, she couldn't stop them. She was terrified and relieved all at once, temporarily liberated from the anguish of bottling it all up inside her. The effect was cathartic, a weight lifting from deep inside her as she handed it over to share. She knew that she had begun something from which she could not return, that she was setting the wheels in motion and she did not know where they would lead.

But afterwards in that moment of silence, when Sir and Miss were taking it all in, when the words were all out, the burden had been shared, she felt afraid again and she wondered, with horror, what she had done. The release she had felt as the words unravelled was almost euphoric, but now she must face the consequences and she was right back where she started, completely alone with her fear and she was so, so frightened.

They were staring at her. Miss Fletcher released her gently and passed her a handful of tissues. Aimee feared that they had duped her. Why didn't they say something? Why didn't they tell her what to do, what was going to happen? They had said everything would be all right and she wanted to know that it would be. It was their fault that she had told them everything, why didn't they do something? They were supposed to be helping her, that's what she'd said, Miss Fletcher had said they would help her!

Deep down, Helen had, of course, known that Aimee was pregnant but she thought that that was the extent of it. But now it appeared that there was much, much more. The poor girl had no idea where her mother was, whether she was dead or alive and in the meantime had virtually taken on the responsibility for not one but two younger sisters. Aimee had said little of the stepfather, but Helen was reading between the lines. There were few women who would walk out on three children and those who did normally did so through fear.

Geoff Ruskin had listened and observed silently. He was shocked. Obviously, Helen had been right to insist on pursuing the matter and he made a mental note that he should apologise for his lack of co-operation. He could see, however, from the expression on Helen's face that she was out of her depth and jaded as he might sometimes appear, his years of experience could not easily be replaced.

He moved from behind his desk and his tone was gentle.

"Aimee. There are two separate issues here. Firstly, you are pregnant. Have you seen a doctor?"

Aimee shook her head.

"Do you know how far . . ." He was not quite sure of the correct terminology. "when the baby is due?"

Aimee had made many mental calculations, she wasn't exactly certain how to work it out but she reckoned that it must be around about August time.

Geoff and Helen exchanged surprised glances, they could not help resting their eyes on the girl's middle. There was a definite

103

thickness about her which anyone more familiar with her normal shape would have observed, but her outline was well obscured by her baggy sweatshirt.

"Aimee. You must understand that you can no longer continue to ignore your condition. If your calculations are accurate, then you have left yourself with no choice but to go ahead with this pregnancy. Do you understand that, Aimee?"

Aimee nodded. Yes, she had been aware in the beginning that there could have been other options but the reality had been that she had been in denial of her condition for so long that termination had not seemed relevant to her, as though somehow the baby would simply never become a reality.

"We have to let your parents know about this, Aimee." Geoff Ruskin was gentle but firm. "Because of the current situation, it will have to be your stepfather we speak to."

"No!" She had known she could not trust them. They were just going to interfere and make things worse for her.

"Aimee, try to stay calm." It was Helen talking to her, her voice soothing. "If you really don't want us to talk to your stepfather first then you must agree to tell him yourself and then we'll take it from there."

Take what from there? Why were they suddenly taking over her life? Aimee was in the grip of panic.

Helen reached out and touched her arm lightly. "Aimee, we want to help you." She reminded her.

Aimee took a deep breath. "Okay. I'll tell him myself. I'll do it." How, she did not know, but she had no choice.

"Aimee, are you in any danger at home?"

Aimee could feel her cheeks reddening beneath their gaze.

"If you are, then you should not deal with your stepfather by yourself."

"I'll be all right, Miss, honest, I'll speak to him."

She heard them breath quiet sighs of relief. If only she could feel the same. She looked at them and stood up carefully. "Can I go now?"

Helen too stood up, she looked briefly towards Geoff and then back to Aimee. "Look, Aimee, I'm here from 8 o'clock in the morning. Come and see me as soon as you arrive." She threw Geoff another glance. "And we'll come to Mr Ruskin's office together. Okay?"

Aimee nodded. "Yes, Miss."

* * *

She had decided that straight after tea would be the best time, before he got too drunk. She had prepared the girls in advance by telling them that they must go upstairs to play quietly after their meal and they accepted her instruction without fuss. Over and over in her head she practised how she would begin the conversation but as she watched her stepfather finishing off his meal, still she had no idea what she would say to him. She herself had eaten little, her stomach churned over and over, her whole body tense with a sick feeling of dread. It was not an unfamiliar feeling to her but it was probably the worst she had known. She realised with sad irony that it was probably better that Sheryl was not around. At least she did not have to endure the guilt of knowing that he would take it out on her mother. No, this time it would be her and her alone who bore the brunt of his fury.

Her heart raced as he mopped up the last traces of gravy from his plate and sucked his lips satisfactorily. She watched as he placed together his knife and fork and pushed away his plate. She knew what his routine would be, he would finish off his cup of tea, lean back in his chair and belch before making his way to the living room where he would slump in his chair for half an

105

hour in front of the TV before adjourning to the pub to waste what precious, little money they had. It had been exactly the same each night since Sheryl had gone. It would be best in the living room, she decided; safer. She rose to clear the table as he left the room and she rinsed the dirty plates before piling them into the washing up bowl. She was conscious of the time drawing closer to the awful moment when she would have, somehow, to tell him. She cleared and wiped the table. She would have to go, she could not afford to wait until after she had washed up and risk him going out before she had had chance to speak to him. It had to be now. She wrung her hands and then ran them over her face. It had to be now. Her insides felt as though they were about to fall out. She rubbed at her bump. Poor baby, poor, poor baby.

He did not look up as she entered the room, his eyes fixed passively on the TV screen. She stood just inside the door. She tried to clear her throat but it materialised in no more than an inaudible gulp. Eventually, he turned towards her with evident disinterest and yet he felt a stirring of curiosity to know what it was she wanted.

She bit her lip. It was impossible. She should have let Miss Fletcher do it. Anything would be better than this. She could not do it. She simply could not do it. He was looking at her now, wondering what the hell was wrong with her. Her face was deathly white.

Jim stared at his stepdaughter and thought suddenly that it must be Sheryl. She must know what had happened to her. Jesus Christ , something awful had happened to her. He was sitting forward now on the sofa, looking at his Aimee intently. Both of them saying nothing, their eyes fixed firmly on each other.

"Tell me. What's happened to her?"

For a moment, Aimee did not understand him, she was so absorbed in her own situation that Sheryl was not in her thoughts and she gazed at him blankly.

106

"For Christ's sake, speak to me! Tell me what's happened to her!" Aimee was vaguely conscious that his tone was more desperate than aggressive. She recalled the pathetic snivelling scene she had recently witnessed and she tried to open her lips to speak. Her mouth was dry. She was shaking her head, trying to tell him that she didn't know anything about Sheryl. She wanted to tell him, while he was still calm; it's me, I'm pregnant. I'm going to have a baby.

She was confused. Had she spoken the words or merely thought them? She hoped she'd said them, finally, but she wasn't sure because he was still staring at her, his face reflecting nothing.

He did not understand. The girl was muttering almost inaudibly. Was Sheryl pregnant? Was that why she had left? Where was she?

"Where is she?"

She was bewildered. Why was he still going on about Sheryl?

"I'm pregnant. Me. Not my mom . . . me . . . I'm having a baby." She had heard herself this time. She had said the words. They were out. She stood, frozen in fear of his reaction. Her hands covered her stomach instinctively. He was getting out of his chair. He stood up. She tried to read his expression. What was he going to do? Dear, dear God, what was he going to do . . .?

It was too much for him to take in. Unexpectedly, he sat back down. The stupid girl was telling him she was pregnant. How the fuck had that happened? She hardly ever left the house apart from to do her paper round. So who the bloody hell was the father? He'd kill him, dirty little bastard. It was bad enough feeding and clothing his own lot, there was no way he was going to start providing for anyone else's bastard. It would have to be got rid of, there was no doubt about it. That was all there was to it. But he'd still kill the bloody bugger who'd done it. He could bloody well do without this hassle. They'd have the bloody authorities round at this rate.

She read his mind. "it's too late. It's due in August."

He screwed up his face in horror. "August!" he spluttered. He was staring at her middle. Jesus fucking Christ, how could he have failed to notice that she was . . . he tried to work it out . . . five, maybe six months up gone.

The penny was dropping. So that was why Sheryl had pissed off. She knew. The fucking bitch, if she thought that he was going to sort this lot out then she could think again. The little slag was nothing to do with him, not *his* flesh and blood. He was stabbing his finger towards her. "Your bloody mother can sort this out." He shook his head vehemently. This is nowt to do with me. Absolutely nowt, I'll have no part of it. She can bloody well get back here and start sorting it out . . . tomorrow."

Aimee was still expecting him to strike her and yet it appeared his anger was now directed once more towards her mother. He did not or would not accept that she had no idea where Sheryl was or whether she was coming back.

"She doesn't know anything about this." Aimee told him wearily.

He was looking at her as though he had never seen her before. It was too much for him to take in. He stood up once more. Aimee stiffened and moved backwards.

"I'm going out."

"Jim!" She hated using his name. "Th . . . they want you to go and see them . . . at school, I mean."

"What? You mean the school knows about this?" He was standing right in front of her and he was seething.

Aimee was shaking inside. "It's not my fault . . . they guessed." Her voice rose hysterically. "Look at me for God's sake!" She pressed the bottom of her jumper so that it lay flat against the outline of her belly and he stared, aghast at her distended shape. She breathed in in an effort to calm herself. "They know that mom's not here. You're responsible for me . . . and for Kayleigh and Stacey and if they think you're not taking care of us then they'll have us taken away." She was gabbling desperately. She didn't know whether it mattered to him whether they were taken into care or not, but it mattered to her and she had to convince him to go and see her teachers, make out everything was under control.

"You just need to tell them that Mom's gone away for a while but that she'll be back . . ."

He did not like the idea of her telling him what to do, little bitch, who did she think she was? But neither did he like the idea of the bloody authorities poking their noses in his business. He sniffed noisily and curled his lip as he looked at her with hatred. He was going to the pub, that was all he could think of right now. Bloody, bloody Sheryl, this was her fucking fault. Like mother, like daughter, fucking sluts the pair of them. He shoved past her and grabbed his jacket from where it was hanging over the bannister. He slammed the door and the house shook.

Aimee was trembling more than ever and she gripped the door frame for support. She felt as though her legs would not support her and she made her way unsteadily into the living room where she sank on to the sofa. She could no longer hold back the tears and she wept uncontrollably, great racking sobs that ripped her heart apart and left her choking for breath.

She was not aware of her sisters approaching her side until eventually she became conscious of their voices, calling her name.

"Aimee, what's the matter? What's happened?"

"Has something happened to mom? Aimee, please don't cry."

She focused on the two little girls, their faces reflecting their distress at the sight of her own. She could not allow them to suffer any more than they did already, she had to be strong for them. She wiped her face with her sleeve and sat up straight.

"It's all right. Don't worry . . . nothing's happened. I was just feeling a bit sad. Come on, I'll get you a drink and some biscuits."

Being strong for her sisters somehow gave her the strength to pull herself together and Aimee felt much calmer after reading them a story and cuddling them up in their beds. She could not feel positive about what was happening and what was to come but nevertheless she attempted to convince herself that the fact that her secret was out was surely one hurdle overcome.

She slept badly, jumbled recollections of the day's events and imagined scenes between her stepfather and her teachers troubled her conscious and unconscious mind so she rose with the feeling that she had not rested at all. She had decided to leave Jim a note since she knew that there would be no chance of her seeing him before she left for school.

The note began without any greeting, simply asking him bluntly if he would go to the school at lunch time and she reminded him of the consequences of him not turning up. She re-read the note several times, astonished at her boldness but she knew that there was no choice.

As promised, she called in on Miss Fletcher as soon as she arrived at school. Helen had been awaiting her arrival anxiously, she too had had little rest since she had last seen the girl. She feared for her mental state, not to mention her physical safety. She had seen the expression on Aimee's face as she had spoken of her stepfather – a mixture of dread and hatred. She had been over and over the situation in her own mind, asking herself whether she could have handled things differently. She imagined how the poor girl had felt throughout the previous months, living with her silent secret. Secrets. She had speculated for a long time about the goings on in the Parkinson household and the middle of the night had found her contemplating the darkest possibilities of Aimee's suffering. She was relieved however to learn that Aimee was expecting her stepfather to call at the school at lunch time.

"How are you feeling, Aimee?"

110

She looked dreadful. Aimee managed a small smile. "I'm all right, Miss . . . got to be. I've got my two little sisters to look after . . . not to mention . . . " She glanced down at her stomach.

Helen was beginning to understand the enormity of the responsibility which Aimee assumed at home. Helen herself could not yet imagine being responsible for two small children, not to mention bringing her own into the world and yet this young girl . . . She was filled with compassion for Aimee and wanted desperately, somehow, she didn't know how, to help her.

Helen could not concentrate, her lessons went badly as her mind was elsewhere. Finally, it was lunch time and there was the stepfather, standing at reception. Helen surveyed him with disguised distaste as she approached from the corridor; he looked what he was: a drunken bully. He looked as though he had slept in his jeans and his coat was shabby. As he turned towards her, it became evident, however, that he had made some effort with his appearance; he was freshly shaven, a fact which was confirmed by the small piece of blood soaked tissue still stuck to the side of his chin. His thinning hair, which was badly in need of a wash, not to mention a trim, was combed flat against his head in an apparent feeble attempt at personal grooming on his stepdaughter's behalf.

Reluctantly, she offered a hand and forced a smile, as she introduced herself.

He mumbled an indecipherable reply.

"I'll take you to Mr Ruskin's office . . . Aimee should be there too."

She led the way in silence, hoping that Geoff and Aimee would already be there so that they could get straight down to business; she could not imagine making small talk with the individual who shuffled along, slightly behind her. As they approached, she could see that Geoff's door was ajar, indicating his presence inside and on stepping inside, she saw, thankfully that Aimee too had arrived.

Geoff, as planned, took the lead in the conversation. Aimee sat frozen in fear. She had no idea how this discussion would develop. She could see that Jim had made a pathetic attempt to smarten himself up and she sensed his nervousness in the company of her teachers. She hoped that he would stay calm, otherwise who knew what might happen. Right now he was looking uncomfortably at Mr Ruskin, who was explaining, much as he might to a year seven student, she thought, that the school took Aimee's situation very seriously indeed and they had to consider that, at fifteen, Aimee's pregnancy may have been the result of a criminal offence.

Aimee realised with horror, as they looked intently at her stepfather, what they were considering, suggesting even, and the idea was unbearable to her. She shook her head in disbelief. There was no way that she was going to give away Jack's identity, but she had to convince them that she had not been abused in the way they were imagining. Whatever else she had had to endure, she thanked God that she had at least been spared that.

"Our concern right now is for Aimee's immediate welfare." Mr Ruskin continued, still looking thoughtfully at the girl's stepfather. "It's vital that she sees a doctor straightaway . . . I understand that your wife is not living at home at present?" He raised his eyebrows questioningly.

"Well . . . no . . . but it's only temporary. She'll be back any day now."

"Is there any way of contacting her . . . letting her know what's going on?"

"Mmm . . . yeah . . . it's not a problem. . ."

"So, when are you expecting your wife back exactly? You see, Aimee needs to see a doctor quite urgently, Mr Parkinson, and I imagine she would want her mother to be there." He turned towards Aimee, who did not meet his gaze.

Jim shuffled awkwardly in his seat. They made *him* feel bloody fifteen again, in trouble with the head. "Yeah, well, like I say, Sheryl, her mother'll be back any day now." He forced a note of brightness into his voice and nodded confidently. "Anyway, we're getting along fine, me and my girls, no problem."

Geoff released a small sigh. He was not getting through to this man. He looked towards Helen, raising his eyes in slight desperation.

"I could go with her." Helen spoke quietly, directing her words towards Geoff. She was unsure of the legalities of the situation in terms of her being Aimee's teacher.

Geoff raised an eyebrow pensively before looking back towards Jim Parkinson. "Is there nobody else? An aunt or family friend?" He watched as the stepfather shook his head; poor girl. He supposed that Miss Fletcher might be the only option. He couldn't let the wretched girl go to the doctors alone.

"Aimee, how do you feel about Miss Fletcher going with you to the doctors? To help you explain and find out what you need to do."

Aimee really couldn't care less, she just wanted to be out of Mr Ruskin's stifling office, away from her stepfather's pitiful act at being the concerned and dutiful parent. He made her want to puke. She nodded her agreement.

"Right then" Geoff stated definitively, "that's that then. I think it's probably best if we leave it there for the moment. Perhaps we could meet again in a couple of days."

Jim rose quickly to his feet, he could not get away fast enough. Bloody interfering, nosy teachers. Who did they think they were?

Helen looked at him without smiling. "I'll show you out."

113

Chapter Nine

Helen's blood was boiling. She and Geoff Ruskin were sat in the head's office. Geoff had given her the news. It was not the first time that Mrs Derwent had had to deal with a pregnancy amongst her students and she knew that it would not be the last.

"I don't suppose we know who the father is?"

Geoff Ruskin shook his head. "We've been trying to gain Aimee's confidence, get things sorted out for her first. We didn't really think it was the time to start interrogating her about the hows and the whys of the matter."

"No, of course." Mrs Derwent was solemn, "You don't think there's any possibility of abuse?"

"We wouldn't like to say for sure."

Geoff glanced at Helen, who chipped in cautiously, "The mother's missing and the stepfather's not exactly up for parent of the year. He drinks, from what I've heard . . . I don't think it's the best of situations."

"We need to inform social services. I'm concerned for the two little girls as well. Helen, it might be best if you leave this to the experts and let one of them go with her, to the doctors, I mean."

"But, I've given her my word now!" Helen was outraged. There was no way that she was going to leave the poor girl in the hands of a stranger. She at least deserved some support from someone she was familiar with. She said as much to the head, conscious that she was allowing her emotions to get the better of her and that she was not expressing herself as respectfully as she might do.

Mrs Derwent sniffed self-importantly. "Helen, you must try to not get so involved. There's a limit to how much we can do as teachers. After that, there are other people qualified to help. Now, I suggest . . ."

Helen was not going to be bullied into letting Aimee down. She was seething inside but she spoke quietly and firmly. "I have given Aimee my word. Now, I'm going to go with her to the doctors and I'm going to help her in whatever way I can. The girl has no one else. If you consider that I'm doing anything wrong which constitutes misconduct, then I'm sure you'll let me know."

Mrs Derwent was visibly shocked, she was not accustomed to having her word questioned and certainly not by one of Helen Fletcher's tender years and limited experience. Geoff, too, was surprised, although in hindsight, he should have known better; it was only because of Helen's tenacity that the matter had come to light at all. He admired her gumption and her sense of righteousness and he didn't want to see her on the wrong side of the boss. He attempted to de-fuse the situation. "Helen . . ."

But Mrs Derwent interrupted him with a wave of her hand. She considered Helen thoughtfully, "You must understand that I am duty-bound to advise the social services of the various circumstances at the Parkinson home. However, in the meantime, it may be appropriate for a member of staff to support Aimee by going with her to the doctors. Since you seem to have fostered a positive relationship with the girl, then I don't see any reason why that person should not be you."

Geoff fought the wry smile, which threatened to betray him.

"Thank you." Helen was gracious in victory.

* * *

The waiting room was full of the usual characters; an elderly lady sat engrossed in a well-thumbed magazine, a young man who looked as though he had just crawled out of bed and a row of young mothers lined up with their babies in front of the nurse's surgery. Helen noticed Aimee's gaze wandering over to the infants in their mothers' arms.

"Are you okay?"

Aimee nodded. It was a bit odd having Miss there but she was grateful. She felt sure that she would never have been able to face this alone.

"Do you still want me to come in with you?" They had discussed this earlier and Aimee had said that she would like Helen to stay with her and help her to talk to the doctor but Helen wanted the girl to be certain.

"If you don't mind, Miss." Aimee whispered politely.

"You don't need to call me "Miss" here. Helen whispered back with a smile.

Aimee nodded. She didn't know what else to call her.

"Helen." Helen gave her an encouraging smile.

"Aimee Parkinson." They both rose swiftly as the receptionist called the next patient.

"Here goes." Aimee had never even visited a doctor by herself before; she was not looking forward to the next few minutes.

"Don't worry. The doctor's job is to help you Aimee, not to judge you."

But Aimee felt his deep brown eyes boring into her with disapproval as he listened to Helen's summary of the situation.

She felt her face flushing with embarrassment as the doctor nodded silently, his face grim. She answered his questions automatically and waited wordlessly whilst he worked out dates.

117

She could not be certain of the exact date of her last period and he advised her that the calculations were merely an estimation of when the baby would be due. "Around about the middle of August from what you tell me but the scan will give us a better idea. I'll try to get you a cancellation . . ."

Aimee did not want a scan, she didn't see why there needed to be such a fuss. She had coped perfectly well until now. As far as she was concerned, she just wanted to know that there would be someone to deliver the baby . . . surely that was all they needed to do.

"I don't need a scan. The baby's fine, he's kicking and everything. I've got my exams to do, I haven't got time for scans and ante-natal classes and . . ."

"Aimee," Helen began kindly. "Don't worry, it's just normal procedure. You want to make sure the baby's healthy don't you?"

Aimee swallowed hard as she nodded. Everything seemed to be moving so fast. Facing the doctor was hard enough, now he was talking about her seeing midwives and consultants. It was not her secret any more, it was out in the open and suddenly very real. Soon, she would be the talk of the school, the estate. Her stomach seemed to be increasing in size daily and the baby's regular kicking served as a constant reminder of the reality of her situation as her life sped more and more out of control.

"Aimee," Helen faced her soon–to-be ex-pupil as they stood outside the doctor's surgery a short while later, "You must try not to worry . . . let's go for a coffee . . . there's no point rushing back to school, it will be lunch time by the time we get there."

Aimee allowed Miss Fletcher to propel her in the direction of the small bakery-cum-coffee shop which was across the precinct from the doctor's surgery. Helen ordered cappuccinos and two chocolate eclairs.

"You could do with putting some weight on." She continued, pushing the cake towards Aimee who looked at her, wide eyed in

118

response. "I mean it." She lowered her voice, conscious of eavesdroppers, "Apart from your bump, you're skin and bone. You have to take care of yourself and your baby."

To Aimee, it felt surreal, sitting in a coffee shop eating cream cakes with her teacher, who was talking about her baby as though everything were perfectly normal.

"Aimee," Helen continued, keeping her voice low, "you're not the first young girl to get "into trouble," she fluttered her fingers and raised her eyes. "And you won't be the last." She bit into her chocolate eclair enthusiastically. "Mmm . . . delicious . . . I know you wouldn't have planned things this way, Aimee and right now you're probably thinking that your life's ruined but everyone makes mistakes. You've been unlucky and it's going to be tough . . . but not impossible."

"But . . . I just don't know how I'm going to cope."

"I know. Look, if I'm honest with you, I wouldn't know how I'd cope with a baby either . . . and I'm twenty seven."

"You don't look it." Aimee said shyly. At sixteen, a whole decade seemed more like a century.

Helen smiled. "No, I feel more like ninety some days after teaching all day."

"Did you always want to be a teacher?"

Aimee was beginning to relax a little and was suddenly curious to know more about the one person who appeared, for no obvious reason, to give a damn about her.

"I think I did. I can't imagine doing anything else really. How about you? What are you going to do?"

Aimee gave a small, wry laugh. Who would want to employ a sixteen year old single mother?"

"You could go to college next year. The baby will be a year old by then. There are crèche facilities at the tech, you know."

A glimmer of hope seemed to flicker in Aimee's eyes and Helen continued earnestly. "The best thing you can do is to take one step at a time. Right now, your priorities should be revision, get the best possible grades you can. After that, forget studying and getting jobs, all you need to think about is getting ready for the baby. Then, when you've had the baby and are settled into a routine, you can start to think about your future."

She made it all sound so simple and straightforward and Aimee knew that it wouldn't be. Nevertheless, somehow, it seemed to make sense and Aimee experienced an unfamiliar wave of optimism as she listened to her teacher.

Helen glanced at her watch. "Suppose we'd better make a move." She opened her handbag and took out an old envelope from which she tore a small section of paper. After another rummage in her bag, she found a pen. "This is my phone number, Aimee. Keep it and ring me, anytime."

Aimee took the number, blushing slightly, as she considered the huge amount of trust that Miss Fletcher was placing in her. Thanks, Mi . . . I mean, Helen."

"I want you to promise, me, Aimee, that you'll ring me if ever you need someone to talk to, either before or after the baby's born." She arched her eyebrows. "Promise?"

Aimee nodded. She felt a strange sensation and acknowledged with some surprise that she felt almost cheerful.

* * *

Geoff Ruskin tapped his colleague lightly on the shoulder in the staff room.

"Everything go all right this morning?"

120

"Fine," Helen nodded. "she's seeing the midwife in a couple of days and they're trying to get her a scan appointment as soon as possible." She spoke quietly. As far as she knew , there were only a handful of staff who were aware of the situation and for Aimee's sake, she wanted it to stay that way.

"The Head's talking about letting her start her study leave early."

Helen felt her hackles rising. "Why?"

Geoff shrugged. He knew what she was thinking. "I don't think it's just the scandal thing, I think she was thinking it might be less stressful for Aimee."

"Well, maybe Aimee should be the one to decide that." Helen was already half way towards the door.

Mrs Derwent's door was shut, an indication that she was not available. Frustrated, Helen made enquiries in the secretary's office.

"She's probably going to be tied up all lunch time, Helen. Can I give her a message?"

Helen breathed deeply in order to avoid saying anything she might regret. "No thanks, Pat, I'll try later." She was teaching all afternoon, she'd just have to leave it until after school. Helen decided to make the most of the time in between and sent a note to the office asking them to send Aimee to see her at break time.

Aimee dutifully arrived not long after the break time bell. She was, Helen noticed, looking slightly less drained, a little more relaxed.

"You wanted to see me, Miss?" She slipped easily back into a respectful greeting.

"Hi Aimee, how are you feeling?"

"Ok, thanks."

"I didn't really want to ask earlier but I just wondered how things are at home?"

Aimee shrugged, clearly embarrassed. "Just the same"

"Have you heard from your mum yet?"

Aimee shook her head silently.

Helen chose her words carefully. "And how's your stepfather treating you?"

"What do you mean?" Aimee was immediately on the defensive. What did Miss Fletcher know about how Jim treated them?

"Well," Helen began casually, "it was obviously a big shock for him . . . the baby, I mean. So I just wondered if he was ok with you."

"Oh, yeah. He hasn't said much really." It was not untrue. Jim continued to brood menacingly, ticking away quietly like a time bomb. But Aimee clung to the hope that as long as he realised that he needed her, which was basically as long as Sheryl was away, then he would leave her alone.

"I see." Helen tried not to appear too inquisitive. She sensed Aimee's guard going up at the slightest mention of her family. She picked up a pile of books from her desk and placed them into her box, ready to take home for marking. "Phew . . . I'll be glad of two weeks off, how about you?"

"Suppose so." Aimee had never exactly looked forward to holidays at home and this was going to be the most testing yet. She was desperate to revise for her exams, but with Kayleigh and Stacey to keep entertained, Jim to keep happy and no sign of Sheryl . . . On the other hand, she had begun to wonder lately whether it was actually easier in some ways without Sheryl there winding Jim up with her very existence. Whilst there was the ever-constant threat of Jim's temper erupting, the last few weeks at least had been the least violent she had ever known. There was a sense of nervous tension about the house but

122

generally it was calm, which it rarely was when Sheryl and Jim were together.

Aimee hated the ambivalence of her feelings regarding her mother's absence. She longed to know that she was safe, ached for her to return and yet she dreaded it too.

Miss Fletcher's voice interrupted her thoughts. "At least you only have another two weeks to do after Easter, then you'll be on study leave." Helen was testing the water, trying to find out how Aimee felt about coming back to school after the holidays.

"I know. But sometimes I find it easier to study at school." Aimee broke off abruptly, she was wary of confiding too much even in Miss Fletcher – Helen – who was the nearest she had to a friend.

"I heard some year eleven kids saying they think they should finish at Easter and just come in for their exams."

"Oh no, I'd much rather be here."

The bell concluded their chat and Helen smiled cheerfully as Aimee walked towards the door. She was gone but within seconds she was back. "Erm . . . Miss, what did you want me for?"

"Oh, nothing, just wanted to check you were okay. See you later." Miss Fletcher was smug. She was glad the Head had not been free earlier. It had given her chance to calm down and what's more, she now had just the ammunition she needed to support her argument. With renewed energy, she called in her year seven group.

An hour or so later, she was again knocking on Mrs Derwent's door, which was now slightly ajar.

"Ah, Helen, I was hoping to see you. About Aimee, now I've been thinking. The girl obviously has a great deal on her plate at the moment and she would probably welcome some extra study leave. So, I think we'll propose that she finishes on Friday and just come in for exams . . . assuming she's going to turn up for her exams. . ." Her voice tailed off distractedly, "I mean, it's too late to withdraw her now, I suppose . . ."

"You know," Helen interrupted keenly, "that's just what I was thinking."

Miss Derwent smiled with relief. At least Helen wasn't going to start kicking up a fuss this time. "Oh good . . . I mean, great minds think alike."

"But, " Helen persisted innocuously, "I was chatting to Aimee at break and she categorically said that she would rather be at school. In fact, considering how her home life is, we'd be doing her a huge favour if she didn't have to take study leave at all!"

Mrs Derwent was speechless. Was the woman proposing that Aimee Parkinson walk around school until the end of the exams, probably a mere six weeks or so away from her due date? "But . . ." She realised that, once again, Helen Fletcher had manipulated the situation to get exactly what she wanted.

* * *

Aimee awoke on the first morning of the Easter holidays with a heavy heart. She could not see how she was possibly going to entertain the two little girls for a fortnight, look after the house, the washing, the ironing, the cooking *and* revise for her GCSEs. Maybe she should just forget about her exams, it would certainly be a huge weight off her shoulders. Perhaps she should just not bother going back to school. It was tempting. But then she thought of Miss Fletcher. What would she say? She would say that she was being a defeatist. Well, that would be easy for her, she didn't have *her* problems to contend with. Helen had admitted to her, that, at twenty-seven, she had never had to worry about anything other than passing exams and finding a job, none of which had proved particularly difficult for her. She had had nothing but encouragement from her parents

124

throughout her life and now she had the support of her fiancé. Hers had been a comfortable and care-free existence and she could not imagine coping with Aimee's problems. So, thought Aimee, what right did she have to expect her to do her exams, go to college . . .

Aimee looked at her school bag and felt a sense of triumph as she pushed it under her bed. Out of sight, out of mind. There was no point, she might as well not bother trying. She pushed the bag further under the bed. There – sorted – one less problem to deal with.

"Aimee, is it the holidays today?" Stacey was pulling on her big sister's pyjama top excitedly. Aimee nodded.

"Will you take us to the park, Aimee?"

Inwardly sighing, Aimee found herself assuring her little sister that, in between tidying the house and doing her paper round, she'd take them to the park.

"Yippee!" The two girls were delighted.

"Ssshh!" Aimee hated to dampen their enthusiasm but if they woke Jim, then there would be hell to pay. "Go and get dressed. I'll make your breakfast. Kayleigh, help Stace."

Aimee managed to put together what would have to pass for a picnic. Since Sheryl's departure, Aimee had had to constantly remind Jim that she needed money if she were to buy food. She had become an expert in seeking out bargains, items on which the sell-by-date was about to expire, together with the bread and fresh fruit and veg, which was sold off cheaply as they lost their freshness.

Everything was packed up ready and Aimee told the girls to get their coats.

"But it's sunny!" insisted Kayleigh.

"It is," agreed Aimee, "but it's still April and the wind will be cold in the park. Do as you're told."

The sound of a letter being pushed through the door caused her to look up. She walked across the small hallway and picked up the single white envelope that had fallen on the mat. She was surprised to see her own name and held it in front of her curiously for a moment before turning it over and sliding her finger under the seal.

"We're ready!"

Aimee looked down at the two girls, beaming brightly. It was so good to see them looking relaxed for a change. A twinge of resentment stirred in her heart as she thought about their absent mother. How could she have deserted these precious babies? How could she have deserted her, her first born? Why couldn't she have taken them all away? So that they could all be free from his tyranny, for ever? She pushed the envelope into her pocket.

"Okay then, let's go."

Aimee had been right to insist on their coats. The sky was blue and the clouds were a perfect fluffy white and yet the breeze was cool. But it was good to feel the fresh air and Aimee felt less troubled as she pushed her sisters on the swings. She placed one hand inside her pocket and fingered the folded envelope that she had placed there a short while earlier. It was her scan appointment and it was for tomorrow morning; ten past eleven at the hospital. She really did not see why she had to go. It was just more hassle. Who was going to look after her sisters? She would have to take them with her. She wouldn't go. What could they do, if she didn't go? She thought again of Helen Fletcher. This was all her fault, why did she have to go interfering?

"Aimee, you're not looking at us." Stacey admonished reproachfully. "Look! Look how high I'm going. Whheeeee!"

"I'm higher than you!" Claimed Kayleigh competitively.

126

"No, I'm highest, aren't I Aimee?"

Aimee laughed, "You're both highest, one after the other. Come on, do you want to go on the slide now?"

"I want to go on the roundabout!"

Aimee tried hard to dismiss her troubled thoughts and give the girls a happy day but her heart was still heavy as they made their way towards the precinct later that afternoon.

"I'm cold." moaned Stacey, tired after a few hours' playing and picnicking. "I don't want to do the papers Aimee."

"Neither do I." Aimee retorted matter-of-factly, "but we have to, so that's the end of it. Wait here for a moment and don't move."

Aimee positioned the two girls outside the phone booth, away from the road. She had a few coins in her pocket, she had been toying with an idea all afternoon and only on seeing the phone booth, did she make up her mind.

She dialled carefully and listened to the sound of the phone ringing out, waiting anxiously for a voice at the other end of the line.

Aimee was relieved to hear Helen's voice, she was not sure whether Helen lived alone and had been dreading speaking to anyone else.

"Aimee – are you okay?" Helen sounded pleased to hear her and yet her tone was also one of concern.

Aimee was conscious of not having much change and quickly gabbled the reason for phoning. Helen did not hesitate to agree to Aimee's request.

"Are you sure it's no trouble?" Aimee continued humbly.

"It's no trouble!" Helen was quite excited, not only was she delighted that Aimee was finally beginning to trust her but she was also curious to be present at the scan. "Shall I pick you up?"

As she expected, Aimee declined and they arranged to meet by the school.

"I'm probably going to have to bring my sisters with me." Aimee finished apologetically.

"Lovely, I'd like to meet them. " Helen sounded genuinely unfazed by the prospect.

Aimee was smiling as she took her sisters' hands. At last there was someone she could rely on. "Come on you two, I'll buy you some sweeties for you to eat on the way."

* * *

Aimee turned the key in the lock. Jim was talking to someone. His voice was low and Aimee could make out neither his words nor his tone. The living room door was slightly ajar and Aimee motioned for Kayleigh and Stacey to be quiet, pushing them gently towards the stairs. "I'll be up in minute," she whispered. She stood still, straining her ears. Still she could only hear Jim's voice. She caught only disjointed words.

"been awful. . . they need you."

Aimee's stomach turned a somersault and then she burst into the living room where she came face to face with her mother.

She looked well, she was wearing a coat that Aimee did not recognise and her hair had been cut into a more flattering bob. She looked like she'd been on bloody holiday! Aimee's emotions rocketed to elation, her mom was home safe and well, then plummeted to resentment, anger and fear. What right did she have to just waltz back in, looking like that whilst her own life was falling apart? Where had she been when she had needed her? They hadn't known whether she was dead or alive and Sheryl hadn't cared enough to let them know that at least she was safe. Well, she could go to hell! Aimee didn't care that she'd come back, they were just fine without her thank you very much. No! They were better than just fine, in fact, they were bloody better off. Jim had not been violent in the whole time she'd been away. Now, what was going to happen? Everything would just go back to normal. Aimee shuddered as she battled to control her emotions.

"Aimee, I . . ." Sheryl took a step towards her.

"Don't touch me!" Aimee was seething with anger.

"Aimee . . . please . . . let me explain . . ."

Aimee turned before her mother could see the tears and fled to the top of the stairs, almost tripping over Kayleigh and Stacey who looked at her in shocked silence.

Aimee flung herself on her bed, shaking with emotion. Her sisters had followed her anxiously, Kayleigh stroked her big sister's hair. "Aimee, what's the matter?"

Aimee fought to quell her sobs in front of her sisters. She sat up and brushed her hair from her face, which was already wet with her tears.

"Are you okay, Aimee?" Stacey looked at her with big eyes, full of concern.

"Who's downstairs, Aimee?" Aimee suspected that Kayleigh already knew the answer.

"It's mom." She studied their reactions, confusion, fear, happiness and doubt crossed their faces.

"Is . . . is she staying?" Kayleigh ventured hopefully.

"You'd better go and ask her." Aimee could not prevent the hint of bitterness from colouring her tone.

"Can we?" Stacey was eager to see her mommy.

Aimee nodded. It was clear that Kayleigh and Stacey were going to be much more forgiving of their mother than she was and she felt guilty and alone as they rushed away eagerly. Kayleigh turned at the door and looked anxiously towards Aimee, who was still on the bed. "Are you coming?"

"In a minute."

"Will you be okay?"

Aimee smiled and nodded. They were so sweet. What had they done to deserve Jim and Sheryl as parents? They would be so happy to see Sheryl but what terrible fate awaited them? Aimee held her face in her hands, for several moments, lost in her despair. She wondered how long it would be before the peace would be shattered.

Some long moments later, however, somehow Aimee became determined to focus her mind on something positive and she found herself reaching under her bed for her school books, resolute that her future would not be entirely in other people's hands.

It was about half an hour later when Sheryl tentatively came into the room. Aimee was sitting on her bed with her back against the wall. Her school books scattered around her. She sensed her mother's nervousness and she did not look up – unwilling to do anything that would make it easier for her.

"Aimee . . . I'm sorry."

"Don't be!" Aimee exploded bitterly, "We've been just fine without you. By the way, have you had a nice time?"

"Not really." Sheryl's tone was flat.

"Where have you been?" Aimee disguised her curiosity with angry resentment.

Sheryl shrugged. "I stayed in a refuge . . . for women."

Aimee was incredulous; she had believed that she had tried every hostel in the area. "Why didn't you let us know you were okay?" Her mind raced back over all the phone calls she had made, the letter she had written, the hours of worry and misery. One minute believing her to be dead, that they would never see her again, the next convinced that she would return and that things would be better. She burst into tears as the recollections bubbled over in her mind. She resented her need of this weak and selfish woman and her anger caused her to cry so hard that she thought her heart would break.

She felt too weak to resist as Sheryl clambered towards her and took her gently in her arms. "Sshh . . . Aimee , don't cry . . . it'll be all right . . . come on." Briefly, Aimee succumbed to the feeling of protection that enveloped her in her mother's hug. For a few moments, she was the little girl who was "Aimee", loved by her mother.

But she was no longer a little girl and it had been so long since she had felt truly loved, cherished and protected and now it was too late. Her childhood had ended long ago and now she herself was to become responsible for another human being.

She pushed her mother away and wiped away her tears as she regained her composure.

"Has he told you?"

"Yes, love, I know. He's told me."

Aimee realised with shame that she had wanted to be the one to tell her mother, to wound her in some way, to get her own back for the pain that Sheryl had caused her.

"Why didn't you tell me?"

"You weren't here!"

"I mean before I went."

Aimee snorted, her voice filled with contempt, "You mean it would have made a difference?"

"Of course." Sheryl's voice was barely audible. She knew that it was not true. She remembered vaguely her state of mind when she had left; she had not cared whether she lived or died, she just had to get away. She had been incapable of caring for her children or even herself. She had no idea now whether it had been her instinct to survive which had forced her to escape or whether she had just been so confused that she had simply walked out.

Sheryl was quiet as she remembered how she had left the house empty handed in the early hours; she didn't think that it was her intention to leave; she just wanted to be safe for a while. She had not known where she was going, she simply wandered away from the estate, with hardly the energy to put one foot in front of the other. Her clothing was torn and her face and body battered from Jim's beating which she had thought would finish her off this time. She didn't know how long she had been walking and she felt no fear of the dark and empty streets. It was almost light when she became aware of a car that had stopped just ahead of her. She was walking beside a main road out of the town and she had not been aware of any traffic until now. She hesitated as she wondered whether to turn round, she trembled with fear, doubting that she would have the strength to run. She squinted in the half-light, the occupant of the car looked to be only slightly built, maybe the person was simply lost. Cautiously, she placed one foot in front of the other until she was almost level with the car, but as far away from the kerb as she could manage without scratching her already sore flesh on the hedges. The driver wound down the electric window on the passenger side and Aimee had her first clear view of the person who it became obvious was female.

"Are you okay?" The woman peered towards her, her expression one of confusion.

Sheryl nodded unconvincingly.

"Can I give you a lift?" The woman could see quite clearly that she was far from all right.

"Have . . . you been attacked?" Her gaze ran over Sheryl's bruises and her torn clothing.

"No." Sheryl shook her head, thinking that the woman suspected that she had been assaulted by a stranger. Then she nodded, confused, she supposed she had been attacked. It was just that she was so accustomed to Jim's abuse that she no longer saw it as an attack, just a way of life.

"Look, love, I'm a nurse. I'm on my way to work now. Hop in, I'll take you to the hospital, get you cleaned up and get someone to take a look at you."

For a moment, Sheryl continued to look doubtful. She should go home. Jim would go berserk if he found out that she'd been to hospital, bringing in the authorities is how he would see it. But then she realised how cold she was and how tired. Her face hurt and her body hurt and the woman was looking at her, waiting for her to get into the car. So she did.

She had had no real intention of leaving; it just kind of happened. She hadn't given them her real name, just in case. You never knew with the authorities where they would go poking their noses next, sending someone round to see if she was looking after her kids properly. Jim would go mental. They were kind at the hospital, the nurse had bathed her bruises and cleaned the cuts. The nurse who had picked her up was called Jean, she was a sister and she said that she could stay for a while in one of the cubicles, "seeing as it's quiet for a change." She even brought her some breakfast and a magazine.

"What are you going to do?" Jean asked gently.

Sheryl supposed that she could simply go home, face the music. He would most probably kill her.

"Kids?" Jean enquired. She looked surprised when Sheryl shook her head. "So why stay then?" she asked incredulously. She had

133

given her a piece of paper with the address of a hostel. "Why don't you go there, they'll let you stay for a little while, until you get yourself sorted."

That had been it and somehow the days had trickled by without her noticing. Everyone was kind to her, there were women who came and went, some of them with their kids and all of them in the same position. She missed her kids and each morning she intended to go home but the thought of just one more night where she felt safe tempted her into staying.

As she held her eldest daughter, she felt stronger than she had in a long, long time. She had failed her daughters and she would have to live with the guilt for ever. She had woken this morning just as she had every morning for the past three weeks, thinking of Aimee, Kayleigh and Stacey, hoping that they were all right and then she would think of Jim and how he would react if she went back. She realised suddenly that she had started to think of "if" she went back and not "when" and the realisation shocked her. Of course she had to go back, she couldn't just desert her kids. She was terrified of what she would be going back to but she could not stay away.

She had walked out of the house with nothing, not even her key and she was forced to knock the front door. She steeled herself. The house was in silence, anxiously she wondered where the children were as the door opened slowly and Jim filled the space. She noted the shocked expression on his face and she was certain there was something else too; he actually looked relieved.

"You're not going to touch me, Jim." Her fortitude surprised her as she looked him in the eye.

He shook his head and he stepped aside to let her in.

She walked into her home like a stranger. "Where are the kids?" It was her only concern.

"At the park." Aimee had left him a note that morning. "They won't be back till after they've done the papers."

It all sounded so normal – life going on without her as though it made no difference whether she were there or not.

"They've missed you." The kindness of his tone was unbearable and tears pricked her eyes. He stood awkwardly, the gulf between them enormous. "I'll put the kettle on."

The house was immaculate. That would be Aimee, of course. Such a good girl, she should be out enjoying herself with her friends, not taking the weight of the world on her shoulders.

He handed her a cup of tea and they sat facing each other across the small living room. His calmness unnerved her, it was so uncharacteristic. Why wasn't he angry? Why wasn't he demanding to know where she had been.

"Are they okay . . . the girls?" It seemed so pitiful to be asking politely after her own children.

He was wearing an odd expression, wanting to tell her something, but not knowing how.

"What is it?" Sheryl was suddenly filled with a sense of foreboding. They were at the park, how could there be anything wrong if they were at the park? "What is it, Jim, tell me."

"It's Aimee." There was a long, heavy silence. "She's gone and got herself pregnant."

"What?" Sheryl was incredulous, her voice hoarse with shock.

He nodded. "Bloody pregnant." Momentarily, he felt the familiar push of anger. He forced it away – not something that came easily to him.

"But . . . who? When?" Sheryl was truly bewildered, she had only been gone three weeks.

"Have you talked to her about it? What's she going to do? I mean . . ." Her voice tailed off in confusion. She couldn't understand how Aimee would have confided this in Jim and she could only imagine that it was in order to arrange a discreet visit to the hospital. She recalled the child that he had forced her to abort just a few months previously and now here she was casually presuming that her daughter would do the same. But this was different, Aimee was still a child. She would be sixteen next week, she had all of her life ahead of her, she could escape this misery and make something of herself. There was no question of her having the child, it just didn't make sense.

"It's too late," Jim stated flatly. "It's due in August."

Sheryl could not take it in. It was May next week, that meant that she was . . . Good God! How could she have failed to notice? What kind of a mother was she? She put her face in her hands and moaned. The pain of knowing what her eldest daughter must have been going through and the realisation that this was the end of her childhood was almost a physical one. She heard him rise from his chair but she felt no fear, she did not care what he did to her. She was worthless.

"Come on Shez." He knelt beside her and pulled her towards him as gently as his rough nature would allow. "It's not your fault. You know what kids are like. They're all bloody at it these days. Christ, we should be grateful she's only pregnant and not on bloody heroin or something."

"Grateful? She's my baby."

"She's sixteen."

"Nearly." Sheryl shook her head in disbelief. "Has she said who the father is?"

He shook his head. He did not even want to admit that he hadn't asked.

Sheryl sat silently cogitating about the few occasions when Aimee had gone to the youth club. Surely . . .

136

Jim interrupted her thoughts. "It's done now. No use crying over spilt milk."

She could not believe that it was Jim speaking. She stared at him. Why was he so calm?

* * *

Now, as she looked at her daughter, the guilt weighed heavily on her shoulders. She had let Aimee down so badly, she had to be there for her now, somehow she had to make it up to her. She thought of how Jim had been since her return. If only, he could have changed for good, she didn't dare hope that it would be possible.

There was very little that she could get out of Aimee that evening but the two little girls were a delight. It was a long time since Sheryl had known Jim to go to bed sober and for once she gave in willingly to his advances. She lay for a long time after he had fallen asleep and she thought of Aimee in the next room, alone with her fears and her secrets.

Chapter Ten

Aimee slept restlessly on and off throughout the night. She had been awakened by the sounds of Jim and Sheryl getting ready for bed and her stomach had clenched into the familiar knot, waiting for sounds of an argument, but they had not come. Instead, she could hear the sounds of the bed creaking beneath their frantic love-making and Aimee pulled the sheet over her head in disgust and bewilderment. She remembered how she had felt in Jack's arms and a longing that she had not felt in weeks consumed her. Her mother was back and she should be glad. She *was* glad. The relief of knowing that she was alive and well overwhelmed her and yet lying in her bed, listening to the sounds of their new-found unity, she felt more alone than ever. And there was another emotion bubbling away inside her, which she did not truly acknowledge, for it made her feel ashamed. She was angry.

Sheryl was already in the kitchen when Aimee arose the next morning. Her mother's bright and cheery greeting re-fuelled the anger that had begun to simmer the previous night and Aimee hated herself for the negative thoughts that tormented her. She wished that she could just be happy that her mother was happy; the last thing that she wanted was for her mother to be the pathetic, down-trodden person who had left them a few weeks earlier but somehow she could not relate to the person who stood smilingly preparing breakfast for them all.

"We'll have to go shopping, Aimee." Sheryl informed her, as if she were the one who had been absent. "I've made some toast. Are the girls up?"

Aimee shrugged disagreeably. She looked resentfully over towards her mother, it was unusual to see her eating first thing in the morning. Something had given her an appetite, she thought with disgust.

"I'm not hungry." It was true. Aimee's stomach was filled with butterflies at the prospect of her scan. At least now she wouldn't have her sisters in tow, she would be able to concentrate on what was going on. She was conscious of something more than curiosity; she was excited about the prospect of seeing her baby. "I'm going for a bath."

"Well, have something when you come down then. Aimee you need to look after yourself you know." Sheryl sighed. Aimee was hurt and she was conscious of the guilty part that she had played in hurting her. She watched sadly as her eldest daughter turned away in silence.

Aimee bathed and dressed herself leisurely. It was good not to have to worry about her sisters for once but the air of cheeriness around the house unnerved her.

"I'm off out."

Sheryl was reading a story to Kayleigh and Stacey, who hung on their mother's every word, delighted not simply to have her back but to have her attention, which was a rare treat.

Sheryl frowned. "Where are you going?"

Aimee glanced cautiously towards her two little sisters. She wanted to say something about the fact that her mother hadn't concerned herself about her whereabouts for the previous three weeks but her innate protection towards her sisters prevented her. "Just a check-up."

Sheryl jumped up quickly. "Why didn't you say. I'll come with you. Aimee, wait, you don't want to go by yourself."

"No, I'll not be by myself." Aimee was conscious of the faint feeling of pleasure in rejecting her mother.

"But . . ."

"See you later." Aimee closed the door carefully behind her. She was inclined to let it slam – but that would have been too risky, Jim was having a lie in and Aimee was not that vindictive. Much as her mother's happy act incited her, the knowledge that Jim could easily revert back to his normal self was never far from her thoughts.

Helen was early and already waiting for her a short distance from the school.

"Hi!" Helen was beaming as Aimee carefully settled herself into the passenger seat, "Where are your sisters?"

Aimee shifted self-consciously in the seat before turning to face her teacher and quietly informing her of her mother's unexpected return.

Helen opened her eyes wide, "Well, that's great . . . isn't it?" She finished hesitantly.

Aimee nodded. "I suppose so."

"Where's she been? I mean . . . is she all right?" As usual, Helen was careful not to appear too nosey.

"She's fine. Anyway, at least it means I didn't have to bring my sisters along. I hope you don't mind coming with me. Well, taking me, I mean." Aimee blushed.

Helen understood that Aimee did not want to talk about her mother and explained that her only other activity for the day would have been marking books and planning lessons, so she definitely didn't mind a change of scenery. "How are you feeling? Nervous?"

She was a bit nervous, she realised. And still embarrassed. She wondered if it were true that motherhood gave you more confidence when you took on the battles of another being. To Aimee, it felt as though she had been responsible for others for a life time already.

"I wonder if they'll tell you if it's a boy or a girl. Do you want to know?"

Aimee smiled. Helen made it all seem so perfectly normal. She treated her like an adult and she liked it. "I don't know. I've hardly thought about it. I suppose it could be useful . . ."

"I think I'd want a surprise if it were me." Helen mused.

Aimee relaxed during the drive to the hospital and she was almost sorry when they pulled on to the car park a short while later.

As she sat with the other mothers-to-be, Aimee again fell silent. She was conscious of how young she must look. The other women chatted happily, some had toddlers with them, a few were with their husbands or partners and a couple were accompanied by older women, who were obviously their own mothers. Aimee wondered what they made of her, so obviously young and Helen certainly didn't look old enough to be her mother, although, she realised with shock, that she was only five or six years younger than Sheryl. Some people might assume they were a couple.

"What are you thinking?" Helen whispered, catching her eye.

Aimee shook her head. It wasn't the place for heart to hearts.

A short while later she surrendered to the various ante-natal procedures and answered the nurse's questions obediently.

"You're slightly underweight for your height, love." The plump midwife informed her with a look of concern. "Are you eating properly?"

Aimee nodded. It was not true. How on earth could she have been eating properly, having been through what she'd been through these past months?

The nurse waved her finger bossily. "I know what you young gi . .. ladies are like. Now then, I'm going to give you a nutrition sheet that will help you to eat properly without putting on any excess weight."

Finally, Aimee was called in to be scanned. This was the bit she'd been waiting for.

She lay down on the bed and Helen took a seat beside her with a reassuring wink. It was a young nurse who explained the procedure to them and Aimee felt nervous but excited as she rubbed the cold gel on to her stomach.

The nurse directed them to the appropriate parts of the screen and at first Aimee could see nothing but blurry lines and shadows but slowly as her eyes adjusted, she realized that she was looking at her baby's head and then an arm . . .

"Oh my God!" She gasped, "I can't believe it . . . wow . . . I just can't believe it!"

Without warning, she burst into tears and then immediately felt completely idiotic.

"Don't worry," the nurse swiftly handed her a box of tissues, "it's quite normal . . . lots of people cry when they see their first scan."

"It's brilliant!" enthused Helen, not noticing the midwife's curious glance at the unusual pair.

"Is he okay?" Aimee asked anxiously.

"He?" questioned the nurse in amusement.

"Well, I mean, you know."

"I know." The nurse laughed. "Well, baby's doing just fine. Look, one arm and another. Two legs, two feet . . ."

As she left the hospital, Aimee could not take her eyes off the small photo of her unborn child. "I can't believe it." She was still shaking her head in disbelief at the sight of the life inside her.

"I know what you mean." Helen leaned over her shoulder. "It's so exciting isn't it?"

"It might be exciting for you. I'm bloody terrified!"

Helen burst out laughing. She had never heard Aimee swear before. Now, she knew for certain that she'd won her trust. "I'm sorry, Aimee," she spluttered as Aimee gazed at her in amazement. "I'm really sorry . . . it's just . . ."

Aimee laughed, understanding suddenly what her teacher had found so amusing. She assumed an air of sincerity. "It's all very well for you, cooing and sighing." She pointed to her stomach in indignation. "I've got to bloody well give birth to it!"

They were still giggling as Helen started the car. "What time are they expecting you back?"

Aimee was brought back to earth with a bump. She shook her head. "Doesn't matter, they're busy playing happy families at the moment. They won't miss me."

Helen picked up the note of bitterness in her voice and she tried to keep her own tone casual. "Fancy going shopping?"

"Well . . ."

"We don't have to buy anything . . . just have a wander around. I normally go out of town where there's no danger of bumping into the kids from school." She smiled at the unintended irony.

Aimee considered her options. "I've got my revision to do" she ventured, "and my papers later."

"You're entitled to a rest . . . it's up to you."

Aimee found herself agreeing on the basis that she would have to be back for four. "I can't afford to lose my paper round."

Helen nodded understandingly although she wanted to tell her that she shouldn't be doing the paper round in her condition.

Unsurprisingly, the shopping centre was busy with pre-Easter shoppers.

"Relax," Helen assured her. "I come here regularly and I've never seen any of the kids from school here. Anyway, who cares? You'll be left in a couple of weeks. "

Aimee was quiet and Helen wondered if she was worrying about her revision, the baby or the whole lot! Helen could hardly begin to imagine what Aimee had been through. She herself had found it hard enough to concentrate on studying and she'd had nothing to worry about. As far as she was concerned, whatever grades Aimee managed would be a considerable achievement. "Hey, let's go in here."

Before she could argue, Aimee found herself being guided into a baby shop.

"Oh! These are just soooo cute!"

Aimee smiled at the sight of her teacher cooing over the new born babygros.

"Oh no, look at this one, this one is even more gorgeous. Will you let me buy it for you, Aimee?"

"But . . ." Aimee blushed. She had absolutely nothing for the baby. Each week, she carefully saved as much of her paper money as she could and had vague ideas about obtaining the essentials second-hand but to date she had done nothing

"It's for my sake really." Helen gushed. "I'm just longing to indulge my maternal instincts."

"Maybe you should have one of your own." Aimee was beginning to feel just a little curious about the woman who seemed intent upon befriending her and she could not help wondering about the man who had given her the lovely engagement ring.

Helen exhaled in an exaggerated sigh. "The nation needs me, I'm afraid, Aimee. Can't go abandoning my students and going off on maternity leave just yet."

Aimee laughed. "Well, if it will make you happy and keep a much needed teacher in the classroom, I suppose I should accept."

"Hurrah." Helen smiled gleefully, moving swiftly to the next aisle. "Ah, look at these gorgeous little things . . ." She threw Aimee an apologetic glance. "Sorry, can't resist, will have to get these too."

A short while later, the pair were walking out of the shop with Helen sporting a large carrier.

"Helen, I can't accept all these. I'll bring you the money at school."

Helen tutted. "Stop fussing, Aimee. They're not even for you, they're for the baby. And I've told you, this is purely an act of selfish indulgence. I've always longed for an excuse to go on a shopping spree in a baby shop."

"Now, I'm absolutely starved. I fancy jacket potato, cheese and salad. How about you?"

Aimee insisted on paying her way. She was touched by Helen's generosity but she was not going to take advantage. Or be seen as a charity case. Whatever people said about teenage mothers, she did not expect hand outs.

* * *

"How did it go?"

Aimee could tell that Sheryl was trying hard to conceal her disappointment at not being present for the scan. Her anger had been diminished by the enjoyment of the day and shyly she produced the scan photograph. "Look, Mom."

Sheryl gazed at the image which brought back so many memories. She had similar pictures of Aimee, Kayleigh and Stacey. But behind the happy recollections, there was so much

145

pain; the recent memory of her own terminated pregnancy not to mention the living hell into which she had brought her three lovely daughters, who deserved so much better. She sat at the kitchen table, the photograph still in her hand, she could only pray that things would be easier for Aimee and for this innocent child that was about to enter the world. Not for the first time, she realised that she had been so dependent on her eldest daughter and now she felt as though she hardly knew her.

"Who went with you – the father?"

Aimee shook her head. So far, there had been few questions asked about the identity of the father and that was the way she liked it. Stubbornly, she returned her mother's gaze. She had no intention of dragging Jack into it. If she ever settled down with a man, it would be because of love, not because she was pregnant. Her mother was still looking at her. Aimee no longer felt the need to widen the gulf that had developed between them in the last twenty four hours.

"A friend came with me. From school."

"Oh, good." Once again, Sheryl acknowledged that she had been so wrapped up in her own life for so long that she knew nothing of her daughter's friendships.

"She's my teacher."

"What? Are you kidding? Good God, Aimee, don't let Jim know. He'll go nuts if he finds out you're associating with the "authorities.""

Aimee shook her head in disgust as she held out her hand for the return of the scan photo. "Don't worry. I won't be discussing anything with *him.*" Her teeth were gritted.

"I'm sorry, love," Sheryl whispered, "but you know what he's like."

Aimee turned away. "I thought he was a changed man since your gracious return." The anger was back and the pleasure of her day had disintegrated.

* * *

Jim was indeed on his very best behaviour. Kayleigh and Stacey enjoyed the happiest Easter Sunday of their lives, their little faces full of delight when their proud mother presented them with what seemed to them to be enormous chocolate eggs.

"There's one for you too." Sheryl handed Aimee the chocolate egg and the now familiar feeling of resentment and shame engulfed her. She could not help but think of all of the Easter Sundays when all that Sheryl had managed was a small cheap egg which didn't even taste like real chocolate. As her mother busied herself preparing a full cooked breakfast, Aimee remembered how not long ago there had only been enough money for a proper breakfast for Jim. Now, her mother marvelled at how far their money stretched when it was not being guzzled by her husband.

For Aimee, it was too little, too late. She loved to see the joy in her little sisters' eyes but somehow she knew that it would not last and as far as her own childhood was concerned – for what it had been worth – it was over. Well and truly over.

It was hard to be any less miserable when she turned sixteen a few days later. Sheryl had made a huge effort, organising Kayleigh and Stacey to make secret cards for their big sister and she had even made a cake, albeit from a packet. But the biggest surprise for Aimee had appeared when she returned from her paper round. She opened the door to find a pretty blue and white pram, filling the small hallway.

"It's hardly been used, love." Sheryl informed her eagerly "Perfect, don't you think?"

147

"Yes . . . thank you . . . it's lovely."

"Mommy, why is Aimee having a baby?" Stacey was pulling at her mother's sweater.

"Because . . ." Sheryl looked at Aimee, lost for words. "Because . . . she's going to be a wonderful mommy. Now, let's go and see if there are any more pressies for Aimee on her big day."

Sheryl had certainly made an effort, Aimee acknowledged, as her mother handed her a large, bulky parcel. As she fingered the cheap but practical pile of vests and babygros, she thanked her mother awkwardly. She could not help but cast her mind back to the beautiful items that Helen had bought, still safely stored in her flat.

Later, alone in her bedroom, surrounded by her revision books, Aimee again took out the baby clothes. She held the tiny items against her face, breathing in the smell of the fabric. Inside her, her baby kicked away, oblivious to the life which lay in store. Aimee rubbed her tummy lovingly. It was her sixteenth birthday. She had often thought of how it would feel to be sixteen, the school leaving age, the age of consent, able to buy a lottery ticket! The reality now was that she felt none of the anticipation and excitement that she had expected to feel. So much, it seemed, had already been decided. There would be no years of dating, playing the field, picking and choosing who she would end up with. Who would be interested in her now? And as for getting a job, it would be the same story. Who would want to employ her? She thought of Helen and her suggestion that she could go to college the following year. It might be possible in theory but to Aimee it seemed as though the up-hill struggle that had been her life for as long as she could remember was just getting steeper and steeper. And she had no one to blame now but herself.

The end of the holidays could not come soon enough as far as Aimee was concerned. She couldn't wait to get away from the stifling atmosphere of the house and she was looking forward to seeing Helen again. She had been so tempted to call her, Helen had insisted that she should if she wanted to, but Aimee had

148

forced herself to resist, not wanting to be thought of as a nuisance.

There were just two weeks left of school before the exams and the atmosphere amongst year eleven was an electric mix of nervous excitement for those who cared about their exam results and boisterous euphoria for those who had little interest in their GCSEs. Aimee had discovered to her horror on the Monday morning that it was now practically impossible to disguise her bump. Wearing her school uniform was out of the question and the weather was growing warmer and warmer, which added to her problem. She had arrived at school wearing a large, baggy, black sweatshirt, which stood out a mile next to the other girls, who were intent upon pushing their luck further each day with even tighter skirts and skimpier white blouses.

Luckily, Jodie Lewis and her cronies had lost interest in Aimee and although she was aware of a few strange looks being cast in her direction, she was no longer the brunt of their sarcastic humour. A few of the kinder girls in her class even seemed to be making a last effort to befriend her and she was touched when they offered her their leaving books to sign. It had not occurred to Aimee to put together any mementos of her school days and self-consciously, she admitted that she didn't have a book of her own.

"What are you doing after the exams, Aimee?" Kelly Stewart enquired amiably at lunch time.

Aimee could feel the blush creeping up her cheeks as Kelly and her two friends looked at her curiously.

"Me and Vicki are going to hairdressing college. Can't wait, can we, Vick? Should be a right laugh. Bet you're stopping for sixth form though ain't ya – seeing as you're quite brainy." Kelly filled the awkward silence herself, remembering why, over the years, they'd stopped bothering with Aimee. But somehow, she couldn't help feeling sorry for her. "You coming to the prom?" There was another long pause.

Vicki didn't really know why Kelly was bothering and she threw Aimee a disinterested smile. God, when did she get so fat? She turned her attention to Sara Turner, who was now telling her about her dress for the biggest event of their lives.

Aimee was wishing that Kelly would leave her alone. With so little time left at school, she had no interest in striking up new friendships; she had survived this long without anyone, she just wanted to be left alone to get on with doing the best that she could with what was left of her education.

Lessons seemed to be flying by at speed, which would have been great if she were still in year nine, Aimee noticed wryly. Now that her school days were numbered, she realised just to what extent they had given her life structure and security. It felt as though she were about to have the rug pulled from beneath her feet and she had no idea how or where she would land.

Kelly's next question startled Aimee. "Are you still going out with Jack?"

"Nnn. . . no." Aimee blushed again. She was not accustomed to chatting about her personal life. She tried to keep her voice casual. "We finished ages ago."

"Oh, shame, I thought you were well suited."

What did that mean, Aimee wondered fleetingly.

"Do you want to come out with us then on Friday? We can call for you if you like. I know where you live."

"Do you?" Aimee was surprised and not pleasantly. She had never invited anyone to her house and she was shamed by the thought of them knowing about the drab little place in which she lived.

"Yeah!" Kelly persisted cheerfully. "Deansfield Crescent. I did my brother's papers for him last year when he went camping."

Great, Aimee had no way of knowing what kind of domestic chaos would have been kicking off. "We don't have a paper delivered," she responded pointlessly.

"Nah, the freebies. Anyway, shall we call for you then, say about seven?"

"I don't know . . . I'll let you know. . . Look, I'll see you later." Aimee smiled weakly as she screwed up her sandwich wrapper and prepared to leave. She could sense that Kelly was just being friendly but somehow she felt lonelier than ever.

"Ouch." She grimaced in pain and her hand shot to her stomach.

"Are you okay?" The girls looked up, startled by her exclamation. She followed their eyes to the hand that was clutching her side, her clothing momentarily flattened to reveal the outline of the bump beneath.

"Christ!"

Aimee hurried away as fast as the cramp in her side would allow her, turning briefly to see the cluster of heads whispering animatedly as they looked sideways in her direction. Her heart sank. It would be all over the school by home time.

Aimee made her way tentatively towards Helen's classroom. As she had half expected, she was not there; she would be having her lunch in the staff room and there was no way she was going up there. Aimee turned to walk away, half contemplating going home. This would make Jodie Lewis's week, probably her year, if not the whole of her time at school, to hear that Aimee Parkinson was up the duff. Aimee really did not think she could handle it.

"Aimee!" Helen was behind her, half running to catch up with her. "Did you want me? I saw you by my room."

Aimee hesitated. Helen had done enough for her already, she was probably really busy; it wasn't right that she should be continually burdened with her problems. "It doesn't matter, Miss, it's nothing."

151

As usual, Helen was not easily discouraged. She could see that Aimee was upset. "Come for a chat, we'll go to my room." Her look implied that she would not be taking no for an answer and Aimee hadn't the energy to argue with her. Helen smiled reassuringly.

"Has something happened?" she enquired sympathetically.

Aimee felt tears pricking her eyes, she couldn't cope with anyone being kind to her right now.

"Hey, come on, what is it?" Helen guided her towards a chair on the far side of the classroom, out of sight from the door.

Aimee sighed heavily. "They know."

"I see." Helen looked serious but not surprised. "Who exactly?"

Aimee repeated her story. "I could see from their faces that they knew I was pregnant and now it will be all over the school. Especially, once Jodie Lewis finds out."

Helen looked pensive. She knew the girls Aimee was referring to. They were decent enough but Jodie Lewis was a different kettle of fish. "Stay here. I'll be back."

It seemed an eternity before the door opened and Helen returned. She was followed by Kelly, Vicki and Sara, all of whom were looking sheepish. Aimee looked away, aware of the blush that was burning her cheeks. She sensed their approach and heard Helen telling them to sit.

"Aimee," Helen began kindly, "the girls want to talk to you."

Aimee turned her head. They were looking at her, all of them, with serious expressions, a mixture of shock and concern. But there was also embarrassment and Aimee knew instantly that even in the short time that had passed since they had come to their conclusion, that the news had been passed on. It didn't matter who they had told, it was hot gossip and by the end of the afternoon, the whole school would know. Including Jack.

152

"It doesn't matter." Aimee sighed jadedly.

Kelly glanced swiftly towards their teacher and took the initiative. "Aimee, we haven't told anyone, that's the truth. But . . . we *were* talking about it and well . . . we could have been overheard. We are truly sorry, honestly."

Aimee chewed at the inside of her cheek. "I told you, it doesn't matter."

"We'll be with you Aimee, we're not gonna let anyone slag you off. Honest. You can count on us." She looked at her friends for support and they both mumbled their agreement.

Helen coughed. "I'm going to go and talk to the year tutors and get a message round that if anyone is overheard spreading rumours, they'll be dealt with severely. It's bullying. Okay?"

Aimee smiled ruefully. She appreciated Helen's good intentions and those of the girls, but there was little anyone could do to prevent people talking. "Thanks." She rose awkwardly from her seat. I need the loo. I'll see you later."

She heard Helen dismissing the girls authoritatively. "Ok, you three, off you go. I'll go and talk to Mr Ruskin." Aimee heard her saying something else which she didn't quite catch but she guessed that she would be reminding them of their promise to keep their mouths shut.

Aimee knew that no matter how determined Helen was to keep a lid on things, even she would not be able to prevent tongues wagging. It would be another obstacle that she would just have to overcome. She had not, however, expected that she would come face to face with the obstacle so soon. She heard the familiar, high pitched voice of Jodie Lewis over the gush of the toilet tank re-filling; she had been on the point of sliding back the lock, but now stood frozen behind the door as Jodie trilled animatedly:

"I just can't get my head round it can you? I mean, Aimee Parkinson! Pregnant! It's hysterical"

Her companion giggled before adding in semi-rebuke, "Aw, Jode, we shouldn't laugh. It's a shame. How would you like it?"

"Actually," Jodie announced haughtily, "I don't think I'd mind. She'll have her own flat in next to no time, you just watch. In fact, " she continued thoughtfully, "she's obviously not that stupid after all, it'll be an improvement on the dump she lives in now. Not to mention getting away from her dad. Step-dad whatever, he's a right drunk . . ."

Aimee froze. But the next words compelled her to confront them.

"So, do you reckon it's Jack Davis's then?"

"Must be," Jodie confirmed, "he's the only one she's been out with isn't he?" Mind you, I never expected *them* to be at it did you?" The pair dissolved into fits of laughter.

Their laughter was halted abruptly as Aimee appeared in front of them.

"SSsshhh! Oh Aimee, shit . . ."

She did at least, Aimee noted, have the decency to look embarrassed. Nevertheless, her blood was boiling at having heard herself the butt of their derision. She walked silently towards the sink and turned on the tap.

"C'mon." Jodie nudged her friend.

Aimee turned round swiftly, not wishing to lose the opportunity of having her say. She held her head high as she called them back. "Jodie, before you go." The two girls eyed her in surprise. "Seeing as you're both so interested in my personal life, you might like to know that Jack Davis is not the father of my baby, so I really would advise you to keep your big mouths shut." Aimee stared hard at their ridiculous, orange faces. "Oh and by the way, I agree with you, a flat of my own is going to be fanfuckingtastic."

She turned towards the hand dryer, rubbing her palms enthusiastically in order that they would not see that she was shaking. It was the first time in five years that she had stood up to Jodie Lewis. She was aware of them moving away silently before she finally allowed the tears to fall. For a moment, she wondered why on earth she was bothering to turn up at school at all. Maybe she would be better off just forgetting the whole thing and spend her energy thinking about how on earth she was going to cope with a little baby. All by herself.

Only the recollection of Helen's support and the advice that she had given her about concentrating on one thing at a time kept her going over the remaining school days. There were looks and whispers but nothing more upsetting than what she had had to contend with all of her life. The dreaded moment when she came face to face with Jack came however as she walked out of school a few days after her confrontation with Jodie. She had, of course, been expecting that the gossip would not be long in reaching him and she had thought long and hard about what she would say to him. However, her mind had been made up on the matter and she was adamant that Jack would not be involved. The sight of him, nevertheless, as he stood before her with a look of hurt and concern etched on his face, pulled momentarily at her heart strings.

He walked silently and purposefully towards her. "We need to talk." His voice was unsteady, full of emotion.

"Okay," Aimee responded with forced composure. "Walk with me to the paper shop."

"Why didn't you tell me?"

"It's nothing to do with you."

"How can you say that?"

"Because it's true."

"What... but?"

"There's no buts, Jack. Think what you like, it's not yours." She met his gaze firmly, defying him to contradict her. "We finished ages ago, Jack."

He opened his mouth to respond. He was not stupid. He knew they had finished ages ago but from what he'd heard, she was six months gone, which put him well and truly in the picture. His mind was racing. He had been so hurt when she had rejected him and he had not stopped missing her. The news of her condition had hit him like a tornado and he was upset that she had not confided in him. But he understood how difficult it must have been for her and he felt sure that she would welcome him back with open arms once she realised that he would stand by her. And now here she was, telling him not only that she didn't want him but that she had been sleeping around. He didn't want to believe this and he longed to be able to rekindle the relationship they had had but to his shame, he was lured by the temptation to take her at her word and simply walk away. She was vindicating him of any wrong-doing, granting him the liberty to continue with his own life without the enormous responsibility that she herself faced. Confusion filled his brain and his emotions raged between a burning desire to love and protect her and the terrifying unknown into which he would be plunged as the father of her child.

"What are you going to do?" He spoke vaguely, whilst desperately trying to conquer his mental mayhem.

Conversely, Aimee's words were clear and concise, just as she had planned. "I'll be fine. I'm planning a year's break with the baby and then I'm hoping to go to college next year."

He saw only resolution in her expression. He could not possibly have known the truth within her heart, the dark fears, the pain, the loneliness and the longing. Aimee gave him no reason to suspect that she wanted him as much as he wanted her. Her rejection was his reprieve and he took it because it was all that she was offering. He told himself that he had no choice. What was he supposed to do? Demand a DNA test? His weakness and her strength overwhelmed him.

"You'd better go, Jack. I've got my papers to do. And I don't want people talking about us and thinking we're still together."

He nodded. There was so much that he wanted to say. His heart and conscience screamed in disapproval but he turned and walked away, just as she asked.

Aimee felt her own heart harden as she watched him becoming smaller and smaller. It had happened just as she had planned it. Why, therefore, was she consumed by disappointment and rejection? She thought of Helen. The plans she had spoken of were Helen's suggestions but she had adopted them for the purpose of creating an illusion of strength and determination. It was an illusion that Jack had believed in, or at least accepted. All she had to do now was to believe in it herself.

Chapter Eleven

Aimee was as ready as she would ever be for the exams and more ready than she had believed that she could be. Somehow, she had managed to free her mind of the turmoil of her life and during the last few weeks prior to the exams, she was able to focus on the task which lay before her. She knew that she could hope for no more than mediocre grades, even in her strongest subjects but she was hoping to achieve the bare minimum in order to avoid future re-sits in English and maths. Years of distraction and half-hearted attempts, she knew, could not be compensated for but she was determined to do the best that she could.

It was Sunday, the day before her first exam; she was on edge, wishing she felt confident enough to do something that would help her to relax but desperate not to waste a minute of the precious little amount of revision time that was left. She was so familiar with the words on the page that lay before her and yet she was convinced that she would never remember them. She felt stifled, wished that she could just do the exam now, get the first one over and done with. She glanced at her watch; two twenty. The weather was glorious, she was reminded that she had not taken Kayleigh and Stacey to the park in weeks and the previous afternoon, she had told them off for persistently nagging her to take them. Surely they could understand that she was too busy right now. There would be lots of time for the park, she had told them, after her exams and then, when the baby was born, they could all go together. Nevertheless, she sighed, she was getting nowhere; she might as well go out for an hour or so and then start again with a clear head later.

Stacey and Kayleigh whooped with delight at their sister's change of heart.

"Yippee!" We're going to the park, we're going to the park!" sang Stacey excitedly.

"Okay, calm down." Aimee laughed. "We're not staying all afternoon. When I say we have to come back, we come back right? I have important work to do for school."

"Yes, Aimee, we promise."

Aimee allowed herself to relax as she pushed her sisters on the swings and caught them at the bottom of the slide; the little girls ran happily from one piece of equipment to the next and for the first time in days, thoughts of her exams slipped briefly from her mind. Eventually, however, she felt ready to return to her studying. "Stacey, Kayleigh! Time to go."

As good as their word, they came running over without complaint. "Aimee! Can we have an ice cream?"

Aimee smiled, they were very good at silently manipulating her and she understood their message that they would come quietly in exchange for a cornet. She felt her pockets, where she thought there were a couple of pound coins. "Go on then, you pair of terrors."

In spite of their best efforts, they were unable to devour all of their ice creams before the hot sun sent them dripping down their hands and by the time they arrived home, they were sticky and grubby. "Right, you pair, I'll get you cleaned up and then I must get back to my revision. No disturbing me, okay?"

"Maybe mommy will read us a story." Suggested Kayleigh hopefully. Aimee had to admit that in the past weeks, the chances of this happening had improved beyond belief. The atmosphere in the house had been as near to what she imagined to be normal as she had ever known it.

And so as they entered the house with optimism, it came as a great shock to the three of them to hear the once familiar sound of Jim's wrath raining down on their mother. The realisation hit Aimee like a thunderbolt; Jim was back on the drink. After weeks of moderation, he had finally succumbed and the effects were evident. She wondered momentarily what had happened to incite him before quickly acknowledging that, once he'd had a drink, he required no provocation.

Quietly, with a sick feeling in the pit of her stomach, Aimee ushered Kayleigh and Stacey though the door, pushing them gently towards the stairs. She glanced towards the kitchen, where she could see Jim, towering menacingly over Sheryl. He was ranting uncontrollably, his face red with rage. The overwhelming emotions of fear, disappointment and despair gripped Aimee as she surveyed the scene. How could she have been so stupid to have believed that this was over? This was the Parkinsons, this was how they lived; nothing was going to change, ever. Anger and hatred towards the source of their misery consumed her.

"Leave her alone!" She screeched as Jim raised his hand above her mother.

He turned, moving slightly away from Sheryl. Aimee could see that her face was already swollen. "For God's sake." Aimee uttered accusingly. "Why can't you just leave her alone? Why can't you let us live in peace?"

He lowered his fist but his manner was threatening as he approached her. "What the fuck has it got to do with you . . . you little whore?" His eyes sank to her swollen middle as he roared. "If you don't like it, then *fuck off*"

Aimee shrank away from him as he raised his arm and brought the back of his hand crashing down on the side of her face. Sheryl, for once, was spurred into action by the sight of her heavily pregnant young daughter being brutalised by her husband.

"Leave her alone, you evil bastard!" She pulled frantically at his T-Shirt, as he raised his fist again to Aimee, who was turned towards the wall, shielding her face and her body . . . her baby. Jim swung round and the blow that was meant for his step-daughter caught Sheryl fully on the jaw. She fell backwards but somehow she found the strength to prevent herself from falling to the floor as she clutched the side of the sink for support. Aimee sensed Jim moving away from her and back towards her mother.

"Go upstairs, Aimee!" Sheryl shrieked, "Leave me! Look after your baby!"

"Baby! Fucking baby! There wouldn't be no fucking baby if you'd been a half decent mother, you good for nothing bloody slut!"

Aimee watched in horror as Jim grabbed Sheryl by the throat and threw her to the floor as though she were neither heavier nor more worthy than an old rag doll.

Aimee screamed as her mother's head hit first the cooker and then the floor, where she lay, limp and lifeless. Aimee's blood ran cold. Jim's fury, however, seemed to be even further incited by the colourless, motionless figure beneath him. He kicked out violently, his face a crimson ball of rage. Aimee barely felt the bruise forming on her own cheek, where he had lashed out at her. She seemed to be rooted to the spot, looking down upon the nightmare vision of her unconscious mother and the maniac of a stepfather. Summoning all of her strength, she fled from the kitchen. She paused at the foot of the stairs. She was not surprised to see her little sisters crouched in fear at the top.

"Go to you room and shut the door." She whispered.

Not for the first time, Aimee cursed the fact that she seemed to be the only person on the planet without a mobile phone. There was one remaining phone box on the estate. She had to make it there and it had to be working. She left the house, tears streaming down her face, desperate and afraid. There was no room for pride. It no longer mattered who saw what. She truly believed that this time he would kill her.

"Are you all right, love?" A middle aged woman, whom she vaguely recognised, had crossed the road at the sight of Aimee's distress.

"I need a phone . . . my mom . . . I need an ambulance."

161

It seemed to Aimee that the woman was reacting in slow motion as she reached into her shopping bag. "I've got my mobile here if you want it. I'm just waiting for my daughter to ring any minute for a lift back from . . ."

Aimee snatched the phone, sick with relief as she dialled 999 with a trembling finger.

Everything seemed to be happening so slowly, Aimee thought of her mother, she could already be dead. And her sisters . . . The woman at the end of the phone seemed to be asking her a lot of unnecessary questions and Aimee wondered desperately why she didn't speak more quickly.

Finally, Aimee ended the call and handed the phone back to the woman.

The woman looked at her, evidently shocked by what she had overheard. "Look, love, why don't you let me come back with you. You can't go back there by yourself. Look at you, you're in no fit state . . . and you in your condition."

"No! No, thank you. Thank you." Aimee turned away, she had to get back as quickly as possible but she certainly didn't want an audience.

Her legs were like lead beneath her as the relief of having help on its way mingled with the dread of returning to whatever hell awaited her. The need to decide whether she should wait for the ambulance to arrive at the house before her or whether she should risk returning first lodged itself in her sub-consciousness as she tried to force her legs to move forwards.

Now that the urgency had been removed from her journey, Aimee felt the weight of her baby inhibiting her progress so that anything beyond snail's pace was impossible. Oblivious to the stares of the occasional passer-by, she moved through the familiar streets, the only streets she had ever known, the route that took her daily to the place of wretchedness that should have been called "home."

* * *

Through the heavy fog that enveloped her brain, she became
aware of a siren growing louder and louder with each step that
she took. As the noise increased, she seemed to find the strength
to increase her pace, eventually making the last turn into
Deansfield Crescent as the police car blasted into sight. A fresh
feeling of panic gripped her. What was that doing here? She
needed an ambulance.

"I sent for an ambulance. We need an ambulance." Aimee blurted
as the police officer stepped out of the car. She saw him taking in
the sight of her, his glance moving slowly up and down, resting
on her prematurely bulging size. She held his gaze defiantly,
refusing to be demeaned by his prejudices.

"It's on its way, love."

Aimee turned to look at the other police officer, a woman of
around thirty, her dark hair was pulled into a severe bun, which
detracted from her pretty features. Her manner was serious, but
Aimee detected a kindness which was absent in her fellow
officer.

"Why don't you show us in?"

Aimee realised that she did not have her key and turned uneasily
towards the path and the back door. She felt the female police
officer's hand steadying her.

"You're Aimee are you?" she asked gently, guiding her towards
the door. "And your two sisters are still in there, as far as you
know?"

Aimee nodded dully in response to the questions. Out of
nowhere, the sound of an ambulance siren filled the air behind
them. Aimee experienced an initial rush of relief and a wave of

163

optimism which was quickly usurped by a chilling moment of dread as she thrust open the door leading directly into the kitchen.

Sheryl lay, lifeless, on the floor. The WPC caught Aimee's arm before she could move any nearer to her mother. "Best to leave her to the experts, Aimee, they're here now."

As she finished speaking, two figures in green filled the door behind them. The police officer moved out of their way and calmly guided Aimee to one side.

Aimee felt a vague detachment from the events around her. She was aware of the WPC speaking in hushed tones to the paramedics. Her head was light and she could not breath; she knew that she was going to faint but somehow she could not get the words out to say anything. Consumed by a nauseous fatigue, she was aware that she was falling.

The harsh fabric lay heavily against her chest, an unfamiliar but not unpleasant masculine aroma filled her nostrils. Slowly, Aimee regained her senses as she came to. She had no idea how she had come to be lying on the sofa of their living room. She tried to raise herself into a sitting position and felt a hand gently restraining her.

She recognised the female police officer's voice and the events of the last few hours came back to her in a wave of panic. "Where's my mom? And Stacey and Kayleigh? What's happened?"

"SSShhh." The WPC's voice was soothing. "The paramedics are just putting your mom into the ambulance, Aimee. She'll be okay, don't worry. They're coming back for you in a moment."

"What do you mean?" Aimee was alarmed.

"You need to get yourself checked over, Aimee. You've had a very stressful afternoon and if George hadn't have caught you, you'd have been unconscious too."

"What do you mean? You mean my mom's unconscious?"

"Yes, love, but try not to worry. She's in safe hands."

"But you said she'd be all right!" Aimee's voice rose to an almost hysterical level and again she felt the soothing touch of the WPC as she held her shoulder reassuringly.

"Aimee, I'm pretty sure she will be. Look, here they are now." A tall male paramedic entered the room, his height exaggerated by the small, slightly plump female colleague who followed him.

The man glanced swiftly from Aimee to the WPC. "How is she?"

"She's quite shaken up . . . she could do with being checked over."

The paramedic nodded decisively. "We'll take her in."

"No!" Aimee was sitting up now, swinging her legs awkwardly off the sofa and pushing away the policeman's jacket that had been draped over her upper body. She couldn't think straight, desperately worried about her mother, she knew also that she had to stay and look after her two little sisters. "Where are Stacey and Kayleigh?" She was close to tears. Her mother was unconscious, about to be rushed into hospital, she herself was in a state of collapse but no one had mentioned her sisters . . . and Jim. "Where's my step-father?" she added quietly. The fist of fear tightened in her stomach as she looked at them for answers.

"It'll be okay, Aimee," the WPC reassured her. "George is with your sisters, upstairs, they're fine. We thought it best they stay out of the way but he'll bring them down in a minute. Mind you, knowing George, he'll be telling them one of his stories and they could be up there for hours."

Aimee was oblivious to her light-heartedness. "Who's George?" she asked blankly.

"The other police officer. The one who caught you . . . and gave you his coat."

Aimee's head was clearing, someone had handed her a glass of water, which she sipped gratefully. "And what about him? My step-father?"

The WPC shook her head. "He's not around, love. But don't worry, we'll find him." She looked at the paramedics, indicating for them to take over.

The female paramedic began to speak. "Now, Aimee, can you manage to walk to the ambulance, if we help you? We need to get going as soon as possible."

The water had helped and Aimee's thoughts were becoming increasingly lucid. "I am not going to hospital." She stated firmly.

"Look, love, Aimee." The WPC persisted, "I'll be here to take care of your sisters . . . you need to get yourself . . ."

Aimee interrupted her. Her mother was lying unconscious in the ambulance and they were wasting time. She looked at the paramedics.

"Would you please get my mother to hospital?" Tears were pricking her eyes and her voice wobbled slightly but her gaze was solid. The male paramedic looked down at his colleague, who nodded silently. They turned to leave but before they left the room, the woman turned back and looked at Aimee. She walked quickly back towards her and stooped to her side. "Don't worry, Aimee we'll look after your mom."

Aimee choked back her tears and closed her eyes briefly in acknowledgment. She drained her glass of water. "Can I go and see my sisters?"

The WPC hesitated. "I need to ask you a few questions first, Aimee. It might be better if the little girls stayed out of the way for the moment."

Aimee nodded as the WPC took out her notebook. "My name's Wendy, Aimee." She told her softly. "First of all, I'm just going to ask you a few general questions about yourself and then about what's happened here this afternoon, okay?"

Aimee's face was grim. She answered Wendy's initial questions as if on auto-pilot, giving her name, age and address whilst all of the time considering the implications of the afternoon's events. Whatever had happened before in the Parkinson household had always remained within the confines of the family. Aimee did not remember ever having been told not to discuss the things that went on with anyone, she had simply grown up with the instinctive knowledge that what went on in their household was not normal or socially acceptable. Now it appeared that everything was spiralling out of control; she had a ghastly vision of her family splashed all over the newspaper.

Quietly, Wendy questioned the sequence of events that afternoon, all of the time scribbling notes and nodding silently as Aimee recalled how she had returned from a trip to the park with her sisters, expecting to get on with her revision.

"I've got my first GCSE exam tomorrow," she explained flatly.

Wendy's eyes were sorrowful. "Try not to worry, Aimee." She uttered, knowing that her words were inadequate. "If you can just try to tell me what was happening between your step-father and mother, then that will be it, I promise."

Aimee visualised Jim's fury, she touched her face as she recalled the blow he had aimed at her, the subsequent attack on her mother and the way that he had knocked her to the floor. "She wanted to protect me and my baby," she ended wretchedly.

"Has your step-father behaved like this before?"

Aimee closed her eyes momentarily against the pain of the question. Wendy scribbled something quickly in her notebook.

"Do you have any idea where he might go?"

"The pub." She spat the name of Jim's local and Wendy recorded it carefully before looking up.

"Okay, Aimee, that's enough . . . thank you." She studied her carefully, God only knew what kind of a life she had led. "You've been very brave." She added quietly. "Now, I'm going to get your sisters down and make a cup of tea."

Kayleigh and Stacey were still giggling nervously at something George had been telling them as they came down the stairs. Aimee heard their laughter subsiding however as they approached the living room and their little faces had assumed an air of seriousness as they peered anxiously through the doorway. Aimee beckoned them closer and hugged them towards her, breathing in the smell of them, silently rejoicing in their safety.

"Where's mommy?" Stacey whispered.

"She's gone to hospital . . ." Aimee did not know what else to tell them.

"Is she going to die?" Stacey was just five years old, she came straight to the point.

Aimee swallowed. Wendy had told her that their mother would be all right. She had to believe her. She looked at Stacey and then shifted her gaze to Kayleigh, who stood silently beside her. "The doctor will make her better, don't worry."

"Has she got to stay there all night?"

"I suppose she will have to, yes."

"Where's Dad?" Kayleigh spoke now, her voice was filled with fear.

Aimee looked up, stalling for time. She did not know how to tell her little sisters that they did not know where Jim was. She knew that they shared her fears, that he would be back when the coast was clear and that he would be very, very angry with them for talking to the authorities. Wendy had just entered the room; she was carrying a tray with three mugs of steaming tea and two beakers of orange squash. She heard Kayleigh's question and saw her expression. Carefully, she set down the tray before

168

stooping in front of the little girls and placing a hand gently on each of their arms. "Listen, I'm going to stay here for a while, make sure you are all safe, okay?"

"Are you going to sleep here?" Stacey's eyes were wide with interest.

"Well, I'll be here until it gets dark and you've gone to bed and then we'll get another police officer to come and look after you."

"What's going to happen to daddy when he comes home?" Kayleigh's little mind was clearly considering the consequences of what was happening. "Are you going to put those cuffs on him and lock him away?" she ventured.

"We'll have to ask him some questions." Wendy answered honestly.

"He'll be very angry."

"Don't worry, sweetheart, we're not going to let him hurt you. Now, what do you want to do. What do you like doing? Colouring? Or shall I read you a story? Do you have any books?"

Stacey giggled. "Of course we do. Santa bought me a pop-up book for Christmas.

"Will you read mine first?" Kayleigh interjected.

The girls hurried back upstairs to fetch their books, arguing amicably about which stories they would ask for first. Wendy passed Aimee her tea. George was in the kitchen, speaking quietly into his radio. "How are you feeling?"

Aimee nodded. "I'm okay. Will you be able to contact the hospital soon to find out how Mom is?"

"Yes, of course. Now, what about you? You need to have a calm evening and a good night's sleep ready for tomorrow. What's your first exam?"

"English."

"I don't envy you."

Aimee shrugged. She would need a miracle now if she were to pass her exams, with all this going on. She grimaced as the baby's foot caught her suddenly in the ribs. She was conscious of Wendy watching her, trying to disguise the pity that she felt towards her. Aimee rubbed at the hardness of her stomach and eased herself to a standing position.

"Better get on with my revision."

Chapter Twelve

It was not a restful night. Aimee had managed to get a little revision done in between feeding her sisters, bathing them and putting them to bed in a mood of forced light-heartedness, all of the time listening out for Jim's return. Wendy and George had finished their shift at ten and Aimee had nodded politely as they introduced their replacement. She herself had checked the doors twice before excusing herself and going to bed, her body so weary that she could hardly climb the stairs. Once in bed, however, sleep had evaded her; she had thought of Sheryl at the hospital, Wendy had received news that she was "stable" and Aimee had brightly told her sisters that she was getting better, silently still fearing the worst.

What they lacked in years, however, Kayleigh and Stacey made up for in experience and they knew that all was far from well. Neither of them slept well. They had insisted upon cuddling up together in the same bed and they disturbed each other further with their restlessness. In the early hours, Aimee crept downstairs to fetch them each a glass of water. The police officer smiled but her eyes were distant, reflecting an arrogance, which implied her understanding that families such as the Parkinsons were a breed apart. Aimee wanted to explain herself. None of this was supposed to be happening to her; she had standards, morals, hopes for the future. Such was her anger towards Jim, the author of her family's sufferings, intensified as it was by fatigue, that she felt certain that, were he to walk through the door, she would take a knife to him herself and snuff out, once and for all, the evil force that reigned over them.

"All right, love?" The officer had enquired as she stood in front of the kitchen sink.

She had not looked at her, simply turning away, returning to take care of her sisters.

"Wonderful." She had replied. "Just wonderful."

As dawn was breaking, Aimee fell into a deep sleep, from which she awoke with a heavy head.

"Is Mommy home?" Stacey was whispering as she tapped her arm.

Kayleigh was fiddling with the alarm clock, trying to turn it off.

"Here, pass it to me, for God's sake." Aimee ordered impatiently, the noise was driving her insane. She apologised immediately as she caught sight of her little sister's crestfallen expression.

"I was trying to help you."

"I know, sweetheart, I'm really sorry. I've just got a bit of a headache." She covered her eyes with her hands. Today was the day of her first exam.

"Me too," chirped Stacey, "I've got a really bad headache. Do we have to go to school today, Aimee?"

"You sure do."

The three of them looked up in surprise as Wendy stepped into the bedroom. "We got our shift changed," she offered by way of explanation, looking slightly embarrassed. "Come on you pair, George is just about to get your rice crispies going snap, crackle and pop."

"Oh goody, George is back too." Stacey was quickly on her feet and half way down the stairs before Aimee had had chance to speak. "Wash your hands!" She called after them.

Wendy smiled. "Now, I'm going to get these two ready and dropped off at school. You just worry about yourself."

"But . . ."

"No buts." Wendy interrupted dismissively.

"But," Aimee insisted "you're not going to take them to school dressed like that are you? . . . and in a police car?"

Wendy looked down at her police officer's uniform, for once lost for words. She rebuked herself for her lack of forethought and sensitivity but in a moment her sparkle had returned. "It's not a problem." She wagged her finger at Aimee. "I've an anorak of my own in the car, I'll make sure none of this lot's visible . . . and . . . we'll walk. That's what we're supposed to do isn't it? Look after the environment, get plenty of exercise."

She smiled triumphantly as she left Aimee to get dressed.

Some time later, Aimee approached the school gate with just a few minutes to spare. She turned and saw Jodie Lewis rushing towards her, out of breath. "Hi, Aimee. Glad I'm not the only one who's late. Oops! Sorry! No pun intended. See ya!" Jodie flashed her a grin as she breezed past in her short skirt, high heels and tight blouse. Aimee felt her spirits sinking further, deflated by the confident sarcasm of the other girl who was everything that she was not.

Aimee crept into the exam room, conscious of her crimson cheeks as practically everyone in the hall turned to see who had dared to arrive even later than Jodie Lewis. She heard George Maccleton's distinctive voice, albeit under his breath, presumably about to make some sarcastic comment; he was immediately and sternly silenced by the Head who was looking extremely severe. An invigilator showed Aimee to her place as the Head informed her in no uncertain terms that she had arrived with seconds, just seconds, to spare and that she must not under any circumstances allow this to happen again. Aimee had simply nodded numbly but not before she had caught sight of Helen at the far side of the hall, who winked and gave her a quick thumbs up.

* * *

The next two hours proved to be a nightmare. There was just half an hour to go now and Aimee knew that there was no way that she was going to finish; she had failed completely to plan her timing and she knew that she had sacrificed a lot of marks by failing to follow the advice that had been drummed into them.

173

She spent the last thirty minutes frantically trying to cram in as much information as possible for each of the remaining questions. She felt cheated; there was so much more in her head that she wanted to get down.

As she allowed herself to be swept along with the crowd as they left the hall, Aimee struggled to hide her emotions. She wondered why she was putting herself through this trauma, what difference would it make if she just walked out of school now and never, ever returned?

"Aimee? Are you okay?" The crowd was dispersing noisily and she barely heard Jack's voice but she felt his hand resting gently on her arm. She burst into tears.

"Hey come on, Aimee, it's just an exam. Jesus, I did shit, I know I did, couldn't think of a thing to write for that last question." He looked momentarily worried, "Come on, it's over with now, no use crying over spilt milk."

Aimee wiped impatiently at her tears. There was an awkward silence before Jack glanced at his watch. "Haven't much time before the next one have we?" He paused uncertainly. "I'm going to the chippy . . . do you fancy coming?"

"I'm okay, I've got my sandwiches." Aimee replied hurriedly.

"Oh, okay." He looked disappointed. ""Well, I'll see you then."

"Jack." He turned back, surprised, as she called after him. "I'll come with you."

"Great!" He had a big grin on his face.

Aimee smiled back and her heart gave a tiny lurch as she realised how much she had missed him. They fell silent for a few minutes, each of them lost in their own thoughts. Jack was battling with mixed emotions. What the hell was he doing, she had given him a reprieve, why was he risking re-kindling any kind of emotion for her? But then he remembered how she had looked outside the exam room, so alone and in such despair and they were only going to share a bag of chips for God's sake.

He coughed awkwardly. "I'm starving are you?"

The chip shop was busy and they kept their conversation casual as they sauntered back in the direction of the school. There were lots of other kids around and there was no chance of a private conversation even if either of them had wanted one. They parted awkwardly.

Later, Aimee realised that she had enjoyed the afternoon's exam. It didn't seem half as bad as the first. Aimee made the conscious decision to plan her time and stick to it and to her relief she achieved what she set out to do.

Her pleasure, however, was short-lived as she came back down to earth on the way back to Deansfield Crescent. Her pace faltered as she neared number 9. There was an unfamiliar car parked outside but there was no sign of the police vehicle that had been there when she had left that morning. She placed her key hesitantly in the lock and breathed deeply as she pushed open the front door. A woman she had never seen before was sitting in the living room; Kayleigh and Stacey were glued to Children's TV, an afternoon treat that was not permissible when Jim was around. They were giggling and did not appear to notice Aimee's entrance. The woman, stood up, smiling. She was about Aimee's height, slim with long, mid-brown hair, which fell loosely over her shoulders. Aimee noticed that she was not exactly smartly dressed and wondered whether she was a plain clothes police officer. She spoke quietly, in a strong regional accent that Aimee did not recognise.

"Hello, you must be Aimee." She held out her hand. "I'm Sophie Roberts, I'm from Social Services."

Aimee felt idiotic shaking the woman's hand. Close up, she looked slightly older than Aimee had first perceived but nevertheless, she could be no older than twenty five. What on earth was she doing in their house and what had happened to the police? And what about Jim? Aimee looked around as if expecting him to suddenly appear.

Sophie opened her mouth to speak and then glanced swiftly at the two young children, still engrossed in the television. "Shall we go into the kitchen?"

Aimee led the way and walked over to the kettle. "Would you like a cup of tea?" she asked politely.

Sophie declined but smiled as she took a seat and watched Aimee take a mug and fill it with tap water. She drank it in one gulp and then re-filled the mug before returning her attention to the young woman.

"You looked as though you needed that." Sophie observed.

"Yeah, well, it's the papers; they wear me out when the weather's hot."

"Papers?" Sophie repeated absently.

"Newspapers. I have to do my newspapers before I get back."

Aimee knew that her tone was unfriendly but she resented this person, this bloody social worker in their home. She could see now the way that she was staring at her "condition" and thinking that she should not be doing a paper round. What did she know? Aimee imagined that she had studied families like hers in books, probably written exam papers about them. Aimee knew that she was only doing her job and that she was there to help – she supposed that it had been Sophie who had brought her sisters home from school but she could not help but feel bitter about the fact that there was yet another stranger involved and goodness knows what they intended to do. Aimee resolved to be as unhelpful as possible. She was perfectly capable of looking after Kayleigh and Stacey and once she'd finished her exams, there would be no problems at all with regard to taking them and fetching them from school.

"Did you pick Kayleigh and Stacey up?"

176

"Yes." Sophie responded brightly, keen to establish a warmer atmosphere.

"I'll be able to do it myself, just as soon as I've finished these few exams. Mind you, mom will probably be back by then . . . I suppose." Aimee's voice trailed off as she wondered whether Sophie had any news of her mother. Or even Jim.

"Yes, I'm sure. Your mom's doing well . . . considering. They say she should be able to have visitors tomorrow."

"Humph! I doubt there'll be time for that." Aimee shocked herself with her bitter tone.

"No, of course. Well, anyway, I could always take the girls."

"Yeah, I'm sure that will be really nice for them. Have a look at their daddy's handiwork."

Sophie blushed but she was determined not to be intimidated by a schoolgirl. She decided that it was probably best to change the subject, re-assert herself as a source of information and assistance. If Aimee chose to ignore it, then that was her decision.

"The police have left an emergency contact number, which we are to use if there are any further problems with . . . well, any further problems. In the meantime, I'm going to be helping out until your mum is out of hospital and well enough to take care of things.

"I'm perfectly capable of taking care of things." Her tone was icy.

"I have no doubt of that, Aimee, but the fact is that you can't be in two places at once and as you still have to be in school for your exams for another couple of weeks, someone needs to be around to help out with the little ones." She faced Aimee squarely; it was in the girl's interest to understand the facts. She cleared her throat before continuing.

"Luckily, at the moment, I can be spared to help out . . . otherwise Kayleigh and Stacey would have to go to foster parents . . . not necessarily the same ones."

"Right," she muttered defiantly, "very lucky aren't we." Aimee digested the information and sighed heavily. "I'll make the tea."

It was obvious to Aimee that the stability of their family was even more tenuous than it had ever been and the balance of control was moving. Part of her wondered why she wasn't relieved. She used to pray that someone or something would save them from Jim's evilness and nothing and no one ever had. Now, it seemed as though everyone everywhere was suddenly concerned for their welfare. But Aimee was not entirely naïve and even more terrifying than Jim was the prospect of being separated from her sisters and the fear of them being separated from each other.

The days that followed were loaded with stress and Aimee found once again that she was more at ease at school than at home. The exams gave her the opportunity to concentrate so intensively that for two or three hours at a time, there was no room for other worries. Whilst her classmates counted down the days, Aimee dreaded the day when she would put down her pen for the last time.

Helen was worried about her. She knew that Aimee was even more troubled than usual but there was little opportunity for contact with students at this stage; they simply came for an exam and went away again as soon it was over. She had made a point of speaking to Aimee at the end of one day but she had responded that "Everything was fine, thanks." and had hurried away before Helen could pursue the conversation. For Aimee's part, it had taken all her willpower not to break down and confide in the one person whom she had come to trust. It was her sense of self-preservation that had fuelled her strength; she knew that Helen considered them to be friends but she was still her teacher and Aimee could not trust that she would not feel it her duty to pass on certain information to others.

Helen was furious when, two days prior to the end of the exams, the Head approached her. "Helen, you may be interested in this, I know you've been involved in the Aimee Parkinson case." She had handed Helen a communication from Social Services advising them that there had been a "domestic disturbance leading to the hospitalisation of the mother and the disappearance of the father."

"For God's sake!" Helen had blurted out. "Do they not think that this information might have been useful a week ago!"

Mrs Derwent had raised an eyebrow. "We'll get this copied to the exam boards. That's about all we can do at this stage. Poor girl."

Helen nodded her agreement. Following this exchange, she had determined to speak to Aimee at the earliest opportunity, but it was not easy. Even with year eleven gone, she had a full day of planning meetings and year ten coursework moderating. She sent a message to the hall that afternoon requesting Aimee to see her after the exam. She was not certain that Aimee would come, there was no reason for her to feel any obligation.

Aimee had received the note with trepidation, she was dreading that she was being summoned to see Mrs Derwent and that there was more bad news from home. Her mother had been out of hospital for almost a week and there was still no sign of Jim. Sheryl was physically recovering from her husband's brutal attack but mentally she was not in good shape, more reliant than ever on her eldest daughter's level headedness and organisation for all that had to be done in the house. For Aimee, such was the relief that it was only Helen who was wanting to see her, that Aimee went willingly.

"Hi Aimee, come in. How's it going?"

Aimee noticed that her teacher seemed nervous, which struck her as being slightly odd. She nodded, "Ok."

"Glad when they're all over?" Helen smiled.

Aimee's lips formed a sardonic smile.

179

"I've got the baby clothes at my flat." Helen said hurriedly. "So, I just wondered about meeting up after you've finished your exams."

Aimee nodded. She felt a sense of unease at the prospect of remaining in contact with Helen after their relationship as teacher and pupil had ended. After all the recent intrusions of the "authorities", Aimee was reluctant to let anyone get too close. Nevertheless, she remembered how much she had enjoyed Helen's company and she knew that if it had not been for the one teacher who had shown an interest in her, then she probably would not have even turned up for her exams, let alone revised for them.

"Do you still have my number?" Helen enquired, interrupting her thoughts.

Again, Aimee nodded.

"You could have called me you know, when things got a bit tough . . . at home." Helen was treading carefully, the last thing she wanted was for Aimee to think that the events at home were common knowledge. On the other hand, she hated for her to think that she was all alone.

"I'm okay, really." Aimee looked curiously at Helen, wondering how much she knew. "What have you heard anyway?" She asked bravely, not sure whether she really wanted to know the answer.

"The school received a letter from Social Services, saying that your mum had had . . . an accident."

"Oh." Aimee felt the colour on her cheeks.

"Has Jim shown up yet?" Helen was feeling a little more confident now. If Aimee was going to tell her to mind her own business, then she suspected that she would have done so by now.

Aimee shook her head. "With a bit of luck, he'll stay away. Well, a lot of luck, I suppose."

"He's wanted by the police now, so perhaps he will . . . if he has any sense."

"He hasn't." Aimee looked away. She would have to go and get her papers done. "I'll have to go."

"Will you call me? Let me know you're ok?"

Aimee nodded and turned to leave.

"When?" Helen tried to pin her down but Aimee would not be drawn further. "Soon. Honest, I will. Just another couple of exams, then I'll have more time than I know what to do with."

"Make the most of it. It won't be for long."

Aimee walked away, she felt very emotional suddenly, so many mixed-up feelings, so many fears and she was so tired.

* * *

The final exam was over; there was a sense of euphoria as students spilled out of the hall. Even Aimee felt herself caught up in the excitement and suddenly it seemed as though some of the weight had been removed from her shoulders. The feeling stayed with her even as she dragged the heavy paper trolley away from the newsagents and as she wandered along the tidy cul-de-sacs and closes, pushing papers through shiny letter boxes into immaculate hallways and porches, she wondered what it would be like to live somewhere that you were proud of, somewhere you could invite people. Aimee was not materialistic and she knew deep down that it was not a big, fancy house that she craved, just simply a home.

Her spirits were still higher than usual, however, when she returned her trolley to the newsagents and she smiled at Mrs Turner as she called a cheery goodbye. She was surprised when the shopkeeper called her back, "Aimee, can I have a word?" Mrs

Turner beckoned her through to the back and Aimee knew what was coming. "You shouldn't still be doing that round you know, Aimee."

Aimee stared towards her feet, barely visible below her bump. Now she was going to have to beg for her paper round. It was the only way she was ever going to get a few bits and bobs for her baby.

Mrs Turner could see the effect her words were having on the girl and hurriedly continued. "So, anyway, we need some help in the shop, just a couple of hours in the afternoon . . . half twelve 'til three . . . nothing heavy, just serving behind the counter. There's a stool you can use to sit on . . . and perhaps stocking the shelves now and then . . . the lower ones, I mean, so . . ."

Aimee was grinning widely; she felt like throwing her arms around the woman. It was too good to be true – she was being offered a job!

She was walking on air as she walked away from the newsagents. She was almost turning into Deansfield Crescent before she realised that she didn't even know how much she would be earning. Probably going to be slave labour, she told herself, but at least it would amount to considerably more than her paper round and it would get her out of the house. Yay! She dismissed the thought that Sheryl had started out working as a shop assistant and look where that had got her! That was Sheryl's story, hers was going to be different. Today, she told herself, was the first day of the rest of her life.

Chapter Thirteen

Helen walked into the hallway of her flat, dropped her bags and checked her phone again. Again, she was disappointed. She moved absently into the kitchen and plugged in the kettle. She was desperate for a coffee. She was thinking of Aimee, as she had thought of her every day since she had last spoken to her a fortnight ago. She had suspected, of course, that Aimee would not call her but thoughts of what might be going on in the girl's life and the knowledge that she had no one to turn to, were driving Helen crazy. She knew that if anything happened to Aimee, she would never forgive herself, knowing that she had no one else to turn to. She switched off the kettle before it had boiled and picked up her keys.

She was conscious of a group of year ten pupils hanging around the precinct nudging and muttering to each other as she walked towards the newsagents. She walked resolutely towards the shop, conscious of the litter and the dirty pavement. The shop assistant looked up at the unfamiliar face, most of their customers were regulars, off the estate, they didn't exactly attract passing trade.

Helen walked towards the counter and realised that she ought to buy something. She picked up a packet of mints and it wasn't until the woman behind the counter had scanned them that she remembered that she had not brought her bag. She coughed in embarrassment, "Ahem, I er, I'll just have to pop to the car . . . I'll be back." The woman nodded, obviously intrigued by the well-spoken stranger.

Helen prayed that she had left some change in her car; the year ten kids were still hanging around and she was beginning to feel a bit of an idiot. Her heart sank as she looked in the various seat pockets, surely she must have an odd pound coin lying around. There was nothing. In desperation, she bent over, conscious of how far her skirt was riding up the back of her legs, but there was nothing under the seats either. She was tempted to just jump back in the car and drive off but she thought of Aimee and she knew that she would have to go back into the shop.

This time the woman smiled a little as Helen walked back in the shop. "Found your bag?" she enquired amicably.

"No." Helen laughed, feeling extremely foolish. She wished she had not rushed out so impulsively. She should have had that coffee and collected her thoughts. She cleared her throat. "Actually, I, er, the reason I came was to see if Aimee still had a paper round here, Aimee Parkinson . . ."

"Oh. I see." Mrs Turner straightened up. She knew that there was no way that the smart young woman had just happened upon the shop. So who was she and what did she want with Aimee? She spoke warily. "No, Aimee doesn't do the papers no more . . . Are you one of those social workers, are yer?" She didn't look like a social worker.

Helen smiled. "No, no. I'm her . . . just a friend. Haven't heard from her and I was wondering if she's ok."

"Right," Mrs Turner was still uncertain. She had been paying Aimee cash and the last thing she wanted was to drop them both in it. "Well, if I see her." She put the mints back on the shelf and turned away.

"Thanks. I'm Helen, Helen Fletcher."

Mrs Turner nodded politely and with a twinge of disappointment, Helen turned to go.

"Hi, Miss!" She nodded curtly towards the year ten lads who were lolling against a wall. A couple of them were smoking. A thought struck her and she turned towards them, a couple of them shifted uncomfortably but the one who had called out grinned cheekily. "What's up Miss, you lost?"

"Nah." Another responded quickly. "She's 'ouse 'unting." They all laughed loudly.

Helen was less intimidated by them than she had been by the shop keeper. She approached them boldly.

"Do any of you know Aimee Parkinson?"

The two at the front shook their heads. Helen sighed. She wondered how to describe her without stating the obvious. "She's just left year eleven, she's . . ."

"Oh yeah, yer know." One of the lads at the back smirked at his mates and gestured to indicate a pregnant belly.

Helen ignored his comment, as she continued optimistically, "Have you seen her lately?"

"Can't miss 'er!" the youth spluttered. "Sorry!" He looked at Helen. He didn't look sorry. "I've seen her working in the shop in the afternoon."

"Oh yeah and what were you doing here? Bunking off as usual?" The lad at the front taunted.

"Nah stupid, lunchtimes . . ."

Helen walked away with a smug smile and the information she was looking for.

Back at the flat, she poured herself a large glass of cold water and drank it in one go before turning on the kettle again. Later, she could hardly contain her excitement as she repeated the story to Paul.

"For Heaven's sake, Helen," Paul responded somewhat sharply, "the girl might just want to be left alone. She'd have phoned you if she'd have wanted to stay in touch."

Helen looked at him, taken aback by his apparent lack of comprehension of the causes of her concern. "Have you any idea what that girl has been through . . . is still going through? Anything could have happened to her for all I know . . . the stepfather's a nutter, the mother's useless . . ." Helen ran out of

185

breath as her annoyance increased. "Haven't you listened to a word I've said about her?"

She was not prepared for the darkness of the look he threw her. "How could I not listen? It's all you bloody seem to talk about these days."

Helen's eyes opened wide in horror as he turned and walked out. "Where are you going?" she asked, suddenly panic-stricken.

"Out"

"But . . ."

The slamming of the door confirmed his departure and Helen stood gazing blankly into the space he had just vacated. Her euphoric mood was gone, replaced by a feeling of utter dejection and disbelief.

He was gone for hours. She repeatedly tried his mobile, each time obtaining his voicemail service. Her stomach churned uneasily, this was not how she and Paul behaved. They had their moments, like any couple but never had she heard him use such a venomous tone. She could not settle to anything that she had planned to do that evening; she found herself checking and re-checking the clock as well as the phone. Mentally, she repeated Paul's words over and over – "It's all you ever seem to talk about these days." Surely, he was exaggerating?

But as the evening wore on, she became less and less sure of anything and to her dismay, she began to acknowledge that she had in fact been almost completely preoccupied with her work for months. Demanding as her job was, and it didn't seem to get any easier, she had always valued the times that she and Paul set aside for each other. Now, however, she was struggling to remember the last time they had had a leisurely evening by themselves. They had been out, with friends, as they always did, but now that she had been forced to reflect upon the way their relationship was heading, she acknowledged, with growing uneasiness that they hardly ever seemed to spend any "quality" time together these days, with just each other for company. But they still made love, she told herself. Or did they? Perhaps they had sex but there was little spontaneity or adventure, not like it had been in the beginning. She tried to tell herself that this was normal for a couple who had been together for a while but then she remembered the look that he had given her as he left and she knew that she had to face the fact that Paul was not happy. His expression was not one of mild irritation or momentary frustration, it was cold and hard and betrayed something far, far deeper. Helen's blood ran cold at the thought of losing Paul. She determined that as soon as he was home, she would start to make it up to him.

Feeling calmer and resolving to put the love and spice back into their relationship, Helen ran herself a bath, poured herself a glass of wine and selected a relaxing CD. There was no time like the present, she smiled in anticipation. She had had a horrible evening but she was so looking forward to making up. . .

She shaved her legs and rubbed a rich moisture lotion all over her body before selecting a set of underwear that Paul had bought her for Christmas. She remembered guiltily now that he had reproached her several months ago for never having worn it.

She was half way down her second glass of wine before she realised the time; it was gone midnight. Her nervousness returning, she picked up the phone once more and hit re-dial. Paul's phone was switched off.

She did not sleep. She was tempted to finish off the bottle of wine but somehow, she restrained herself. She rose before the alarm and studied her reflection in the mirror. Her eyes were puffy and her face pale. She would have to start now if she were to look normal by the time the bell went. Deliberately, she closed her mind to the personal turmoil which raged inside her and turned her mind deliberately to thoughts of the day which lay ahead of her.

No one would have guessed how she was feeling that day. To the outside world, she was simply "Miss Fletcher", a vision of efficiency and poise. Lunchtime came and she sat at her desk; yesterday she had been unable to think of anything but seeing Aimee; that, she realised now was the problem. And yet, there was part of her that refused to accept that her genuine and selfless concern for the young girl, who, after all, really did not have anyone else, could have been the sole cause of Paul's behaviour. Nevertheless, she could not face another trip to the newsagents, not yet. She was too vulnerable; she could not let Aimee see her so low. It was not as though Aimee were expecting her, she reasoned, feeling guilty in spite of herself. Blocking further emotions from her mind, she worked through her lunch break. She could put on a brave face but food she could not stomach.

Somehow, she got through the afternoon; she had been free during the final period of the day and attempted to prepare her lessons but by now her mind had begun to wander and fatigue had started to set in.

Geoff Ruskin glanced at her curiously as she passed him on her way out. He had never seen her leave so early before and she was looking extremely pale. She had responded vaguely when he had asked her if she was okay. She certainly did not look okay, she seemed to be in a world of her own.

Helen had been determined all day not to try Paul's mobile and being at school had somehow given her the strength to maintain her resolve. As soon as she was away from the building however, she fished her mobile from the depths of her handbag; no missed calls, no messages. Setting up the hands free, she pressed the volume button, taking the phone off silent, as if this would miraculously cause it to ring. A short while later, she pulled up at a set of traffic lights. Hating herself for needing him more than he obviously needed her, she looked at the phone again, tears springing to her eyes for the first time that day. She could not believe that this was happening to her; she was well out of practice in playing mind games. But she knew it was more serious than that. She knew Paul; at least she had thought she did, until last night – now she was far from sure. The thought had occurred to her that something awful had happened to him; deep down, she knew that an accident was not the reason for his staying out all night. Nevertheless, she ought to ring, just to be certain . . .

Her heart sank as she heard the answer phone switch on and Paul's voice once again invited her to leave a message.

Even though it was normal for Helen to be the first to arrive home, the flat seemed oddly deserted when she walked into the hallway a short while later. Everything was just as it always was but somehow something had changed, everything had changed. No longer knowing what lay ahead in the hours to come, Helen was aware of a sense of foreboding, she knew that she would be unable to settle to her school work and preparations for an evening meal with Paul, she knew would be futile; this was more than a quarrel and the outcome was becoming increasingly ominous as the hours since she had last spoken to her fiancé slipped treacherously by.

She was kicking herself a while later when a trip to the bathroom caused her to mis a call and she dialled her voicemail in desperation. Several seconds seemed to hang in the air as the quiet, serious tones of the speaker seeped into her consciousness. Helen felt disorientated, confused, the voice she was listening to belonged to the last person she had expected to hear from; the voice – hesitant and polite, belonged to Aimee. Helen had not heard a word Aimee had said; she pressed the re-play button, thinking that perhaps she had missed a contact number but there was none. Helen hated herself for the feeling of relief that she experienced in recognising that there was no onus on her to return the call.

An hour or so passed by before the phone rang again. Helen was still wearing her work clothes. She had been unable to settle to anything and her heart pounded as she grabbed the phone.

"Helen, hello, it's me . . . I called earlier. I wasn't sure what time you got in." Aimee gabbled nervously.

189

"Oh . . . yes . . . hello, Aimee." There was a slight tremble to Helen's voice as once again bitter disappointment kicked in. Aimee did not respond and Helen quickly gathered her thoughts, conscious of the silence along the line and her un-encouraging greeting.

"I'm sorry, Aimee. I was . . . never mind . . . how are you?"

"Great! I've got a job!"

"Yes, I heard. Well done!"

Again there was silence. It was clear that Aimee was expecting Helen to take the lead but she could hardly think straight and for once had nothing to say.

"I, er ." Aimee was forced to try to fill the silence. "I mean, would it be okay for me to meet, for us to . . . " Aimee's voice tailed off, it sounded as though she were asking a favour and Aimee didn't do that too well.

Helen fumbled mentally, her mind filled with thoughts of needing time to sort things out with Paul but at the same time not wanting to let Aimee down. She thought quickly, there was no way of getting in touch with Aimee; she knew well enough that she would hate her to go to her house but right now she felt unable to invite her to the flat. "Can I come into the shop in a couple of days, Aimee? You're there at lunch times aren't you?"

"Er, yes . . . that would be fine." Aimee could not disguise her disappointment in Helen's apparent and sudden lack of interest. "I'll see you then . . . my money's about to run out . . ."

Shit, Helen immediately reproached herself for her handling of the conversation. She should have at least explained to the girl that she had a few problems on her mind. But of course, that was not Helen's style, she was normally so capable of keeping her private life private. "Damn, damn, damn." Suddenly, she was aware of a great weariness and for several moments she was lost in a feeling of total isolation and despondency.

190

She jumped visibly; startled by an unexpected sound behind her and then Paul was standing in the hallway. He was still wearing the clothes that he had been in the previous evening and he was, she noted, looking awful. That, she thought, desperately was surely a good sign. He must have been as upset as she was.

There was an awkward silence. Helen was close to tears, of relief and of anger. She wanted to yell at him, hit out at him even, but at the same time, she longed to be in his arms and for everything to be as it had always been between them. How long ago was that though? She now wondered.

Paul did not speak. He walked into the bathroom and closed the door. Helen stood around feeling foolish as she heard him using the toilet. She walked into the kitchen and absent-mindedly picked up a cloth to wipe down surfaces that didn't need wiping. She tensed again as she heard him come out of the bathroom and she waited for him to join her, dreading the conversation that lay in front of them but at the same time still full of hope that they could sort things out.

She had expected him to join her, believing that he would want to discuss their situation as much as she did. But he did not join her; she heard the slight squeak, which indicated that he was opening their bedroom door and she relaxed slightly – of course he wanted to change into something clean. She wondered whether she should start dinner. She was, she realised, weak with hunger. Perhaps they should get a take-away, open up a bottle of wine and start to make up . . .

She walked towards the bedroom, taking a deep breath to calm the anxiety that bubbled away inside her. She hesitated before pushing the door open, preparing a smile and a conciliatory tone. The smile, however, froze on her face as she saw what he was doing. Her words came out in a high-pitched whine, not at all what she had planned.

"Paul, what are you doing?"

He did not look up. "What does it look like?"

She sat on the bed beside the suitcase, in a grip of fear and desperation. She watched in horror as he calmly removed handfuls of clothes from the wardrobe and placed them, hangers and all inside the suitcase. The thought occurred to her that he must have somewhere in mind to hang them up. "Wh . . . where are you going?"

"It doesn't matter . . . I'll be back to pick up the rest of my stuff and my mail."

"But . . ." She shouted his name hysterically as she rose from the bed and grabbed his arm, which was pressing down the pile of clothes. Her legs were like jelly; she had never truly believed that that could be a physical state. The nightmare was worsening with every passing moment. "For God's sake! You're over-reacting. Let's just talk about it. Look, we had an argument, lots of couples argue . . . lots more than we do . . . Paul!"

He lifted his head to look at her, his face a mixture of coldness and sadness as he calmly shrugged off the grip she had on him.

"It's not about an argument, Helen. In fact I don't really recall having an argument."

"So . . . so, what's going on?" Helen's mind was racing as she realised that she did not want to hear whatever it was that this was really about. "What about us?" She asked weakly, "What about our plans . . . for the future? " She glanced down at the engagement ring which sparkled on her finger.

He shook his head, "I'm sorry, Helen. We're just not right any more"

"What . . . what do you mean? Of course we're right . . . I love you . . . we're engaged." Helen burst into tears, unable to take in what he was saying. The uneasiness that she had felt all day was proving to be justified and the reality was far, far worse than she could ever have imagined. She could not envisage her life without Paul. She did not want to. It was true, she loved him and he was all she wanted. He was her best friend . . .

"I've met someone else."

"What?"

He sighed. "Please don't make this difficult, Helen. You must have known this was on the cards."

What the hell was he talking about? Was she really that stupid? Had she really been so wrapped up in work that she had not noticed that her life was falling apart?

She slumped down on the bed. He had filled the case and was struggling with the zip. His calmness was insulting. Did their relationship mean so little to him that he could end it without so much as a flicker of emotion?

She rubbed her forehead. "You mean you met someone else yesterday? Last night . . . after our . . . our disagreement?" Surely, that was what he was trying to say. That he had gone out in a mood, had too much to drink . . . and . . .

"No," he uttered steadily, "I mean I've been seeing someone else and we . . . I love her," he finished simply.

Helen laughed, almost hysterically, before getting a grip of herself. He was destroying her but she would not allow herself to lose control. She glared incredulously at him. "Well . . . how long?" Surely to God he was only talking a couple of weeks. He was deluding himself, he was infatuated, of course he couldn't be in love with someone else.

He shrugged and for the first time he had the decency to look ashamed. "A couple of months."

She laughed again and her tone was heavy with sarcasm, deliberately intending to belittle his ludicrous declaration of love. "So you've been secretly screwing her for a few weeks and you've decided you're in love . . . very sweet."

"It's not like that." He was now becoming angry and he felt the need to defend himself, even though he knew deep down that he had behaved like a bastard. "We have fun together, we *talk*, have a laugh . . . she enjoys my company - something you haven't done since . . . Christ, I don't know when."

"That's just not true, Paul." Helen was shaking her head.

"Well, that's how it seems, Helen. It was like once you'd got that bloody ring on your finger, you just took me for granted and stopped making an effort. When was the last time you got dressed up just to stay in with me? You're always in those bloody joggers."

She began to cry again. She no longer knew what she wanted from this discussion. How could she continue to want him after what he had just told her? What he had done to her? Everything had changed and yet nothing had changed – she loved him. You couldn't just stop loving someone – could you? Her head throbbed with confusion.

He heaved the suitcase from the bed. "I'll text you . . . or email you . . . or something, to get everything sorted – the flat, the bills, whatever."

Chapter Fourteen

Aimee was used to being let down by people. She had never had anyone in her life on whom she could depend and she was accustomed to dealing with pain and disappointment. That's the way it had been, all of her life, to the point where she had now come to always expect the worst, that way anything else was a bonus. Nevertheless, she had expected more from Helen. Helen had encouraged her to believe that they were more than simply teacher and pupil. She had treated her like a friend.

Aimee could not believe that she had been so foolish as to have been taken in and she was angry; not with Helen but with herself for allowing her defences to have been weakened; allowing someone in. She had never done that before, not even with Jack. He was the father of her child and yet he knew nothing about her. Little by little, she had come to trust Helen, who, over the past months had always made time for her and, having found the confidence in herself and their relationship to have made contact, it was a blow to then be rejected. It was another cruel lesson in life, Aimee decided, as she resolved to ensure that in future she allowed herself to need no one.

She quelled her feelings of isolation and gleaned satisfaction from the fact that her life had fallen into a pleasant pattern of looking after her sisters and working in the shop. She had continued to take responsibility for both school runs and it was she who saw that they and their clothing were clean and presentable. Sheryl had the occasional "good" day when she would clean the house from top to bottom and then take a bath herself before cooking Jim's favourite meal, with plenty left over, just in case . . . but there was no sign of him. On other days, she would do little more than dress herself and sit in front of daytime TV, drinking endless cups of tea and eating very little. She had lost so much weight that Aimee feared for her physical health as well as her mental state, but her attitude towards her mother fluctuated frequently from the caring and thoughtful daughter that she had always been to despair and disgust that she should have allowed herself to have become so wretched and so useless. Aimee dreaded the thought of what would become of her sisters without her and she was aware of the strange irony of events that meant that Jim's disappearance, the culmination of his violence, had brought with it the hope that Aimee would be able to stay with her baby and her sisters. She would look after them all.

It was a typical British summer with no two days alike but when it was hot, it was, to Aimee, unbearably so and she began to long for the freedom of walking around unencumbered by her pregnancy. Mrs Turner was kind to her and she was not overworked but each day took its toll on the girl, barely into womanhood and already juggling so many demands upon her time and energy, mentally and physically. Aimee found her employer rather nosier than she would have liked but she was adept at fending off unwanted questions whilst remaining polite and respectful. Aimee wondered why she bothered to be so discreet and loyal to her parents; there were, she knew, bound to have been rumours, probably always had been. In spite of herself, she still longed for someone to talk to but she could not bring herself to open up.

The days quickly slipped by into weeks and Aimee was conscious that she was getting near her time. One particularly hot afternoon, she arrived home with the girls to find Sheryl still in her dressing gown. Aimee's feet were hot and swollen and she could not disguise her irritation. "For God's sake Mom, can't you at least make an effort." Stacey and Kayleigh looked taken aback by their older sister's sharp words directed towards their mother. They idolised their mother and between them agreed that they were glad that Jim had gone away and they hoped he would stay away. They tried so hard to please Sheryl and did not want her upset - she might leave them again, like she did before and then everything would be horrible again. Kayleigh glared at Aimee and took her mother's hand.

196

"Come on Mommy; take no notice, Aimee's just grumpy cos she's too hot."

"And too fat." giggled Stacey mischievously.

Aimee turned away and after removing her shoes she made her way into the kitchen where she was greeted by her mother's unwashed mugs but, unsurprisingly, there were no preparations for their evening meal. Aimee reflected for a moment on how her little sisters hardly seemed to notice that it was she who kept their household ticking over, ensured that there was food in the cupboards and meals on the table, clothes were washed and ironed and the house cleaned, not to mention getting them to and from school on time each day. It was a thankless task, which would only be appreciated if she withdrew her labours. Only then would they realise just how much they depended on her. Yet Aimee knew that, in spite of the niggle of annoyance that was rearing its head, she would not let them down. They did not deserve that and she loved them too much. It was going to be a long upward struggle, taking charge of her sisters as well as her own new baby, but she had no choice, for her the only option was to do her best for them. She was thankful that, despite social services' continued involvement, stretched resources and manpower meant that their visits were infrequent.

Later that evening after she had read the girls their story and settled them into their beds, she descended the stairs and resolved to have it out with Sheryl. She had to pull herself together. There was less than two weeks left of school before the long summer holiday and her due date was just one week later. Aimee knew that she should be thinking about getting her bag packed in readiness for her labour, which realistically could begin any time now. She needed to know that Kayleigh and Stacey would be looked after and right now she was not sure that Sheryl was capable.

She was surprised to see her mother looking unusually alert when she walked into the living room. Her habitual position of late was slumped in front of the television and irrespective of

197

what was on, she would watch the screen with a vague, lost expression as if swept away into an alternative existence, untouched by her own troubled state.

Tonight, however, Aimee found her mother sitting upright, waiting for her. She had, Aimee noticed, with a small but pleasant shock, tidied away the children's toys, the TV was turned off and there were two mugs of freshly brewed tea in front of her.

Taken aback by the scene, Aimee was lost for words. She had been preparing a little speech about how she needed her mother's support, some help with *her* children, not to mention the one she herself was about to give birth to! She had been all set to convince her that Jim was probably gone for good and that they had a chance to start over, without him wreaking havoc in their lives. She had a vision of a calm, safe family unit, with her sisters and her baby brought up without fear and violence and she wanted her mother to believe in it too.

Aimee picked up one of the mugs and settled her weight awkwardly into the chair opposite Sheryl, who looked embarrassed and a little nervous as she began to speak quietly.

"You're a wonderful daughter, Aimee, far more than I ever deserved."

"Mom . . ." Aimee blushed, self-consciously. Wonderful daughters did not go around getting pregnant before their sixteenth birthday!

"No, Aimee, listen to me." Sheryl, for once, sounded determined in what she was about to say and Aimee did as she was told, unaccustomed to her mother's assertiveness. "I've let you down . . . all of you . . . I'm sorry." She looked down into her lap and there was an uncomfortable silence before she continued. "I'm going to try harder . . . pull myself together and start looking after you all better."

"And yourself."

"Yes." Sheryl smiled tentatively. Aimee had been so unpredictable lately - understandable, she knew, with everything she had had to put up with - but nevertheless, Sheryl was anxious about how her daughter would react. She was relieved to see Aimee returning her smile warmly and, encouraged, she continued. "I'll take the kids to school in the morning . . . you have a lie in. Then we could get the bus into town, go shopping . . . for the baby, I mean, if you want. . ."

Aimee was delighted; it was more than she could have hoped for. It was a trip that she had been resolved to making alone. She had managed to save a small amount of money and had made a list of the necessities, nappies and so on, that she would need straightaway.

"That would be great Mom, really great."

And it was. It was the most enjoyable morning that Aimee could remember having spent with her mother. They did not have a lot to spend but they managed to find a few bargains and stocked up on the basics. They even stretched to a cup of coffee and a cake in one of the smaller, more reasonably priced cafes.

During the bus journey home, Sheryl squeezed her daughter's hand. "I've really enjoyed today, Aimee. We'll do more of this from now on."

Aimee nodded in agreement. The next few weeks were going to be daunting and she would be lying if she said that she was not afraid. But it felt good to be facing it all with her mother at her side. Sheryl continued to chatter excitedly about the new baby all the way to the precinct where Aimee had to get off to go to the newsagents.

"Don't forget, Aimee, I'm picking the girls up. You go straight home and put your feet up after you've finished work."

"Yes Mom." Aimee smiled, "Just make sure you don't leave any of the bags on the bus."

During the ensuing days, Aimee wished that the time would stand still so she could savour the days of peace and normality that had descended upon their household. And yet, at the same time, she wanted the baby to be born, wanted rid of the uncomfortable bump that had taken over her body, wanted to know that her baby was healthy and strong. Her mom had been making a huge effort and had been to see her doctor about her nerves. She had been prescribed anti-depressants and although she had been dubious at first, Aimee could see the positive effect that they appeared to be having on her mental stability and so encouraged her to take them.

It was the last day of term and Kayleigh and Stacey were breaking up early. Sheryl was due to collect them at two thirty whilst Aimee was still in the shop. Mrs Turner had insisted that she should give up or reduce her hours whenever she wanted but Aimee saw no reason not to work. She felt better than she had in months, years probably. Nevertheless, it was another hot day and Aimee was willing the last twenty minutes away so that she could go home and soak her hot feet. She had not taken a lot of notice of the phone ringing briefly in the back; she assumed that Mrs Turner would answer it as usual.

"Aimee, it's for you."

"Me?" Aimee's stomach lurched horribly. Who would be ringing her and why?

She looked at the receiver suspiciously before lifting it to her ear. She vaguely recognised the high pitched, busy voice at the other end of the line and as the woman introduced herself swiftly as the secretary of her sisters' school, alarm bells began to sound in her head.

"Don't worry dear, your sisters are fine. It's just that we've broken up early today and no one has arrived to collect Stacey and Kayleigh. We don't have a telephone number for your mother."

"No." Aimee muttered, her mind going into overdrive. "Er, well, it's odd be . . . because my Mom knew what time to come. I, er, I'll come now, straightaway."

Mrs Turner bustled around her, assuring her that it was no problem, "I'll have to get used to coping without you." she reminded her jovially. She glanced at Aimee's worried expression and tapped her arm gently. "Yer Mom's probably just lost track of time, that's all."

Aimee made her way as quickly as possible to the school where Kayleigh and Stacey were waiting for her in the secretary's office. The excitement of breaking up had withered with the discovery that they had been forgotten and they smiled weakly as Aimee appeared in the doorway.

"Say thank you to Mrs Bentley for having you."

"Thank you Mrs Bentley."

"That's okay, girls, have a nice holiday, be good for your Mom." She smiled at Aimee, who, nevertheless, felt her disapproval. "Good luck, dear."

"Where's Mommy?" Kayleigh demanded as soon as they were outside. "Mommy said she was picking us up."

"Has something happened?" Stacey asked quietly.

Aimee forced a bright smile to her lips. "No, I'm sure everything's fine. I've been at work. Mom probably didn't notice the time." She wished she could believe that that was all there was to it. "Anyway, you two have six weeks off now, isn't that great?"

"Can we go to the park?"

"Of course, tomorrow." She led them to the top of Deansfield Crescent, chattering to them about everything they could do in their holiday but all of the time, looking for some indication of whether Sheryl was at home.

Sheryl was at home. She was sitting in the living room, smoking – she had not smoked for weeks – she was smiling happily across the room. She was not alone. The three of them poured into the doorway of the small room and came face to face with Jim, sitting in "his" chair, with a self-satisfied smirk.

"Come here, you two, give yer old dad a kiss."

Kayleigh and Stacey looked up at Aimee in horror. Aimee ushered them forward, disbelief and revulsion coursing through her. She looked at Sheryl. What the hell was going on? Why was *he* sitting there, as bold as brass? They were getting on with their lives, they were happy, what was she thinking of? Sheryl had been advised by the police that she should contact them if he re-appeared and that an injunction would be taken out, preventing him from making contact with her. And then there was the matter of the charges that she should be bringing against him – had she forgotten that this, this . . . cretin . . . had practically killed her?

Aimee turned and walked upstairs. She felt sick and faint and angry and stupid. She had really believed that this time they were in with a chance of making a happy life for themselves. Jim's return meant only one thing – disaster.

She sat on her bed, her head in her hands and began to weep, tears spilling slowly through her fingers. She fell sideways into a foetal position, clutching her baby. She knew where the arms were, and the legs, so often as she allowed her hands to wander over her body, she had imagined and longed for the moment when she would hold her baby. Now, she wished more than anything that it was not going to happen. With Jim in their lives, they were doomed; she had nothing, nothing to offer her baby.

Sheryl was the last person Aimee wanted to see and when she heard her voice and sensed her approaching the bed, Aimee sat suddenly bolt upright, her hair wet and wild, half covering her tear-stained face. "Get away from me!" she spat angrily.

"Aimee, love, listen . . ." Sheryl began softly.

Aimee knew that voice, knew what was coming next, she had heard it all before, so many times. He's changed, everything's going to be different, give him another chance . . . blah blah blah . . .

Aimee was shaking inwardly with rage. "How can you be so stupid?" She uttered between clenched teeth. "And selfish! Don't you care about Kayleigh and Stacey? We had a chance to be happy, all of us together, without him. He will ruin their lives . . . just like he's ruined mine."

"No, Aimee."

"Yes!" Aimee took a deep, deep breath. She glared at her mother, she was finding it hard not to despise her for her cowardly, stupid, selfish behaviour. "Leave me alone."

Sheryl could see that she meant it; she turned and walked away, her expression apologetic and pathetic.

Aimee sat back down on the bed, smoothing down her hair with her hands and wiping at her face. She was alone. There really was no one on whom she could depend. She was sixteen years old, about to become a mother and she was terrified.

Kayleigh and Stacey burst happily into the room.

"Aimee! Mommy and Daddy are taking us to soft play!"

"We've never been to soft play!"

"Mommy says you can come too, if you want."

Aimee held out her arms and pulled the two girls to her, smothering them in a big hug and planting a kiss on each of their heads. "I'm a bit too tired, darlings. Next time, maybe . . ."

She watched them skip off. They were young enough to live for the moment and trusting enough to believe his every word.

A short while later, she heard the door slam shut. She rose and watched them from the window, hidden from view by the

203

curtain. Sheryl had her arm linked through Jim's and the girls were running excitedly ahead. The sun was still strong and there was just a hint of a breeze nudging at the trees. Children were outside, on their bikes and scooters, laughing excitedly – tomorrow would be the first day of the six weeks' holiday and they had not a care in the world.

A sudden, sharp pain caused Aimee to clutch at her stomach. She moved over towards the bed but then realised that she needed the toilet. Great, she reflected moments later, that was all she needed, an upset stomach. Several trips to the toilet later, Aimee lay on her bed, washed out and thirsty. The pains in her abdomen were growing stronger, she could not lie still. She went downstairs, desperate for a drink. She didn't know what to think – was this it? Or was this just a bad stomach? Or nerves? She didn't know and there was no one to ask. After half an hour of pacing around the house, it was clear that the pains were not going to go away. From under her bed, Aimee pulled out the bag that she had packed with everything on the hospital list in preparation for her labour. Still undecided about what she should do, she unzipped the bag and checked the contents, knowing already that everything she needed was inside. Another strong wave of pain caused her to double up. When it had passed, she opened the drawer of the battered bedside table and took out an envelope, which contained all the money that she had managed to save. With Jim in the house it would be safer to take it with her. She made her way downstairs.

She stepped out of the house, the hot and now sticky air hitting her as she closed the door behind her. She turned in the direction of the bus stop. She had no idea how long she would have to wait for a bus but she breathed deeply, determined to remain calm. First babies normally took ages, she reminded herself. The walk would probably do her good. "Ouch!" A group of children turned to stare as she almost dropped her bag and it was a few moments before she was able to move on. She was almost at the precinct before another contraction took hold of her and she breathed a sigh of relief – the bus stop was just around the corner. Without warning, however, she felt a gush of water and looked down in horror as she realised that her waters had broken. There was no way that she could afford to wait for the bus.

She burst through the door of the newsagents, in the grip of yet another contraction.

"Good Lord! Aimee, are you okay?" Mrs Turner hurried from behind the counter and was instantly at her side.

"I think it's the baby!" Aimee spluttered, gripping her side.

"How often are the contractions coming?"

"I . . . I don't know." Aimee felt foolish; she had known that you were supposed to time them but somehow it just hadn't occurred to her to do so. She hadn't even been sure that they were contractions. How were you supposed to know?

"Gordon!" Mrs Turner called her husband who was in the back, arranging boxes that he had just fetched from the warehouse. "Gooooordon!"

Mr Turner arrived in the doorway between the stock room and the shop. "For pity's sake, woman, do you have to yell like that in the sh . . . Good God . . . Aimee! Shall I call an ambulance?"

"No," his wife stated firmly, "there's no time, bring the van around, I'll take her."

"But . . ."

"Just fetch me my bag! And look lively. Gordon!"

Gordon opened his mouth and closed it again before turning obediently and a few seconds later they heard the slam of the back door and the distant sound of the revving of an engine.

"Come on, love. By the time we get out there, he'll have brought the van round."

The newsagents was at the end of the precinct and with Mrs Turner's support, Aimee stumbled to the edge of the path. Mr

Turner came to an abrupt stop just in front of them. He leaped out of the van and was immediately beside the passenger door, which he opened for Aimee.

"Thanks Gordon, I'll phone you later." Mrs Turner smiled briefly at her husband before hurrying round to the driver's side and shifting her weight into the seat.

She crunched the gears noisily and revved the engine rather too loudly. "Are you okay, Aimee, love?"

Aimee nodded weakly, sitting within the constraints of the car seat was not helping.

"Haven't seen 'im move so fast in years!" Mrs Turner chortled, inclining her head back to where her husband was standing, somewhat bemused on the pavement behind them.

Aimee smiled just before another contraction caused her to gasp in agony.

"Just hold on, love, soon be there." Luckily, Aimee's eyes were screwed up in pain and she was unable to see the worried expression worn by Mary Turner as they slowed down for a red light.

"Come on." Mary muttered impatiently. "Come on." She tapped nervously on the steering wheel, the lights seemed to take an age to change and had barely turned amber before she was accelerating forward, cursing under her breath as the car lurched forward in the wrong gear. She began silently to question her decision to drive Aimee herself as she joined the queue of holiday traffic heading out of town, she had completely forgotten the schools had broken up, as well as a number of local factories.

Aimee had not said a word since getting in the car and Mary could tell that she was totally oblivious to everything else around her, intent as she was on breathing her way through the pain.

"Good girl, Aimee." Mary rubbed her thigh encouragingly, whilst inwardly fighting off the rising panic that told her that there was no way that they were going to get to hospital. She hit another set of lights on red and the line of cars beyond them stretched endlessly up the long, narrow hill towards the hospital.

Desperately, Mary surveyed the scene around her. "Oh! Thank God!" In one movement, she turned off the ignition, pulled on the handbrake and leaped out of the car. The driver of the car behind her looked up incredulously and leaned heavily on his horn as the lights turned to green.

"Stop!" Mary was yelling and waving her arms madly as the police car towards which she was heading began to move off. "Stop!" She saw, with relief that the young female officer in the passenger seat had spotted her and was indicating for the driver to hold on whilst she wound down the window.

"Oh, thank God!" Mary patted her chest in an attempt to regain her breath.

"What is it?" The two police officers were studying her with concern and the woman was about to get out of the car. Mary realised that they probably it was she who was in need of help.

"No." Mary shook her head breathlessly, pointing toward the adjacent road, where her stationary car was causing complete chaos. "It's, it's my . . . friend, she's having a baby. Now!"

"Stay here." The officer instructed her colleague, I'll go over." She moved swiftly out of the car and broke into a run. "Mind the traffic!" She called back over to Mary, who was following at a more comfortable pace, still breathing heavily from her earlier exertions. Mary saw her enter the car through the driver's door and lean over to speak to Aimee. Within seconds, she was on her radio and Mary arrived as she began to talk urgently. "Mike, we need to get her to hospital straightaway, bring the car round." Mary turned back towards the police car and watched as Mike turned on the lights and siren, took the lights on red and turned towards them. "Right, Aimee," the officer spoke softly but firmly, "we're going to move you into the back of the police car. Don't worry, you'll be at the hospital in no time." She turned to Mary. "Help me get her out."

Between them they shuffled Aimee into the back of the car. The young girl was dripping with sweat, her face contorted in pain and fear. The WPC jumped into the back with her and pulled Aimee across her lap so that she was almost lying down with the police officer mopping her face, smoothing away her hair and offering words of comfort. Mike wound down the window and spoke quickly to Mary. "Don't worry, love, she'll be fine. We'll see you at the hospital . . . take your time!" Within seconds, the lights were on, along with the siren and the car sped away. Mary stood rooted to the spot, feeling suddenly redundant, before noticing the now enormous queue of traffic that had built up behind her vehicle.

"Any chance of getting a move on?" The driver in the next vehicle pulled an impatient face.

Mary exhaled deeply as she turned on her ignition. She was getting too old for this kind of excitement.

Chapter Fifteen

Mary glanced at her watch as she walked towards the reception desk. It was well over an hour and a half since Aimee had been bundled into the police car. The traffic had literally crawled the few short miles and then the walk from the car park to the maternity wing must have taken her fifteen minutes. She wondered how long Aimee had already been there. She had seen the police car speeding away along the centre of the road, bringing the traffic on both sides to a halt, so she guessed it would have taken them nowhere near the length of time it had taken her.

The young girl on reception indicated for her to take a seat whilst she checked on Aimee's situation. Mary sat around and allowed her eyes to wander idly around her. A woman of about her own age was waiting opposite, accompanied by a highly excitable toddler.

"Baby, baby, me see baby." The young boy was clearly eager to meet his new sister or brother.

"Okay, Charlie, not long now, darling." explained his grandmother patiently. She smiled amiably towards Mary. "At least, I hope not."

Mary nodded. "Been here long?" She enquired by way of making conversation.

"No, just got here . . . Ah here's my son now."

A man in his late twenties or maybe early thirties was striding towards them; he was beaming widely. "Hi Charlie!" He glanced towards his mother, "Thanks, mum." but quickly his eyes returned to his eldest child, "Coming to meet your baby sister?"

"Yeah! Baby! Me see baby now."

Mary watched them walk away, their delight was almost tangible. God, she hoped Aimee was okay. Not that the future looked so rosy for her, heaven only knew how she was going to cope, poor thing. She checked her watch again. The receptionist seemed to be taking ages. Her thoughts turned to Aimee's family. It was her mum who should be sitting here but Mary knew that the Parkinsons had no phone. Their address, however, was in a book at the back of the shop so she would have to go round there later when they had some proper news. The prospect did not fill her with joy – from what she knew of the family, visitors were not normally greeted enthusiastically, although from what she could gather, Jim himself was not around these days.

"Excuse me." Mary jumped up as her thoughts were interrupted. The receptionist, was, she noted thankfully, smiling brightly. "A little girl! They're both doing fine and mum's just taking a bath so as soon as she's on the ward, I'll let you know."

"Phew! Thank Goodness!"

"Your first grandchild?"

"Oh no, we're not related . . . Aimee works for me . . ." Mary's voice tailed off as she saw the girl's expression change and she started to mumble something about relatives only.

"But . . ." Mary explained how she had been the one who had attempted to bring her into hospital, "I had to flag down a police car in the end and I can't get in touch with her parents at the moment . . ."

The girl looked dubious, she realised that she had made a mistake in not checking the visitor's identity. "Well, I'll do what I can . . . I'll speak to Sister for you."

Left alone once more, Mary blew impatiently. "Bloomin, silly rules," she muttered irritably. She recognised suddenly that she was starving and very thirsty. And Gordon! She'd forgotten all about him! He'd be wondering what on earth had happened to her. She found her mobile phone, switched off to save the battery, at the bottom of her bag. Was she supposed to use her phone in here, she wondered briefly, before switching on the ancient Nokia. Gordon answered the phone swiftly at the other end – he'd clearly been awaiting her call.

"Is that you, Mary? I can hardly hear you. Is everything all right?"

Mary quickly gave her husband the news, conscious that she might be breaking more rules!

"Look, Gordon, we need to let her parents know, they'll be wondering where she is."

"I doubt it." Gordon muttered before comprehending his wife's unspoken request. "Oh no, not me, Mary, I'm not going round there."

"But, Gordon, she's all alone. She should have her family with her. They haven't even decided whether I'm allowed to see her yet; it's strictly relatives only. Please, Gordon, you haven't even got to speak to them, just put a note through the letterbox or something. Poor girl's been through enough . . ."

Gordon let out a defeated sigh. He knew his wife well enough to know that she was not going to take no for an answer and he'd never hear the last of it if he didn't go.

"Bloody hell, woman. All right."

"Thank you Gordon. Gordon? Hello . . . Gordon. Damn signal's gone. Gordon? Gordon, if you're hungry . . ." Too late, Mary turned back towards the reception desk; the young girl had returned and was leaning over her computer. Mary walked boldly towards her. There was no way she was leaving this hospital without seeing Aimee.

"Ah, yes," The girl looked up as Mary approached. "Sister says you can have five minutes as soon as Aimee's settled on the ward."

211

Very generous, Mary did not speak her thoughts aloud but wondered where the patient's best interests had featured in that decision. "Thank you, dear. Now, is there anywhere I can get a drink of water? I've no change for these bloomin' vending machines."

The young receptionist tapped a few keys on her computer but looked up cheerfully. "I'll bring you one."

Mary was pleasantly surprised and a few minutes later sipped the water gratefully. She supposed a biscuit would be out of the question; she was ravenous. She returned to her seat; there was no one else around now and so idly she picked up a well-thumbed and dated magazine. The contents seemed familiar to her; having married a newsagent and worked there for so many years; she had become accustomed to the way magazines seemed to churn out the same kind of drivel and mostly these days she preferred to read a good book. She'd heard that even they were going out of fashion, though – they were all going to be on the computer! Nevertheless, it was better than watching the clock and soon she was lost in a short story. She was just coming to the end when a voice brought her back to reality.

"Excuse me, Sister says you can go and see them now. Just five minutes though." The receptionist's last few words were spoken anxiously; she'd obviously been on the wrong side of Sister before.

Mary followed the signs as instructed by the receptionist and eventually came to a set of double doors. She pressed the buzzer to obtain entrance on the ward and within seconds she saw Aimee looking brighter and happier than she had ever seen her. She was smiling in delight at the bundle in her arms. Mary rushed towards them and gasped joyfully as she caught sight of the sleeping infant. "Oh Aimee! She's beautiful. Absolutely beautiful! You clever, clever girl! Aimee giggled happily and felt a slight blush creep up her cheeks. She didn't suppose cleverness came into it but right now, she had never felt happier, never more proud and never had she had so much to live for.

Mary sat on the edge of the bed. "Have you thought of a name for her" She asked excitedly.

Aimee nodded shyly. She had given the matter quite a lot of thought over the last few weeks and had been unable to come to any final decisions. She had reflected ruefully on the name her own mother had given her, a name which meant "loved." She did not feel loved. Now, as she held her own baby, she realised that there must have been a time when Sheryl had felt such a surge of love towards her and such a desire to cherish and protect. Aimee felt more determined than ever that she would do a better job. She wished that she could bottle these moments for ever and draw upon them whenever things got tough, as she knew they would. Her beautiful daughter had not asked to be brought into this world; she would give her a name that would always remind her of these first, precious moments of joy.

"I'm going to call her Beatrice, it means "bringer of happiness". Trixie for short though. And her middle name is Mary."

Mary blushed slightly. She was a little taken aback. Did she mean ...? Or maybe it was a family name. "That's lovely, Aimee."

"I would never have made it without you Mary. If it hadn't been for you, Trixie would probably have been born in the street! Thank you."

Mary was overcome. She leaned towards the young girl, now a young mother, and hugged her tightly. "Oh lovey."

There was a loud cough behind them. Sister was standing in the doorway, a stern expression on her face. "Aimee needs to rest now."

"Yes," Mary sniffed, emotionally, "I'm just off."

Aimee held out her hand. "Thank you again, Mary ... see you soon?" Her voice rose hopefully.

"Yes, of course ... and ..." she lowered her voice, "Gordon's gone round to tell your parents ... so I expect they'll be in to see you."

213

Aimee nodded silently. "Bye, Mary."

Chapter Sixteen

Mary slumped wearily into the armchair. "Phew, what a day!"

Gordon licked his lips. "Oh well, at least that was a good idea," he murmured, appreciatively, referring to the fish and chips they had just eaten.

"Mmm, well, I knew you wouldn't get yourself anything so I thought it best to pick something up. I was starving. And I'm shattered!"

"You sit there, love," Gordon offered, taking her plate, I'll sort the washing up."

Mary raised her eyes with some derision. Nice of him to offer when there was so much of it! "Before you do that," she called, "come and tell me what happened when you went round Aimee's."

Gordon grunted as he came back into the living room. "Yeah, well, don't expect any thanks from that department. Bloody ignorant sod her father."

"Stepfather." Mary interjected.

"Whatever. Anyway, I told him what had happened and that you'd gone with her to the hospital and that you'd just phoned and told me that she'd had a little girl."

"And what did he say?"

"Well, he looked as though he couldn't give a toss. Just muttered that he'd tell the missus and that was that, door shut in me face. Bloody marvellous! Don't know why you bother with some folk."

Mary sighed. "Well, we've done our best by Aimee, that's all that matters, poor kid . . . both of 'em."

***

Aimee's immediate post natal euphoria diminished slightly as the evening wore on and there was no word from her mother. The midwives were lovely and paid her lots of attention. She had fed Trixie and the baby was sleeping contentedly next to her bed. "I'd get some sleep yourself if I were you, dear." The nurse advised her. "You'll be needing your energy, believe me."

Aimee nodded; she was very tired. She'd been lucky that she had not had a long drawn out labour like some first time mothers but, if anything, it had all been a bit too quick and now that it was all over, she felt exhausted. Even so, her mind raced furiously as she lay back on her pillows. The days ahead were filled with mystery. If only Jim had not come back she felt sure that she would be feeling different, her mother would have been in to see her, probably would have been there for the birth and she would be looking forward to taking Trixie home. As it was, she didn't know what the future held, for either of them.

Finally, she must have fallen into a deep sleep from which she was awakened by the sound of her baby's cries. The lights in the ward were now dimmed and Aimee experienced a moment's confusion during which she had no idea where she was. She sat up quickly and tried to move swiftly out of bed. Automatically, she placed her hand to her shrunken tummy and this, together with the soreness of her body, reminded her that she had had the baby. She reached into the plastic, hospital cot and carefully lifted Trixie towards her.

"There, there, what's all this? It's all right, mommy's here." Words of comfort sprang automatically to Aimee's lips and the child's cries subsided as she felt her mother's arms around her. Aimee settled herself back against the pillows and offered her breast to her baby as one of the midwives had shown her earlier. Trixie had not been very interested and Aimee couldn't help

216

worrying that she would be unable to master feeding her baby herself in spite of the nurses' reassurances. This time, however, there was no such hesitation as Trixie immediately began to suckle greedily. Aimee sighed with a mixture of relief and contentment. She could not take her eyes off her baby. She studied her tiny hands with their delicate fingers and minute nails. She had weighed in at a respectable seven pounds and six ounces but nevertheless the first size babygro seemed to bury her. Aimee smoothed her hand over Trixie's fine hair; it was dark, like her own. She had tried to work out if she had Jack's nose but she could not help hoping that her daughter would not grow up to look too much like her father, she had tried so hard to bury her feelings for Jack and did not welcome the prospect of a permanent reminder. Over the days to follow, however, as she watched the other mothers joined by their doting partners and in some cases older children, Aimee could not ignore the twinge of loneliness that tugged at her heart. She had to be strong, she told herself severely, even if she were to include Jack now, there would only be heartache later, they were so young and unlike her, Jack had been cushioned from any type of responsibility, there was no way that it would work.

Following her feed, both mother and child slept peacefully until dawn. It was light by the time Trixie awoke again and Aimee herself awoke feeling surprisingly refreshed.

"Hi there!" A nurse called cheerily as she entered the ward. "Everything ok? You'll have some company in a bit, we'll be bringing another lady along."

Aimee smiled politely. She was not sure she wanted company. Especially if it meant being surrounded by someone else and their loving family.

By mid-morning, Aimee was painfully aware that she had still heard nothing from her mother; visiting time was almost over and the lady who had arrived earlier had had a steady supply of visitors, evidently oblivious to the fact that there was supposed to be a limit of two visitors per bed. She was surrounded by cards and cuddly toys and the ward was filled with excited chatter. Aimee suffered their smiles and the way they peered politely into the cot beside her. Their words were kind, but they were strangers and it was all completely meaningless. Aimee and Trixie had each other – it had to be enough.

Trixie needed her nappy changing again. It was going to be panic stations shortly; she had packed only the minimum that she thought she would require immediately following the birth and at this rate she wondered whether what she had would last another day and night.

"Hello Aimee." Aimee had been engrossed in the task of re-dressing Trixie and had not noticed anyone approaching her bed.

"Mom!"

Sheryl moved awkwardly toward the bed. "Oh Aimee, she's beautiful. She looks just like you did."

Aimee saw that her mother had a tear in her eye and looked away feeling oddly embarrassed. Her emotions were in turmoil, anger towards her mother bubbled away inside her but at the same time, she was glad to see her. Sheryl was holding a pink envelope and she gestured towards a bag that she had placed on the floor. "I've brought a few things I thought you might need."

"More nappies?"

"Yes and a couple of clean outfits. I wasn't sure how long they'd be keeping you in."

Aimee was pleased that for once Sheryl was behaving like a normal mother and had come to her rescue in bringing the things she needed but her last comment reminded her that at some point she would be leaving the hospital.

"They said I can stay for another couple of nights if I want, 'til I feel confident you know with feeding and everything."

Sheryl nodded.

"Is he still there?" Aimee could not keep the note of resentment out of her voice.

Sheryl sighed. "Oh, Aimee, give him a chance, love."

"What?" She blushed, the people opposite had looked up suddenly as Aimee raised her voice.

"How many more chances does he get before he kills you?" She had lowered her tone to a whisper, but the words spilled out forcefully.

A bell rang, indicating that it was the end of the visiting session. Only partners were allowed to stay on. A nurse approached the bed and spoke to Sheryl. "You don't need to rush off, as there's no one else with Aimee." She intended the words kindly but again Aimee blushed, her single status was patently obvious to everyone.

Sheryl looked awkward and Aimee sensed that she would not be staying long. "Can I hold her?" Her mother enquired, breaking the ice that was threatening to settle between them.

Aimee softened as her gaze turned once again to her daughter and she handed Trixie carefully over to her mother.

Sheryl cooed softly as she took her grandchild and the tension dissolved as Sheryl asked eager questions, which Aimee delighted in answering. By the time she waved goodbye to her mother, Aimee was feeling considerably more positive. Sheryl had promised to return the following day with the girls and Aimee realised how much she had missed them; she couldn't wait to show her daughter off to their aunties! She resolved to dismiss all thoughts of Jim from her mind; she had two whole nights of indulging herself in the company of her baby without the intrusions of the outside world and for this short time at least, she could pretend that life was perfect.

Later that evening, Aimee showed her daughter off to her second visitor.

"She's perfect Aimee!" Mary was sitting beside the bed rocking the baby in her arms. She had arrived promptly, first through the door in fact, for the evening's visiting session, bringing with her a gorgeous pink teddy bear and an enormous, gift-wrapped box of chocolates.

"Thought you'd need these, lovey, I know what hospital food's like!" she had whispered.

"But I've got to get my figure back!" Aimee protested.

"Pah!" Mary scoffed, "Look at you, there's nothing to you."

"You haven't seen my belly – it's like a blancmange!"

"What rubbish. Anyway look at her, she's worth it, aren't you sweetheart? Yes, you are."

For a moment, Mary had looked so wistful that Aimee caught her breath. It suddenly occurred to her that she knew nothing of her employers' lives. Mary looked up and met her gaze. "Me and Gordon couldn't have kids," she offered softly. "They never had all this IVF business in our day. Still, que sera and all that. She sniffed noisily. You're very lucky."

Aimee sighed inwardly, not knowing what to say. No-one had ever been able to say that about her before. Lucky, was not the way she would have described her situation, she pondered guiltily.

"Sorry, love." Mary too felt embarrassed. Momentarily, she had been filled with envy; with age she had come to accept her childlessness, although the yearning had never quite gone away and yet she knew too that no-one in their right mind would

220

exchange places with Aimee and she guessed that the little she knew was only half of it, if that.

"Shall we start the chocolates?" Aimee suggested.

Mary nodded, pulling herself together. "Thought you'd never ask!"

That night Aimee was woken frequently but it was not by her own baby, who slept like an angel between midnight and the early hours. She could only hope that this was a sign of things to come. It was apparent, however, that not all of the new mothers in her own and the surrounding wards were going to be as lucky and it seemed as though as soon as one stopped, another one started.

Her poor night's sleep left Aimee feeling edgy the following morning and she could barely eat her breakfast. Her determination to enjoy her couple of days hiding from the world was waning. She was supposed to be going home in twenty-four hours' time, but what kind of reception would there be from Jim? To him, she had always been the outsider, the evidence of Sheryl's life before she had met him. So, how would he view Trixie?

By the time visiting time arrived, Aimee had spent several anxious hours with thoughts of her future whirling around uncontrollably in her head. She did not trust Jim and even if she went back there now, his mood could change at any moment. She had vowed to herself that she would not subject her baby to the traumas that she and her sisters had been forced to endure. This, after all, would render her as weak as Sheryl. She was consumed with an overwhelming love for her new daughter and the desire to protect her was so strong it was almost frightening. She could not imagine how she would feel when Trixie so much as grazed her knee and so the thought of subjecting her to the horrors of a life under Jim's roof was insufferable. But what choice did she have? Eventually, she would be eligible for a council flat but how long that would take she did not know. So, in the meantime, they would be at the mercy of Jim's good nature. Anger towards her mother returned and now it was greater than ever. How could she let him back into their lives, where were *her* protective instincts?

And where in fact was she? Sheryl had promised to return with her sisters and it was now almost half an hour since visiting time had begun.

By the time her mother walked through the double doors, Aimee was livid. She knew that she was being over-emotional and for a split second, she felt guilty. Then, she took in the sight of her mother's pale, worried expression. She realised with a sense of dread and fear that she faced the future alone.

Aimee steeled herself as Sheryl approached the bed. Her expression challenged her mother to speak, to tell whatever it was that she had come to tell her.

"Where are the girls?"

Sheryl was thrown briefly; it was not what she had been thinking about. "Oh, I thought . . . look , Aimee . . . it's Jim . . ."

"Well," Aimee returned heavily, "there's a turn up."

"He just needs to get used to the idea, that's all . . . give me time, love, I'll talk him round."

"*Jim! Talk him round?*" Aimee spluttered incredulously. She was reeling inside, panic stricken, what exactly was Sheryl saying?

"So, what you're saying is, I can't come home."

"Not, *can't* love. . . well, I mean *not you.*"

"*What?*"

"Aimee, you're so young. You don't know what you're taking on. You . . . you could have your life back, another chance . . . go to college."

"My life! What life? I never had a life!"

Sheryl was clearly determined to proceed with her suggestion but Aimee was nothing less than incensed. "You said that we would all be together, without him." Her voice was boiling with resentment and Sheryl visibly cowered. "Now, you're choosing *him* over me!"

"It's not like that, Aimee, love."

"It's exactly like that!"

"There are lots of couples wanting to . . . adopt . . . you're so young . . . why ruin your life?"

"Ruin my life? So, is that what I did? Ruin your life? Well, guess what, Mom? I'm out of it, out of your life. If that's what you want."

"Aimee . . ."

"Just go, Mom, just GO!"

"Ahem, excuse me, is . . . is everything all right?" A nurse had approached the two of them unnoticed but now it was obvious that their heated exchange was attracting considerable interest. To make matters worse, Trixie began to holler at full lung capacity.

Aimee glanced at her mother. "Just leave us alone."

She did not take her eyes away from her mother and to her disgust she saw that Sheryl looked relieved; all she actually wanted was to get out of there.

Aimee realised that the nurse had picked up Trixie, whose cries were beginning to subside.

"There, there, come on, then, sweetie, that's it."

Aimee wiped angrily at the tears that were falling freely down her face. The nurse cradled Trixie in her one arm and with her free hand on her other arm she swiftly drew the curtains around Aimee's bed. Still making soothing noises in the infant's direction, the nurse handed Trixie to her mother. Holding her baby against her own body had an immediate positive effect upon Aimee; at once she felt calmer and she let out a deep, heavy breath, suddenly conscious that she had been holding herself rigid.

The nurse shifted somewhat awkwardly. "It's a strange time, this. You imagine you're going to be full of the joys of spring once baby arrives, but somehow it doesn't always happen that way. Don't' worry, everything will sort itself out in time."

Aimee's expression hardened once more. "In time? I'm supposed to be getting out of here tomorrow and" her face crumpled, "and I've nowhere to go."

Aimee buried her head to her chest and sobbed. Trixie too began to cry, clearly distressed.

The nurse clucked around her making soothing noises and passed her a tissue whilst once again attempting to take Trixie into her own arms. "Give baby to me, love, let's get you calmed down."

"No!" Aimee turned away, pulling Trixie protectively towards her breast. "I'm her mom, I'll take care of her."

"Okay, okay. Look, I'm going to go and get you a cup of tea. You sort baby out and I'll be back in a tick." She did not wait for Aimee's response, she disappeared quietly through the curtains and Aimee was left to placate her daughter.

"I'm sorry, darling. I didn't mean to frighten you. Mommy's here now. That's it, everything's going to be all right."

Somehow, it just had to be all right. Somehow, Trixie's life had to be different. But how?

By the time the nurse returned, Aimee was sitting calmly feeding Trixie, who was half feeding, half dozing.

"That's more like it." The nurse smiled. "Now, I've even managed to find you a couple of choccy biscuits but don't get telling anybody else." She winked pleasantly and settled the cup and saucer on the bedside table. "She's happy enough now, by the look of her." She inclined her head in Trixie's direction and Aimee nodded her agreement.

The nurse settled herself on the end of the bed. "So, you've had a bust up with your mom?" Again, Aimee nodded. "And you reckon you can't go home?"

"Oh yes, I can go." Aimee explained acidly. "Just not Trixie." The tears pricked hard and she fought them off.

The nurse's expression changed slightly but she quickly attempted to hide her surprise. It was clear that she had not thought the situation so serious. "I see. So, there's nowhere else you can go?"

Aimee shook her head and she felt the colour seeping to her cheeks. A feeling of worthlessness engulfed her and she shrank under the nurse's look of pity as she nodded brusquely towards Trixie. "She's nodded off. Let me pop her in her cot for you and I'll pass you your tea." This time Aimee did not argue as the nurse took Trixie gently from her. The tea was hot and sweet and welcome.

The nurse sat down again. "Aimee, you'll not do yourself any good, or Trixie for that matter, by getting yourself in a state. Now, listen, I want you to promise me that you'll not worry yourself about what's going to happen to you. This is the twenty first century." She rubbed Aimee's arm reassuringly, "No one gets thrown out of here on to the streets." She smiled, before standing up and smoothing down her blue nurse's polo shirt over the regulation trousers. "Now, I'm going to see what arrangements can be made for you and then I'll be back. You're not to worry. Promise?"

Aimee nodded obediently and watched the nurse retreat again behind the curtains, her lip quivered sorrowfully as she bit into a

225

chocolate biscuit. The sweet, sugary taste should have brought her some comfort but charity left a bitter taste in your mouth and after swallowing hard, Aimee cast the treat to one side.

Chapter Seventeen

Aimee endured another restless night and when she slept she dreamt, dreams she could not quite recall upon waking but which left her uneasy, fretful and fearful for the future.

The following morning, the nurse on duty paid her little attention and it was clear that she knew nothing of the events of the previous day. Aimee tried to ignore the butterflies in her stomach and wondered anxiously about what the day would bring. She did not even know whether yesterday's nurse would be on duty today or whether she had passed on any message to the staff on duty. Aimee was not to know that the kind-hearted nurse had looked in on her before going off duty but, finding her patient asleep, had left her in peace.

The morning's visiting hour began and Aimee did not expect to see any familiar faces and she was filled with surprise and relief therefore when she heard Mary's friendly voice calling out a cheerful greeting as she approached her bed.

"Mary! What are you doing here?" Aimee was conscious that today was the day that she had told Mary that she would be going home. She was puzzled.

"That's a fine welcome, I must say!" Mary remarked playfully. "Hello, my darling." She cooed as she leaned over Trixie's cot, "and are *you* pleased to see me?"

She turned, still smiling, towards Aimee. "Are you all right, lovey?" She sat herself down on the bed before adopting a slightly sheepish expression. "I had a call from the hospital yesterday evening. They had my details from when I came in with you, I'd given them to the receptionist, just in case," she explained hurriedly. "Anyway, she . . . well, told me what had happened with your mum, sort of thing."

227

Mary, Aimee noticed, looked mildly embarrassed, as if she reluctantly had become privy to confidential information. At that moment, they both turned to see the nurse bustling towards them.

"You must be Mary." She smiled professionally. "I'm Anna. " Aimee realised at that point that she hadn't thought about her having a name. Anna turned to Aimee, her voice adopting a more sympathetic note. "How are you feeling?"

Aimee nodded unconvincingly. "Fine."

"Good." Nurse Anna smiled encouragingly. "Now, we've managed to sort you and Trixie out with somewhere to go, as soon as you're ready."

Aimee's stomach pitched horribly. Was she supposed to feel relieved? She realised that Anna was awaiting her response and she attempted a grateful smile. "That's great." Her voice was flat, "Wh . . . where are we going?"

"Don't look so worried. You'll be fine there. I know the place. It's a kind of half-way house type of thing if you like. For young mums like yourself . . . before they get a place of their own. The council will have to find you somewhere . . . eventually." She smiled again, conscious that the news was not being received with quite the enthusiasm that she had hoped for, expected even. After all, what other choice did Aimee have? And she'd put in a lot of time and effort finding her this place. She glanced at Mary, hopeful of some support.

Mary cleared her throat awkwardly. "You'll be fine pet. And I'll be around, you won't be on your own."

Aimee nodded. They were both being very kind. She began to cry. It was crazy, she told herself. Logically, she knew that she should be jumping at the chance to escape Jim and the misery of the house that she had never been able to call home. Yet, she felt so unbearably lonely, so unwanted, dependent on the charity and compassion of strangers. And she could not help but grieve for the one part of her life that she was afraid of leaving behind – her sisters – God only knew what would happen to them without her looking out for them. "I'm sorry," she murmured guiltily, tasting the salt of her tears as she spoke, "I . . . just . . ."

"I know, I know . . ." Nurse Anna passed her a tissue. "It's all right, you're entitled to a cry if you want one. Everything's changing for you. It's quite normal for you to feel like this . . . but you'll be fine, you'll see. And you're going to be a great mum." She beamed brightly, again glancing at Mary.

"Yes, Aimee. You are." Mary reached over and squeezed her hand.

Aimee blew her nose gently. She hoped so. She wanted more than anything to be a good mother and one thing was certain, having seen the mistakes her mother had made, she at least knew for sure that she would never subject Trixie to the fear and uncertainty that had governed her own childhood. She wiped away the last of her tears and looked lovingly at her daughter, it was her job to protect her and silently she vowed that this was the last time that she would cry in front of her precious baby.

"I can take you today, in the car, if you like." Mary offered tentatively, "I'll help you get settled in, make sure you've got everything you need."

"Thanks." Aimee smiled, determined now to embrace her future positively. "That'll be great." Her mind, however, began to race. She had very few things at the hospital. She would have to make contact with Sheryl if only to arrange to collect her clothes and the few bits and pieces that she could call her possessions. Most importantly, she needed the rest of Trixie's things. "Would you be able to take a note to my mother?" She asked Mary.

"Of course."

"It's just that I need to sort out about collecting my stuff . . . and Trixie's".

229

The thought had occurred to Mary only seconds earlier. "No problem. We've got Gordon's niece staying with us at the minute. On holiday from college so she's come over to help out in the shop, earn herself a bit of pocket money. So," she announced cheerfully, "I'm completely at your disposal."

Nurse Anna stole a quick look at her watch. "Best get on," she stated simply, "You'll be ok?"

Aimee nodded, this time with greater conviction. "Thank you . . . you've been really kind." She added shyly.

"My pleasure. I'll see you before you go."

Aimee felt overwhelmed with the enormity of what lay ahead, simply getting through the day was going to be a major challenge. She had never spent any time away from Deansfield Crescent, never been on any overnight school trips, never even slept at a classmate's house. Being in hospital had been her first night of anything resembling independence but that, she felt sure, was nothing compared to the now immediate prospect of moving away from her family, for good. Somehow, she had to summon the strength to face the future confidently. She was a mother, she was responsible for another human being. She *would* be responsible, it was her duty and what she wanted more than anything else in the world. In this, she would not fail.

"Right," Mary ventured tentatively, "there's no time like the present, I say. So, I suggest we get over to this place ASAP and then take it from there. Once we get you settled in, we can make a list of what needs fetching from your mother's and see what else you need."

Aimee twisted herself round and dropped her legs on to the floor. "I'll get my things packed." She smiled and held Mary's gaze for a tiny moment. Mary smiled back.

They were almost packed up when Nurse Anna re-appeared.

"You'll be needing one of these. You can't take Trixie in the car without one."

"God, yes, of course, I completely forgot. " Aimee looked horrified as she realised her oversight and gratefully reached out to accept the car seat.

"This one's the hospital's spare. You'll need to get it back to us, I'm afraid. But you'll pick up a second hand one no problem."

Aimee nodded. God, this was so difficult. What else had she not thought of?

Nurse Anna handed her a sheet of paper on which were written the details of the Mother and Baby Hostel. "Now then, a midwife will be visiting you every day for a week or so – that's always the case, whatever the circumstances, but there will also be a social worker contacting you within the next couple of days."

Aimee looked momentarily alarmed.

"It's ok, nothing to worry about. They're going to make sure you have all the help you need getting the benefits you're entitled to and putting you on the right track for getting registered for somewhere of your own. Don't worry, Aimee, they're there to help you – nothing else."

Aimee nodded. She did actually feel a lot better for knowing that there were going to be people around to help her. She was not completely alone after all. A tingle of excitement crept over her, maybe just maybe everything would be all right after all. For her, and, most importantly, for Trixie.

Chapter Eighteen

Mary stepped out of the bath and wrapped herself in the thick bath sheet. It had been another hot day and she was weary. She dried herself quickly before pulling on her dressing gown. She fancied a drop of something to help her sleep, her mind was still racing with the events of the day. Needless to say, she could not get the image of Aimee out of her mind. She hoped she was okay, poor kid.

Gordon was doing the books on the dining room table. He raised an eyebrow inquisitively as she handed him a brandy.

"I need something to wind down with." Mary explained, "And I don't like drinking on my own."

Gordon nodded simply but held out his arm to hug his wife towards him. She had a heart of gold, Mary, and it wouldn't be the first time she'd taken on other people's problems. He hoped she knew what she was doing, getting involved this time. Jim Parkinson was not someone he wished to have anything to do with if he could help it.

He took off his glasses, put down his pen and rubbed his forehead. "Ah, that's enough for one night. Come on let's sit somewhere comfy." He led Mary towards the living room, he could tell that she needed to talk and that she would have no chance of sleeping unless she got it all off her chest.

"Oh Jim, poor girl, she's been so brave. I don't' know how she's managed it."

"Come on, tell me all about it."

Mary took a sip of her brandy, wincing slightly, it was good stuff. "Well, that place she's staying Jim, I just feel so sorry for her. I mean, it's clean enough and there's everything she needs – pots and pans and things in the kitchen and sheets for the bed but . . .

well, it's just not like being in your own home and with a new baby . . ."

"Love," Gordon interrupted gently, "it's probably a darn sight better than taking the poor mite back to the Parkinson place."

Mary bit her lip thoughtfully. He had a point. She'd been there herself only that afternoon to collect Aimee's belongings. She had not exactly received a warm welcome. Sheryl, the mother, seemed a nervous wreck and those poor little girls. She had seen him – Jim – he had been sitting glowering in the living room whilst she had stood in the hallway. No one had invited her to take a seat, she had just stood there, listening to the sounds of Sheryl packing up her daughter's possessions. It had not taken long. Sheryl had re-appeared with a battered, brown suitcase and a few carrier bags. "There's just the pram after this," she had explained quietly.

"And tell her we want our bloody suitcase back." Jim had barked moodily.

Mary had said nothing. He could bloody well fetch it if he wanted it. As requested by Aimee, Mary had slipped Sheryl a note of the hostel's address. She had merely nodded and pushed it into her pocket. Mary had wanted to shake her, she was such a pathetic sight, she wondered about the safety of the two little girls in a house with that madman and a mouse . . .

"I just feel as though I should do something," she explained to Gordon.

"Love, you *are* doing something, now stop worrying."

Mary nodded absently, she had meant about the two little girls, but she did not expand on this to Gordon.

"How's Natasha getting on in the shop?" She enquired, referring to her niece who was currently out with a group of friends.

"Fine. She's a good girl, pity she's got to go back to school."

"Gordon," Mary admonished, "She's a sight more capable than selling newspapers."

Gordon widened his eyes in mock indignation.

"Ah, it's different for you . . . and me come to that, but she's young and ambitious." She sighed, Natasha was not much older than Aimee but their lives had been and, no doubt, would be very different. She wondered what Aimee would end up doing with her life – she too was a bright girl.

"Gordon?"

"Yes, dear." Gordon knew that tone. Mary had some plot or other going round in her head.

"I've been thinking about the flat above the shop."

"Yes, dear." Here we go. Gordon had always maintained that it was not worth the hassle of letting out the flat, he had enough to do with being a shopkeeper without turning into a landlord as well. You never knew these days, no thank you very much, he didn't need the hassle and he wasn't desperate for the money.

"Well, Aimee can't stay in that place for ever, so . . ."

Gordon smiled ruefully. "Let's just see what happens, shall we. It's early days yet."

So that was that, thought Mary, feeling a lot more comfortable about Aimee's living arrangements. It wouldn't take too much to do the place up, there were two small bedrooms, a little kitchen and bathroom and a modest living room. It would be perfect. She would be independent but near enough for Mary to keep her eye on her - after all, if she didn't look out for her and little Trixie, then who would?

Mary slept easier that night for feeling that matters were under control. There was, of course, the small issue of furniture, but Mary had an eye for a bargain and it was not as though she'd need much to begin with, she told herself. She remembered how she and Gordon had started out with not even a sofa to sit on. Things had been different in those days. None of this buy now pay later business. If you couldn't afford it, you didn't have it. But they'd managed and they'd done all right in the end. They had everything they needed. And more; but the one thing they had never had, money couldn't buy. It made her mad to think of people like the Parkinsons, having babies willy nilly and then abusing and neglecting them. In her book, emotional abuse was no better than any other kind and she knew, instinctively, that Aimee and her innocent little sisters were such victims.

The following morning, Mary rose early, bright eyed and bushy tailed as Gordon would say. He knew that when she had something up her sleeve, there would be no stopping her. Over breakfast, he again voiced his concerns.

"Mary, love, just be careful. Don't go getting yourself attached to the girl, you hardly know her and . . ."

"Gordon, I'll be fine. I know what I'm doing. Aimee needs a friend that's all . . . and well, a bit of help. She's a good girl. She's had it rough, love."

"What about the father?"

Mary paused. "Trixie's you mean?" She shrugged and then sighed. She had tried not to dwell on those thoughts. "I don't know, I haven't asked. Dread to think, to be honest . . ."

Later that morning, Mary arrived at Aimee's door, laden with carrier bags, she'd been having a sort out and brought Aimee a few towels and tea towels and she'd also brought along an old radio that they never played.

Aimee opened her door cautiously but then it became clear that she was delighted to see Mary."

"Wow! What have you got there?"

Mary shrugged her shoulders. "Oh, just a few old towels and things you might need, I was about to throw them out."

235

Aimee smiled; somehow, she didn't feel like a charity case with Mary, she had a way of giving that made you feel as though you were doing *her* a favour.

"How're things?"

Again, Aimee smiled. "Fine."

Mary looked at her. "Really?"

"Well, you know . . ." Aimee shrugged. "We're okay. Trixie seems quite content."

"Yes," Mary stated knowingly, "but she's not the one sharing a bathroom and kitchen, is she?"

Aimee looked at her earnestly. "It's not too bad, honestly."

Mary nodded. She was dying to tell her about her little scheme, but resisted. It was best not to build Aimee's hopes up, not until she had everything sorted. She walked into Aimee's room, everything the girl owned was there – there wasn't much but the jumble of baby equipment, the pram and the hospital car seat meant that there was little spare space. There was the bare minimum of furniture: a bed settee and a small table on which stood a battered old alarm clock and a few odds and ends.

Trixie was asleep in the pram and Mary bent over her with a sigh. "She gets more beautiful every day, Aimee."

Mary had brought along some food too, noting that already Aimee was looking decidedly skinny. "If you're going to carry on feeding that baby, you're going to need your strength." she reminded Aimee. "Do you fancy some cheese on toast?"

Aimee nodded obediently, realising how hungry she was. She'd managed to get into the communal kitchen the previous evening whilst Trixie was asleep but had only grabbed a quick sandwich. To be honest, she had felt nervous of meeting the other mothers and hadn't wanted to hang around too long; she didn't feel quite up to being sociable just yet. Aimee could not help but wonder what the other young mothers would be like but felt sure that, just as she had not fitted in at school, so too would she be the outsider here. She was so grateful to Mary; she could only imagine how she would feel if she'd had to do this without her support. Nevertheless, she knew that somehow, she would have to eventually find the strength to go it completely alone. Mary had her own life to lead; at the end of the six weeks' holiday, her niece would be gone and she would be needed in the shop again. She could not help remembering how Helen had appeared to lose interest so suddenly. Who was to say it would not be the same with Mary? If she had learned one thing, it was not to trust people. Even so, right now, she was indebted to Mary for the support she had given her.

Over the following days, Aimee became acclimatised to her new surroundings and discovered that there were three other young mums and their babies sharing the house. They seemed eager to be friends and Aimee quickly found that they were all keen to help each other out, sharing the cooking and washing up, so that they could take turns to mind the little ones, whilst their chores were done. One of the girls, Angela, had been there three months and was due to be moving out the following week. The council had found her a flat and Angela and her baby had to go. She was not looking forward to it. "It's the pits!" She had confided to Aimee, "Compared to this place. At least it's clean here. It'll take me weeks to clean the place up, there's carpet in there but I swear there's things living in it, I think I'll end up chucking it out and living with floorboards 'til I can afford new stuff." She rolled her eyes, "God knows when that'll be."

Aimee had smiled grimly. So that's what she'd be faced with three months down the line . . . and that's if she were lucky. There were all sorts of things in the news about the government's plans to reform housing benefit, not to mention poor children dying from mould infested walls. She hardly dared listen.

Mary, in the meantime, busied herself with her plans. Her first visit to the flat had caused a mixture of dismay and delight. Her initial impression, upon entering, had not been encouraging, the place had been unused for years, there was a pile of stuff up there that would need sorting out, most of it was probably rubbish. The whole flat would need a thorough clean and preferably a lick of paint. There were, however, a few pleasant surprises, things that they'd moved up there, out of the way, intending to get rid of and then had simply forgotten about. There was their old telly and dvd, still working, just a bit out of date, and there was even a sofa she'd forgotten about! Brilliant!

Mary had set to work straight away with her rubber gloves and disinfectant and several hours of back-breaking scrubbing later, she felt a lot happier about the prospect of Aimee and her new baby being able to make a home there. She would have liked to have got the decorators in and really gone to town on the place, but she reckoned that could come later on. Once she'd got the cobwebs down and scrubbed the walls, they did not look too bad - a few cheap pictures would soon cheer the place up.

Mary's next mission was to scour the second-hand furniture shops with a list of requirements. Within a fortnight, she'd located everything she needed and paid the necessary deposits. All she had to do was find a few off cuts of carpets and then arrange delivery of the furniture. She was so tempted to let Aimee in on what she was doing; she knew how worried she was about the prospect of what the council would come up with for her. On the other hand, she did not want Aimee to know how much effort she had put in and even though she had actually spent very little, she knew that Aimee would feel awkward if she discovered that the furniture and contents of the kitchen cupboards had been obtained solely on her behalf. No, it would be far better to let Aimee think that the flat had already been furnished and simply needed a bit of a clean.

The weather took a turn for the worst and they had had a week of heavy showers interspersed with hot, humid spells. One such afternoon, Mary arrived home weary from another shopping trip. She had had a successful day, having procured a bed, ex-display and slightly scuffed but otherwise perfect. She was

238

delighted, the idea of a second-hand bed had not appealed to her and she doubted whether it would appeal to Aimee either, although she knew that the girl would have been grateful even for that.

The flat was almost ready and Mary was filled with nervous excitement at the prospect of revealing it to Aimee. Aimee had been telling her about one of the other girls, Angela, who had moved out into a council place and it sounded horrific but Aimee had so obviously been trying hard to sound positive about her own future, thinking ahead to a time when she would be working and able to save for something better. Mary could see that Aimee was no scrounger who expected to exist entirely on benefits and this made her all the more willing to help her out.

Later that evening, Gordon listened patiently as his wife told him of yet another bargain find. Having Aimee to look out for had given Mary a sense of purpose. She was never happier than when she was helping somebody out, but Gordon still couldn't help worrying that she would end up getting her fingers burned somehow. He was more cynical than his wife and less trusting. He remembered suddenly a visitor that he had had earlier that afternoon in the shop.

"Oh, there was a woman called in today, looking for Aimee."

"Oh?" Mary was immediately curious and suspicious. "Who? Her mother?"

"No, no. She wasn't a relative by the look of her. Not from round here I would say, although she did look familiar."

"Well, what did she say?"

"Not much, just asked if Aimee still worked here and whether she'd had the baby."

"What did you tell her? You didn't give her Aimee's address, did you?" Mary was alarmed.

"Course not." Gordon rolled his eyes, what did she take him for? "She wrote her name and number on a piece of paper and asked me if I'd pass it on to Aimee."

"So where is it then, this piece of paper?"

Gordon looked sheepish. "I left it at the shop."

"Oh, for goodness' sake, Gordon!"

"It's okay, I know exactly where it is, I put it safe and then it just slipped my mind. I'll bring it back tomorrow."

Mary tutted. "I'll call in for it first thing, on my way to see Aimee." She wondered who it could be and continued to fire a string of questions at Gordon in an attempt to solve the mystery; it had been weeks since Mary herself had served the young teacher and it had slipped her mind. It was no use her trying to fathom it out, it was time for the evening news and Gordon was no longer listening.

Mary studied Aimee's face as she took the piece of paper, wondering what the girl's reaction would be. To her relief, Aimee's expression was wide eyed with delight. "She was my teacher at school." She explained to Mary and she began immediately to ask eager questions about the unexpected visitor. Mary, however, had little to tell. "Go and 'phone her now if you like," she offered, "I'll watch Trixie." But, to her surprise, Aimee hesitated. Mary frowned, she had seemed so pleased; it occurred to Mary that it was a little odd that her teacher should go to the trouble of seeking out her ex-pupil and her naturally curious nature was somewhat disappointed when Aimee muttered something about calling her later and then changed the subject.

That afternoon, Aimee got Trixie ready for a trip to the park. She was now three weeks' old and, unlike some newborn babies, had taken well to her pram. The weather was more pleasant after the previous days of humidity; a light breeze had brought the temperature down to a more tolerable level, but Aimee took great care to ensure Trixie was protected behind her canopy

240

from the afternoon sun. She herself had begun to feel quite recovered from the birth and was eager for some activity even if it were just a leisurely stroll.

As she ambled towards the park, talking animatedly to her little daughter, she was aware of the telephone booth just around the corner and sub-consciously rubbed her hand over her pocket, which contained the little slip of paper on which Helen had written her number. It had not been necessary for her to bring it, Aimee did not know many 'phone numbers but months ago she had quickly learned Helen's by heart and she had not forgotten it. She knew, however, that she would never have dialled it again had Helen not re-initiated contact and the hurt that Aimee had felt from Helen's sudden lack of communication caused her to wonder whether she should bother to call her now. A little voice of caution inside her head reminded her that Helen had been the one to encourage their friendship, only to relinquish it at a later date. Nevertheless, Aimee reasoned with herself that there could be no harm in simply making the 'phone call if only to share the wonderful news of Trixie's safe arrival. Coming to a halt outside the phone booth, she carefully engaged the brake on Trixie's pram before gathering a handful of coins. As always, whenever she used a public phone, she was half-surprised to hear the dialling tone, indicating that the machine appeared to be in working order, in spite of the uninviting smell and the grime embedded in the handset. She was aware that she was probably the only teenager on the planet who was not conjoined to the latest mobile phone but right now it was hardly on her list of priorities. The line connected quickly and Aimee realised that she had butterflies in her tummy.

"Hello!" Helen answered after just a couple of rings and Aimee caught her breath nervously, suddenly shy of the woman who had been her teacher for years.

"It's Aimee," she faltered.

"Aimee!" Helen sounded genuinely delighted. "Oh, I'm so glad you've called. How are you? Congratulations! Where are you?"

241

Aimee laughed nervously at Helen's babbled reaction. "I'm fine!" She moved her eyes towards Trixie. *"We're fine!"*

"Oh, thank goodness. Where are you?" Helen's tone was persistent.

"Just going to the park."

"Can I join you?"

"Well . . . of course, yes!" Aimee smiled. Helen sounded really keen to see her and suddenly Aimee was filled with happy anticipation.

"Great! I'll be about fifteen minutes."

Aimee replaced the receiver and retrieved her change. She rubbed her hands together with some distaste before spotting the changing bag beneath the pram. "Can your mummy pinch one of your wipes, darling?" She smiled down at her baby who, she realised, had fallen fast asleep.

Aimee spotted Helen's car approaching the park entrance and she smiled brightly as Helen spoke through the wound down window. "I'll just park over there, won't be a tic."

Soon Helen was at her side and, to Aimee's surprise, she embraced her in a great big hug. "Oh, Aimee, I'm so glad you're okay." She held her ex-pupil at arm's length and studied her for a moment as if to convince herself. "You look really well . . and . . ." she turned towards the pram, gasping with delight. "Oh! She's beautiful!" She looked back into Aimee's face and nodded knowingly, "She looks like you," she confirmed approvingly. Aimee felt herself blush slightly. It was what everyone said but then no one knew what the other option was!

"Shall we go in?" Helen pointed towards the park gate. "It's a lovely day, isn't it?"

For a few moments, they walked in companionable silence. The sun was bright but cooled to a pleasant temperature by the slight

August breeze, the strong scent from the summer flowers in the neatly laid-out gardens wafted lazily towards them and the, as yet, distant sound of children's laughter mingling with the quiet buzz of a bumble bee was all that they could hear. At the same time, Helen and Aimee met each other's eye and smiled shyly.

"Aimee," Helen began quietly, "I'm really sorry I haven't been in touch."

"It's okay." Aimee responded generously.

"No, it isn't. I should have been there for you, and I wasn't."

Aimee was touched by her sincerity and for a brief moment felt as though her emotions would overwhelm her. She had been hurt by Helen's disappearance from her life and there had been times during the past weeks when she had felt anger towards the woman who had offered her friendship, only to withdraw it without a word of explanation. She smiled solemnly. She didn't understand why Helen had behaved that way, but she had the feeling that she was about to find out. Helen, however, appeared to change her mind and she held back whatever it was that she had been going to say. It had, in fact, occurred to Helen, just as she was about to confide her troubles in her young friend that what she had been through had been nothing compared to her experiences, not just those of the last few months, but probably during the entire of her life.

"So . . . what happened, how did it go? The birth, I mean. Was your mum with you?" This was a question that had been on Helen's mind above all others. The idea of Aimee enduring her labour alone had filled her with guilt.

Aimee smiled shyly. "It was okay. Actually, I think I got off pretty lightly compared to some women." Aimee then proceeded to tell the story of how Mary and then her police escort had basically just about got her to the hospital in time. She went on to tell her how good Mary had been and how she had moved into the hostel. Helen was conscious that Aimee said nothing at all about any involvement on the part of her mum and stepdad. It horrified her to think of the young girl having had to face it all without the support of her parents, but she had too much respect for Aimee to pry. Listening to her tale, sounding so worldly-wise and in control, it was hard to believe that she was just sixteen years old.

By the time Aimee had finished talking, they had found themselves a bench, a short distance from the children's playground.

"So, how long do you think it will be before you get somewhere of your own?" Helen enquired tentatively, silently wondering about the possibilities of Aimee returning to her own home. She had no idea what the current situation was, whether the stepfather was still around or whether it would be feasible for Aimee to live there with her baby. She simply knew that at sixteen, Aimee was very young to be confronted with the prospect of running a home and taking charge of a child alone. If anyone could cope, it was Aimee, Helen was well aware of this fact and yet it was still more than a young girl should be expected to deal with. Not for the first time in Aimee's company, Helen remembered how she herself had been at her age. Stress had been sitting her GCSE's - little had she known! Her thoughts turned now to this summer's results.

"Will you be going into school on Thursday?"

For a few moments, Aimee looked puzzled. Why on earth would she want to do that? The penny, however, quickly dropped. Nevertheless, going into school was the last thing she intended to do. She vaguely remembered that she was supposed to have left a self-addressed envelope at the school if she wanted her results to be posted to her. Needless to say, this had slipped her mind.

"I don't think there's much point in me collecting them really." Aimee shrugged glumly.

"Oh Aimee, you worked hard."

"Well, maybe but I was not exactly, well, you know, focused at the time."

Helen studied Aimee's face. "Shall I get them for you?"

Again, Aimee shrugged. "If you want. It doesn't really matter."

Helen thought for a moment before she spoke. "Well, it won't be the end of the world if they're not good, but aren't you just a little curious?"

"I suppose so. But I'm telling you, they'll be crap."

"So, I have your permission to get them for you?"

Aimee laughed. Trixie began to stir. "I'll have to feed her soon." Aimee sounded regretful; she was relaxed here with Helen and was in no rush to return to the hostel. Although she and Trixie had taken to breastfeeding, she was not yet ready to go public.

Helen looked thoughtful. "I've got the baby clothes we bought back at the flat."

Aimee noted the way she had said "we" and not "I" and nodded appreciatively.

"Do you fancy coming back with me? We could have something to eat and I'll drop you back home later."

Aimee was not sure how she felt about going to Helen's with the prospect of maybe meeting her boyfriend. She knew she would feel awkward.

"I don't know." She faltered, looking into her lap, thinking of how shabby and shapeless she must look.

Helen looked disappointed and Aimee felt a warm thrill to feel that someone wanted to spend time with her. "What time will your fiancé be back?" She enquired cautiously.

Helen's expression hardened and instantly Aimee knew why Helen had lost touch. She'd had troubles of her own to contend with. "He's gone." Helen explained. "He won't be back." It still hurt her to admit it and the words, spoken aloud caused her now to catch her breath but she had resolved not to wallow in her own problems. She was here for Aimee now and she would not allow herself to indulge her self-pity.

Aimee did not know what to say and for a few seconds, there was silence. She tried not to allow her eyes to wander towards Helen's ringless finger.

Helen brightened deliberately. "Will you come?"

It was not charity, Aimee acknowledged, Helen *wanted* to go back with her. Suddenly, she was eager to go but she was brought down to earth by the practicalities of her new position. "I won't be able to stay for long - I've only one spare nappy with me."

Helen shook her head. "Not a problem. Why don't we stop at the supermarket on the way, pick up a couple of pizzas and whatever else you need?"

Aimee grinned. It wouldn't hurt to buy a big pack of nappies whilst she had the luxury of a lift in Helen's car. Trixie certainly got through them at an impressive rate. "Okay." She nodded enthusiastically.

Trixie now was wide awake and concentrating hard, her face contorted intensely. "Looks like we're going to need that nappy sooner rather than later!" Helen observed.

As they made their way towards the car, Aimee thanked her lucky stars that the pram doubled as a car seat and soon she was swiftly dismantling it and strapping Trixie carefully into the back of Helen's car. She sat slightly awkwardly next to Helen but soon Helen had helped her to relax with her chatter and questions about Trixie's routine; there was no mention of Jim, or her mother and Aimee cast them out of her mind.

The few hours spent at Helen's flat were a revelation to Aimee. Helen presented her with the baby clothes. "I've washed them, so Trixie will be able to wear them straightaway." Helen had announced eagerly. They ate Pizza followed by chocolate ice cream and they cooed delightedly over the baby, who also seemed very relaxed in the new surroundings. Helen cuddled her and Trixie adored the attention. Helen was amazed. "Babies normally cry the minute they come near me," she admitted.

Aimee was incredulous to discover that it was nine o'clock. Helen glanced regretfully at the clock. "Next time, you could stay over," she invited simply.

Aimee nodded. She had had a lovely time, but she just could not help but wonder if Helen would tire of her company. Surely she must have other people she would rather be spending time with. She was a professional, e. ated woman, whilst she, Aimee, was . . .

"What do you think?"

Aimee realised that she had not heard whatever it was that Helen had said.

"About Thursday?" Helen repeated. "I could go and get your results and then pick you up, say about eleven and then we could go for a drive somewhere, maybe take a picnic or something?"

"Well . . ." Aimee hesitated; she was still not sure she even wanted her results. "The picnic part sounds fine but . . ."

"Great! That's arranged then." Helen laughed happily. She too had enjoyed herself for the first time in weeks, months even. "Look, Aimee, don't even think about the results. If they're bad, forget about them for now, you can always re-take them later. And if they're good . . ."

"They won't be." Aimee interrupted stubbornly.

The following morning Aimee answered a knock on her door, expecting to see one of the other girls. Mary had said that she would pop in at around lunch time and it was not yet eleven. To her surprise, it was Helen, who looked both animated and sheepish. "Sorry to intrude. Can I come in?"

247

"Of course." Aimee moved aside.

"I won't stay long. I'm meeting up with an old friend but there's something I wanted to ask you."

Aimee nodded curiously and then listened as Helen launched into an explanation of how she would be going away on Friday for a week and how she would be really, really grateful if Aimee would go and stay in her flat. "Just so I've got peace of mind, you know."

Aimee suspected that Helen did not really need a flat sitter but that she was trying to give her a break from the hostel. Before, she could get her breath, however, Helen continued.

"And if you like it, maybe you could stay for a little while. I mean, I've been thinking about advertising for a flatmate." She had begun to gabble rather nervously, seeking out Aimee's reaction in her face.

Aimee was stunned into silence.

Helen reached out and touched her arm. "Don't say anything. Just have a think." She pushed up the sleeve of her light, cotton shirt and glanced at the time. "Must go. I'll see you on Thursday."

"See you!" Aimee called after Helen's retreating back. She closed the door and something resembling a combination of a smile and a frown crossed her face. She was flattered that Helen trusted her with the run of her home, but she was also baffled. There must be other people Helen could ask. Aimee knew that Helen's family were not local, but she had friends. And had she imagined that Helen had just hinted that they could become flatmates? It seemed absurd. She could hardly get her head round the idea of moving in with her teacher, ex-teacher, let alone consider how she actually felt about it. Odd, wasn't the word! Aimee found herself wondering about what had happened between Helen and her boyfriend; they had been engaged to be married and now it was all off. Aimee felt a twinge of sadness at the frailty of human relationships. How could things turn so sour between people who say they love each other?

Just before twelve o'clock there was a second knock at the door and Aimee leapt up, eager to share her news. Mary greeted her enthusiastically as Aimee took her jacket and offered her her usual cup of tea.

"You look bright eyed and bushy tailed this morning." Mary remarked. "Did you 'phone your friend yesterday?"

Aimee eagerly poured out the events of the previous afternoon and evening as Mary listened attentively. The older woman was delighted that Aimee had enjoyed herself so much, she often worried that the poor girl had no one other than herself and she was no company for a young girl.

"I'm really glad you had a good time, Aimee." she told her warmly.

"Anyway," Aimee continued excitedly, "listen to this! Helen called round unexpectedly this morning and guess what?"

Mary shook her head with a laugh. "I give up, tell me!"

"She wants me to be her new flatmate!" Once again, Aimee found herself giggling at the prospect. "What do you think about that? Amazing isn't it? I mean, it's incredible, why would she want *me* as a flatmate?"

Mary pushed her cheek out with her tongue solemnly. "I . . . er, I don't know dear."

Aimee's smile faded as she took in Mary's expression. She had not meant it to be a question that required an answer. "Don't you think it's a good idea, then?"

It was not often that Mary felt at a loss for something to say, but as she stood there, watching the excitement shrink from Aimee's smile, she felt a surge of irritation towards this Helen, who had burst back into Aimee's life with her impetuous ideas. She

249

thought with despair now of the flat above the shop, which she had been lovingly restoring and was almost ready to present to Aimee. Mary's frustration with this unexpected situation turned inwards and she felt foolish – a silly, interfering old woman whose moment of glory had now been usurped by someone younger, more exciting. Mary's immediate, subsequent thought was of the selfishness of her own reaction. The whole idea of the flat above the shop had been for Aimee's benefit. Hadn't it? So now, her intentions should remain the same, that Aimee find somewhere suitable and safe to live and who was she to choose where that should be?

"Mary?" Aimee was mystified and disappointed by Mary's silence. She had expected her to share her excitement.

"I . . . I'm sorry, dear." Mary looked up apologetically. Deliberately, she pulled herself together. "I think it's a great idea . . . if you do . . ." she added. She smiled at Aimee. "I just want you to be happy. You and Trixie, you deserve it."

Aimee returned her smile, relieved but still not entirely reassured.

"Look, Aimee." Mary continued hastily. She had decided, given the turn of events, that now was the time to reveal all to Aimee. "There's something I want to show you."

Aimee nodded curiously.

"We'll need to go in the car. So, when you're ready, there's no rush."

Mary sat down and waited nervously whilst Aimee gathered her things and got herself and Trixie ready for the mystery trip. Mary, she noted, was uncharacteristically quiet and her edginess was contagious.

Mary tried not to be disappointed. She had been so looking forward to this moment. She had had plans to buy fresh flowers for the flat and for it to be totally ready. There were still one or two bits and pieces that needed sorting out before the place was just as she wanted it, prior to showing it to Aimee. She had never contemplated for one moment that Aimee would make arrangements of her own and again she forced herself to remember that Aimee's best interests had to take priority. If Aimee decided to move in with Helen, then so be it.

Aimee glanced at Mary, deep in thought. "We're ready."

Mary forced a smile and took a final sip of her tea. "Right then, off we go." She tried to ignore the butterflies in her stomach. She felt foolish, bloody foolish.

They were a few minutes away from the flat before either of them spoke. Mary, temporarily stationary at a red light, turned to Aimee and cleared her throat.

"Aimee. The thing is, I had this idea and now I think I might have been a bit hasty." She thought of Gordon and his warnings. "A bit of an interfering old bat, probably." A small, embarrassed laugh escaped her and she stalled the car as she brought out the clutch rather too rapidly. She sighed. "I was just trying to help really. Anyway, you'll have to make up your own mind. It's entirely up to you and I don't want you to feel under any pressure. You have to think of yourself and Trixie of course and what's going to be the best thing for the two of you."

Aimee had absolutely no idea what Mary was going on about and simply looked at her blankly.

"What I mean is," Mary finished as they pulled up in front of the precinct. "You have to decide whether you want to go and live with Helen or ..."

"Or?" The only other option as far as Aimee was concerned was to be whatever the council came up with and she was pretty sure there would be no competition.

"Or ... here." Mary's tone was almost apologetic.

Aimee was still unclear. The precinct? What did Mary mean? Slowly, she followed the older woman's gaze. She was staring at

251

the newsagents, well not exactly at the newsagents, just above it. Something had changed, Aimee noticed vaguely. There was a window on the second floor of the building and Aimee had never really looked at it before, but something was different, she felt sure. Was it the curtains? She couldn't be certain.

"Come with me." Mary insisted, trying to sound more confident than she felt. She snapped off the ignition and stepped out of the car. Aimee leant over and took Trixie out of her car seat, carrying her in her arms as they began to walk around the back of the line of shops.

Mary had the key ready and they walked in silence. Aimee was unfamiliar with the back entrance to the shop. There was a door which Mary unlocked using one key and then two more doors, one to the left, leading, Aimee assumed, to the shop and another which Mary now opened using a second key. The door opened almost immediately on to a staircase, which Mary began to climb. "Just close the door behind you, love." She instructed before leading the way. At the top of the stairs, they came to another door, which again Mary opened. Aimee peered ahead, intrigued.

Aimee again shut the door behind her. They were in a small hallway; it smelled of lemon cleaning fluid.

"It's the flat above the shop." Mary explained unnecessarily.

Aimee giggled, suddenly nervous, not quite sure what they were doing there.

"Come through." Mary invited. She led the way and soon they had entered the small living room. Aimee glanced around her, there was a sofa, a television, a small table with a lamp on. Was someone living here? She wondered. As far as she had been aware, the flat had always been empty.

"Sit down." Mary waved Aimee towards the sofa and waited for her to settle herself before perching cautiously next to her.

"The thing is, Aimee." Mary began, "I thought, well . . . I thought you and Trixie could live here."

Aimee's eyes opened incredulously. "How?" She was thinking immediately of the cost of course.

"Easy." Mary rushed on, this part she had thought out already. "It's no different to the council finding you somewhere, you're still entitled to the same benefits. You just get somewhere decent to live instead . . . oh and a friendly landlady!"

The penny was beginning to drop for Aimee. She saw now what Mary had been up to these past weeks. She had done all this for her. She looked around her at the modest but clean and functional furniture.

"Come and look!" Mary was excited now, still nervous of Aimee's reaction but desperate to show her the rest of the flat. First of all, she led Aimee, still holding Trixie in her carrier, through to the tiny but spotlessly clean kitchen. There was a cooker, old fashioned, but scrubbed until it was gleaming and likewise the sink and taps. On the work surface there was a neat row of jars which were labelled tea, coffee and sugar. Mary indicated these and apologised. I haven't got round to filling these up yet or I'd offer you a cuppa." Aimee shook her head in disbelief.

"Come on, I'll show you the rest." Mary ushered Aimee back out and they turned towards another door, the bathroom. This, too, was spotless. The toilet pedestal neatly surrounded by a fluffy light blue mat and a matching rug lay next to the bath. Finally, Aimee noticed, these details were complemented by the neat blue curtain which hung at the small window. Aimee shook her head again, she was speechless.

Finally, Mary revealed the two small bedrooms. One, the slightly larger of the two, was furnished simply with a bed and a wardrobe. The other room was empty. "This could be for Trixie, when you're ready for her to be by herself." Mary whispered, anxious and eager.

"Mary . . . I . . . have you bought all these things . . . for me?" Aimee was blushing and flustered. She was deeply shocked. She had had no idea that Mary had been organising all of this.

"No, no." Mary assured her. "Most of it was here already. I've just cleaned it up a bit." Aimee turned towards her, dubious.

"Well," Mary relented, "I bought a few little bits and pieces, you know . . . for the kitchen and the bathroom, just to get you started.

Why? Aimee wondered, why would anyone do that for her. "Mary, really, you shouldn't have done all this."

Mary's expression became serious. "I know. I see that now. I should have spoken to you first. I didn't mean to interfere with your life. I was just trying to help, but if you prefer to live with Helen, then really, it's no problem at all. I just thought you should have the choice, now that I have done it."

Choice! Aimee was stupefied. Not very long ago, she was facing the prospect of homelessness. Now she had a choice!

"You don't have to give me an answer straightaway." Mary told her reassuringly. "Take your time. It's a big decision."

Aimee walked back into the living room and moved around as if in a daze. Could she really live here? Just her and Trixie? Was it really possible? Mary seemed to think so. She walked to the window. She moved the net curtain aside and looked out on to the precinct, there were a few youths hanging around aimlessly as usual, but it was quiet enough. But then, Aimee wondered, was it a bit too close to Deansfield Crescent? So many people round here knew her business. Would it not be better to go where she could make a clean start? And what was it like at nighttime when the shops were shut? She thought of Helen's flat, modern, luxurious even, compared to this and tucked away in a "nice" neighbourhood. It would be great to have a flatmate. Even at the hostel she felt lonely and isolated once her own door was shut. But what if Helen got fed up with having her around? Not to mention Trixie. Surely, Helen had not thought the matter through properly? But what about Mary, Aimee wondered. She too seemed to have become carried away with her plans; what would she expect in return? Did she want her to continue working at the newsagents and, if so, how did she feel about that? Her thoughts lingered for a moment on the exam results which would be available in a few days' time. At some point, Aimee needed to make some decisions about her future. Her mind was beginning to whirl with confused thoughts and ideas, worries and concerns which had shot up from choices that a few hours earlier she had not had.

Mary, disconcerted by Aimee's silence, interrupted her thoughts. "Shall we go and have a coffee somewhere? You look a bit shell-shocked."

Aimee nodded. "I am," she agreed. "Oh, Mary, I'm sorry." She realised suddenly how ungrateful she had appeared. She stepped forward and with the arm that was not carrying Trixie, she pulled Mary towards her. "Honestly, this is just fantastic. I'm so grateful for everything you've done and . . ."

Mary returned her hug but then pulled away and wagged her finger sternly. "I don't want to hear any more about it. Now, you have a think about what you want to do and let me know when you're ready. There's no rush. Not as far as I'm concerned."

Aimee smiled her gratitude. "You're an angel, Mary, you really are."

Mary sniffed. "Well, if I am, then you deserve me. It's about time you had a bit of luck."

Later that afternoon, Aimee found herself sharing her news with Kelly, one of the other young mums at the hostel. "A bit of luck!" Kelly repeated, when Aimee had finished her tale. "You're a right jammy sod, more like! Tell you what, you go and live with your teacher mate and I'll take the flat above the shop, then we're both happy!"

For a moment, Aimee wished she hadn't said anything, she had been hoping for a bit of advice, but obviously that was not going to be the case, not everyone's motives were as selfless as Mary's it seemed. Nevertheless, believing in Mary's genuine intentions did not make her decision any easier. There were pros and cons to both scenarios and Aimee seemed unable to contemplate them without being utterly confused. That night she fell into bed thinking that she might just as well toss a coin because she felt completely incapable of reaching a decision and sticking to it.

Chapter Nineteen

Aimee's results were neither as bad as she had anticipated nor as good as they could have been, given a different set of circumstances. She had fared reasonably well in English, Maths and IT and not too badly in a couple of other subjects, but her French grade was dismal, as was her chemistry result. Helen maintained that she should be proud of herself, that there were plenty of kids out there who had taken their exams without another care in the world and had not done so well.

"And the important thing is, you've got your English and Maths, so, if you're going to go on to college later, they're the main things you need to worry about. So, I say, we go celebrate."

Helen had packed a tasty picnic and they drove to a spot by a river, about half an hour out of town. It was so peaceful and Aimee found herself relaxing. There were few people around and she was able to feed Trixie without worrying about anyone else. She savoured the air and the moments of tranquillity. This is how she wanted Trixie's life to be. She could not help but think of her sisters; they would love it here. She wondered how they were, how things were. The usual clutch of fear gripped her as she thought of Sheryl and Jim and what was going on back in Deansfield Crescent.

Helen chatted to her about her week away with an old university friend and again brought up her plan for Aimee to stay at her flat.

"I'll pick you up and bring everything you need over before I go and I'll take you back when you're ready. You can stay as long as you like after I get back, though, to see how we get along. You probably just have to tell your social worker, so they know where you both are. Don't want to start a panic!"

Aimee could not believe that Helen was serious about the idea of them becoming flatmates. She was quiet, imagining what it would be like to share a flat with someone like Helen. She realised that no matter how close they became, Aimee would always feel indebted to Helen and no matter how relaxed she had become in her company, living in her flat, with a screaming baby and all of the untidiness that went with having Trixie would be a pressure that she would not have if she chose the flat above the shop. But then, she thought of the precinct and its depressing outlook, its proximity to Deansfield Crescent . . . and Jim.

Aimee told Helen slowly about Mary's proposition. Helen was surprised and, Aimee noted, a little deflated. "Wouldn't you be lonely, though, Aimee?" And, well, it's not the nicest of neighbourhoods . . ."

"It's what I've grown up with." Aimee reminded her.

"Yes, but . . ."

"I think it would be best." Aimee was suddenly sure of her decision. "I need to face up to my responsibilities and I don't want to be a burden to anyone else."

"You wouldn't be a burden. I'd love a flatmate." Helen could sense that she was defeated and, in her heart, she knew that Aimee was right, for all the right reasons."

"You're very brave, Aimee." She reached out and hugged her former pupil. "I'll only be a phone call away if you ever need me, you know that don't you? And we'll stay friends."

"Of course. Thank you, Helen."

Mary was delighted with Aimee's decision when Aimee called her later that day and she was full of the final arrangements to get the place completely ready. "We could get you moved in at the weekend, if you like."

It was a big move, away from the hostel and the security of having other people around her but Aimee knew it was the right thing to do and she agreed. As she gave Trixie her final feed that evening, she looked lovingly down at her daughter. Maybe they had a chance after all.

It was a busy few days of preparations, Aimee realised that there were so many things that she would not have thought of without Mary, organising gas and electric, council tax, not to mention making sure she had basic supplies such as light bulbs. Aimee knew that things would be tight living on benefits and it was not her intention long term, but she felt sure she would cope. She had no choice and it was not as though she were accustomed to luxuries in her life.

By the end of Saturday, everything was ready and Aimee sat in her room at the hostel, waiting for Mary to pick her up. There were just the last few remaining essentials that she had kept with her for Trixie, everything else, such as it was, had gone to the flat. Aimee looked around her, for a while this had been "home", a place of refuge for the first time in her life, but she was not sad to be going, she was ready to start a new life with her baby. She owed Mary so much and yet she knew also that Mary truly enjoyed helping her, the daughter she had never had. Not for the first time, Aimee reflected on the cruel hand of nature that sometimes gave children to those who shouldn't have them and denied those who should. She hoped that her own daughter would never feel that she, Aimee was undeserving of her.

The other mums gathered around to wave her off; envious as they were, their kind words were genuine and Aimee felt quite emotional as Mary drove them away from the hostel and the small group of well-wishers.

Later, after Mary had left her with instructions that she should let them know if there was anything they needed, Aimee cried. Trixie lay sleeping in her cot, without a care in the world, Aimee thought. Once again, she thought of her sisters and she realised that what she now felt was guilt. Let down by her parents, she too had now abandoned them. The overwhelming sense of relief and happiness that she felt for herself and Trixie was marred by the anguish she felt on their behalf. Notwithstanding this pain, however, Aimee fell into a happy routine, during the following days, taking care of Trixie and the flat. There was little time left for herself at the end of each day but each night she went to bed happy that she and her daughter were safe.

It had been a glorious summer and the weather showed no sign of letting up. Aimee generally took a walk each day with Trixie in her pram and often she ended up at the park. It was the final week of the six weeks' holiday; the park was still filled with the happy shouts of children playing. Aimee was heading out of the park, down the long path that led to the exit and she took no notice of the young couple on the bench as she passed by. The moment she had done so, however, something made her turn to look at them, there had been something familiar which caused her to look directly at the boy with his arm around the slim girl with the carefree smile. As soon as she turned, she wished that she had not. Jack was as shocked as she was and the smile on his lips faded instantly. She saw his mouth move but he did not speak.

Aimee looked away, her face flaming, her footsteps quickening and her heart racing. God, what an idiot, he must have thought that she was staring at him because he was with another girl.

"Aimee! Wait!" She had not expected him to speak to her and was alarmed when she realised that he was running after her.

"Hey, Aimee! Hold on." She did not dare to look round; momentarily she wondered about the other girl. She had not recognised her; what on earth must she be thinking?

He caught up with her, but she did not stop. Gently, he touched her arm.

"Just a sec, Aimee. I only want to talk to you."

Reluctantly, Aimee stopped walking, but she shuffled uncomfortably. Her mouth was dry and her heart was pounding almost audibly in her chest.

"Are you ok?" His voice was just as she remembered it – full of kindness.

She nodded but no words came out. He looked down at the baby shyly.

"She's lovely," he whispered. "What have you called her?"

Aimee smiled, relaxing as she too gazed at their lovely daughter. "She's called Trixie."

He did not take his eyes off the little girl and Aimee felt the emotion pushing at her throat, threatening to choke her.

"Wow, I can't imagine . . . it must be amazing. . ."

"Not that amazing at two o'clock in the morning."

He looked at Aimee now, genuinely concerned. "How are you managing?"

"Fine." Aimee announced proudly, regaining her composure. "I've left . . . I've got my own place now." It was the first time she had spoken the words, it sounded unreal to her and she smiled in spite of herself. Aimee found herself telling Jack about the flat and she could see that he was impressed.

"Wow! That's fantastic." He hesitated. "Maybe, I could pop round and see you." Unless things had changed dramatically, he did not imagine that she had many visitors.

Aimee's smile faded, she half turned towards the girl who was still sitting some way off on the bench.

"I don't think so, Jack." She started to move away from him.

"Aimee, wait, look . . . damn . . ." He cursed and turned and was actually relieved to see that his date was now heading in the opposite direction. He walked slowly towards the bench. He needed to sit down.

Aimee quickened her pace and exhaled deeply. She could not wait to get back to the flat. She was barely through the door a short while later when Mary appeared, out of breath.

"Oh, thank God! There you are Aimee; I've been waiting for you. I was going to come and find you if you hadn't got back soon."

She was gabbling and flustered and Aimee looked at her in bewilderment. "Mary, what's wrong? What's going on?"

Years of dread and fear hurtled back and immediately Aimee's thoughts flew to her sisters, her mother . . . it had to be something to do with them . . . with Jim . . .

"It's your mom and dad, they've been taken to hospital. I don't know much else."

Aimee's stomach somersaulted uncontrollably. "What about my sisters?"

"I'm sorry, love. I don't know anything else."

"Oh my God. I've got to go." Aimee's mind raced. Trixie was crying for her feed. She would have to do that first.

"Feed her, love and then I'll have her while you go round."

Feeding Trixie, Aimee's nerves were in bits and guiltily she thought of how this would affect her baby who needed calm and stability. There was, she realised, no escape from the miseries of the Parkinson household. Even now, Jim was ruining her life and the peace she was striving for, for herself and her daughter.

It was not long before she rounded the corner of Deansfield Crescent and all the familiar feelings rushed back as if she had never been away, as if nothing had changed.

There was just one police car outside. Aimee's pace slowed down as she reached the path. What lay ahead of her? Please God, let Stacey and Kayleigh be okay.

She pushed open the back door. The house was quiet. The scene that greeted her was one that she had seen many times but, having been away and having lived in her own orderly space, the disarray of the kitchen shocked and unnerved her. As she walked towards the living room, she heard an unfamiliar, female voice followed by Kayleigh, or was it Stacey? Aimee rushed forward. The two young girls sat at either side of the female police officer on the sofa, a book on the woman's lap fell off as the sisters jumped up at the sight of their sister.

Aimee clutched her little sisters to her. "Oh, thank God, you're safe. Thank God." Tears sprang to her eyes as they held her desperately. "Are you going to stay, Aimee?"

Aimee gathered her senses quickly and looked at the policewoman, who said nothing.

"What's happened?" Aimee's voice was dull.

The officer eyed the young girls. "There's been an accident. You're Aimee, right?"

Aimee nodded.

"Your parents have been taken to hospital."

Aimee now looked at the two little girls. "Will you two be very good girls for Aimee and go and choose some toys. I think you might have to come and stay with me tonight."

Dutifully, Stacey and Kayleigh turned towards the door.

"Is Mommy going to be ok?"

"I hope so darling." Aimee heaved a huge sigh as they left the room. "What's happened?"

The officer pressed her lips together, she wore a grim expression, which filled Aimee with a sense of dread.

"There was a fight."

"A fight?" That was an interesting perspective. "You mean he attacked her. What's he done this time?" Her voice was hard, but inside she was trembling as she waited for the news of how far he'd gone.

The officer eyed her carefully. "Your father's been stabbed, Aimee. He's in intensive care."

Aimee felt the room spinning as she heard the words in what appeared to be slow motion. She staggered towards the sofa and seated herself on the edge.

"Oh my God! What about my mom? Where's my mom?"

"She appears to have taken an overdose. She's under observation."

Aimee buried her head in her hands. "What has she taken? How many? Is she going to be okay?"

"We think paracetamol, but we don't know how many."

"Oh God! She was on anti-depressants, I think, still. She could have taken those too. Would that make it worse?" Aimee was horrified as she recalled how she had encouraged her mother to take the doctor's advice in the hope that it would improve her state of mind. "I'll have to go to the hospital . . . I can't . . . What about Stacey and Kayleigh? And Trixie. Oh my God, Trixie, I've got to get back to Trixie, my baby."

"Look, Aimee, you've had a shock. Have a cup of tea and then we'll decide what's the best thing to do, for everyone."

"No!" The thought of drinking tea in this house was abhorrent to Aimee. "I'm going to get my sisters. They will have to stay with me." Aimee's mind raced from one thought to the next. She had to look after her sisters. Finding out about Sheryl and Jim would have to wait. God, she hoped he was dead. A cold shiver crept down Aimee's spine. That would make her mother a murderer . . . Aimee closed her eyes in horror.

"Look, Aimee, I can't just let the girls go with you. I have to get it all cleared with social services."

Aimee gave her address to the police officer and waited whilst she made some calls. To her relief, it was not long before they were able to lock up the house and climbed into the police car for a lift to Aimee's flat. Trixie had just woken and Mary greeted them at the door with the baby in her arms. Her expression did not change as she took in the sight of Aimee, the policewoman and the two young girls. Gordon had been right. The Parkinson's were trouble. But these were the innocent victims and she reminded herself that they had no one else to turn to.

The police officer saw them safely inside. "I'll find out what's happening at the hospital and I'll call round later." Aimee nodded her thanks and ushered her sisters indoors.

"Oh Aimee, it's lovely." Kayleigh whispered, shy in front of Mary.

"Where are we going to sleep?" Stacey tugged at her big sister's arm.

"Sssh, you two, don't worry, everything will be fine." Aimee had spent years reassuring her sisters when things were bad and she fell back into the role with ease.

"We've a big airbed somewhere." Mary pondered. "I'm sure I'll be able to find it and pop it round."

Aimee smiled with sad appreciation.

"Don't worry, Aimee, I'm here to help."

Aimee knew that she had to be strong for her sisters, but she could feel the emotion welling up inside her. "Come on you two, let's make you some sandwiches."

The hours dragged by. Stacey and Kayleigh were excited by their new surroundings, but Aimee could sense their underlying tension. God only knew what they had seen and heard happening between their parents.

Mary, true to her word, found the airbed and brought along bedding to go with it. To the girls' delight, she had also brought comics and sweets from the newsagents, both of which were a treat which cheered them up considerably.

By bedtime, the two little girls were worn out and fell readily into the makeshift bed, but as Aimee kissed their cheeks, she could see the worries that lay beneath their brave smiles. "Are we going to see mommy, tomorrow, Aimee?"

"I don't want *him* to come back ever again," confided Stacey.

"SShh. Don't worry now. Come on, cuddle up and go to sleep." Aimee stroked each one of her little sisters lovingly. How she wished she could take away their pain and their fears.

Darkness was falling by the time there was a knock at the door. Mary had resolutely insisted on staying with Aimee until there was news of her mother and stepfather and it was she who opened the door to the same police officer they'd seen earlier. Aimee could hear their hushed tones and dread and fear squeezed her from inside, creeping outwards to cover her in a cold shudder of terror.

The police officer wore a serious expression and Aimee willed her to speak.

"It's not good news, I'm afraid."

"Please." Aimee begged quietly, "Just tell me."

The police officer nodded; this girl was not your average sixteen-year-old, she could see that. "Your mum's in intensive care. She's stable and they're optimistic that she will pull through with no long-term damage."

Aimee nodded and breathed deeply as she acknowledged with relief that Sheryl, once again, had survived.

"And?" Aimee's thoughts turned to Jim.

The officer stepped forward, her voice quiet and respectful. "I'm afraid your stepfather died on the way to the hospital. He had lost too much blood, there was nothing they could do . . . I'm sorry."

Aimee closed her eyes, sure that she would pass out; her whole body was consumed with weakness. Confused thoughts raced through her head. Deep inside, part of her was laughing hysterically. Jim Parkinson was dead. He was dead. She wanted to shout it from the roof tops. She wanted to wake her sisters and tell them it was a day for celebration, never again would they suffer at his hands, never again would their lives be blighted by his cruelty and evilness. The bastard was dead.

But it was not a day for celebration. Their mother was a murderer. How could she possibly explain that to her innocent little sisters. Where did she begin to justify what she had done?

Mary was leading her towards the sofa, supporting her weight, soothing her with gentle words of reassurance. Aimee realised that she was sobbing uncontrollably and she could not get her breath. Mary held her and stroked her hair. "Come on, love, that's it, let it out."

She was glad he was dead. Wicked as that was, she could not pretend that it was not so. But her mother, her stupid mother! What had she done to their family now? Why could she not have just made him stay away? Or left – gone away, anywhere, it wouldn't have mattered as long as they were together - safe. How were they ever going to get over this? Her mother would have to go to prison. How would she survive?

As if reading her thoughts, Mary spoke. "Aimee, love . . . your mother was provoked. She'd suffered a lifetime of abuse. That will be taken into account, you'll see. Come on. We have to be strong now for the children."

Maybe it was the way she had said "we" that gave Aimee the strength to take control of herself. For the first time, she realised that she was facing the Parkinson's problems with someone else.

Someone else now was in on the dreadful secrets of the way that their lives had been and Aimee no longer had to pretend.

"It's no reflection on you and the girls, love. You've been a wonderful daughter and sister and you're a great mum. No one's going to judge you because of your parents." Mary wished these words could be true. All that she could guarantee was that she and Gordon would be there to help them.

All her life, Aimee had felt the shame of who she was, where she lived, what she wore and most of all what went on behind closed doors. She looked up and saw the photo of her baby. She thought of her little sisters upstairs. She had never let them down and she never would. They had all of their lives ahead of them and whatever happened, they would stay together and hold their heads high.

Chapter Twenty

It was the first day of the new term. Kayleigh and Stacey were excited about going back to school and Aimee was anticipating the relative peace of there being just herself and Trixie. With September had come a cooling of the air and there was little to amuse Kayleigh and Stacey at the flat. The last week had been hectic and the flat was beginning to feel crowded and a little chaotic. It would be good for the girls to get back to a routine, she told herself, feeling a little guilty for looking forward to them being at school.

The girls had accepted the news of Jim's death with little emotion. They had not encountered death before and were full of questions about what would happen to him now but there was little chance that either of them would be weeping for the loss of their father. It had been harder to explain about what would become of Sheryl. No one had been able to tell Aimee how soon a date would be set for the trial, all that was known was that until then, their mother would remain in custody. Her solicitor was building a solid case for self-defence and everyone Aimee spoke to – social workers, Mary, Helen, they all reassured her that Sheryl was most likely to receive a suspended sentence.

Aimee had spoken to her mother on the phone and it was clear that Sheryl's emotions were in turmoil, devastated by what she had done and the effect that it would have upon her children. Aimee, however, feared that it was Sheryl, who once more would be scarred by the latest turn of events. Aimee had assured her that she would take care of Kayleigh and Stacey, but she told her nothing of the complications that she feared due to the fact that she herself was still only sixteen years old and would not normally be considered responsible enough to take on the role of foster parent. So much of their future lay in the hands of the courts and with the exhausting task of taking care of her sisters and her baby, Aimee had little time or energy for worrying about her mother. Her one goal was to provide a secure and loving environment for her sisters and her daughter. She knew that she was under the close scrutiny of social workers and that there were those who felt the girls should be taken immediately to trained and experienced foster carers, to experience a "normal" family environment. The prospect of this happening filled Aimee with dread and fuelled her energy and patience each day.

Somehow, Aimee managed to get the girls to school on time and hugged them tightly before they skipped through the school gate. It was the first time that they had been out of her sight since they had left Deansfield Crescent. Aimee sighed slightly as she pushed Trixie's pram up the hill away from the primary school. There was so much to do. The house in Deansfield Crescent had to be emptied. None of them wanted to go back there, ever. In spite of her own crowded conditions in the flat, they were happy there and every day they found something to laugh and smile at.

"Hi, Aimee!"

She was startled from her thoughts by a soft, familiar voice. Jack had caught up with her and was now walking beside her.

"Hello, Trixie!" He peered into her pram. "She's growing."

He had remembered her name, Aimee noted, pleased in spite of herself. She nodded, feeling a blush creep to her cheeks. She knew that practically everyone around knew what had happened in her family. The newspapers had made sure of that.

"I'm really sorry to hear about . . . well . . . you know . . . everything that's happened." Jack felt the colour creep to his own cheeks.

Aimee shrugged awkwardly and mumbled something that he could not hear.

"I'm just off to college. First day," he offered brightly.

"Good. That's great! Look, Jack, I'm sorry, I have to go. Trixie will be wanting her feed soon."

"Yeah, right." He was reluctant to let her go. They had reached the point where he must go in one direction and she another. He plucked up the courage. "Aimee, do you think we could meet up sometime?"

"I don't think so Jack. I don't have time."

"I could come round after college. Give you a hand . . ."

Aimee looked at him levelly. "There are three kids in my flat, Jack."

He looked surprised. "Three? Oh, yes, I'm sorry . . . I know...but..."

She laughed. He had no idea. "Go on, you're going to be late for college."

She watched him walk away and he turned again and waved. A warm feeling washed over her, but Aimee was eager to dismiss any notion of getting involved. Not yet, at least. She had to believe that she could stand on her own two feet first. Trixie opened her eyes sleepily and smiled up at her mother.

"Girl power, Trixie, that's us." Aimee beamed happily at her daughter. "Come on, we have to get back . . . home."

DISCUSSION POINTS

- WHY DO YOU THINK THAT AIMEE OFTEN FEELS SO GUILTY, EG WHEN SHE DOESN'T GET JACK A CHRISTMAS PRESENT?

- WHY DO YOU THINK NEIGHBOURS DO NOT INTERFERE?

- DO YOU THINK THAT SHERYL IS AS MUCH TO BLAME FOR THE FAMILY'S SUFFERING AS JIM?

- WHY DOES AIMEE NOT HAVE AN ABORTION?

- AIMEE DOES NOT CONSIDER HERSELF TO BE A NORMAL TEENAGER, BUT ARE THERE OCCASIONS WHEN SHE DOES BEHAVE AS A "NORMAL TEENAGER?"

- WHY DOES AIMEE GROW UP WITH SUCH LOYALTY TOWARDS HER MOTHER? THERE HAD BEEN TIMES WHEN AIMEE HAD BEGGED TO LEAVE, EVEN BEFORE THE TWO SISTERS WERE BORN.

- WHAT DO YOU THINK OF HELEN'S DECISION TO GIVE AIMEE HER PHONNUMBER EVEN THOUGHTHEY ARE STILL TEACHER/PUPIL?

- DID YOU NOTICE THE USE OF THE WORDS "MOM" AND "MUM"? WHAT SIGNIFICANCE DO YOU THINK THIS HAS?

- DO YOU THINK AIMEE IS RIGHT TO EXCLUDE JACK FROM HIS DAUGHTER?

- WHAT DO YOU THINK SHOULD HAPPEN NEXT, IF YOU WERE TO WRITE THE NEXT CHAPTER?

Printed in Great Britain
by Amazon

41037640R00155